Chemistry

To Kate for her enthusiasm

Chemistry

K.B.McGowan

Presta

Copyright © K.B.McGowan 2010

The right of K B McGowan to be identified as Author of this Work has been asserted in accordance with the UK Copyright, Designs and Patents Act 1988.

First published in 2010 by Presta
Reprinted 2011

20 Grafton Street, London

ISBN-13: 978-0-9567275-0-3

Typeset in 10.5 on 13.5 pt Palatino
by Servis Filmsetting Ltd, Stockport, Cheshire
Printed and bound in Great Britain by MPG Books Group Limited,
Bodmin, Cornwall

www.prestabookproduction.com

1

With one bound he was by her side, her heaving bosom ... this from the dowdy woman on Olly's left, and ... *if, as implied by the inoculation theory, the refutational defence derives immunising efficacy from the motivational arguments against the truism ...* from the book held open rather ostentatiously by the American – you could tell by his shoes – on Olly's right. Oh God ... Olly's gaze returned to the plain woman for salvation, her eyes, judging from her slowly moving finger, had settled satisfyingly on *her heaving bosom, testament to her burning desire....* He checked her for excess heat and heave, but the only outward sign of her vicarious pleasure was the clenching of her toes.

The American had gotten to the bit about *the refutational defence confers resistance even to novel attacks ...* What do these words mean? Novel attacks – that's novel; the man was clearly some sort of shrink, but what was she? Mentally shrunk, judging by her choice of reading. These were just weightless thoughts, fluttering in Olly's head. He was in the lightest of moods, musing on the infinite variety of city dwellers down there in the London clay.

Crossing the city by tube seemed to Olly the intelligent way. Perhaps not for short journeys, when travel was often more vertical than horizontal, especially in London's deep tunnels, but today Olly was relaxed, unperturbed by the press of the fellow tunnellers, all mortals just sharing his space for a few minutes, sharing the short passage of time,

1

and ultimately also his epoch. Sometimes positive thoughts were best to overcome less than savoury encounters, but in any event Olly, and presumably most of them, had the ability to moderate their spatial empathy, to switch off and get on with their lives internally.

Not to be late, have a full bladder, or be in dread of an encounter was the way to enjoy this mode of travel, and even more to do it after office hours. An evening journey with a benign British crowd could be quite uplifting, and so it was today.

Olly was quietly abstracting – idle thoughts: for example, what is slower, a second or an hour – surely the smaller goes faster – no they are both travelling along the same beam of time, or is it light, am I just particles of light, or some other matter, ah well does it … concern me? What happens to all these thoughts, do they all disappear in puffs of smoke blown like cotton bubbles from a speeding steam train? What about the forty people in this carriage? That's nearer three hundred on the whole train. Imagine the fug of notions trailing behind each person's head, a vapour trail of vacuous ideas all real in the moment but blown away by the onrush of time – perhaps we need the Big Friendly Giant and his dream-catching net. Speaking of dreaming … Olly now was dreaming.

He was dreaming of all the molecules, biochemicals, and electric charges brought together in unimaginable combinations to create a human being; of the infinite possible outcomes to bring about a personality, and the incredibly stretched chain of variables leading to attraction. He was floating on one of those puffy cotton clouds looking down. Everything was clear from up there, the numbers were actually quite manageable, time was quite slow, he could see how things coalesced, how matter assembled itself seemingly randomly, but when numbers are large enough how patterns emerged to defy anarchy.

He watched as a formula as long as a train – figures and images, numbers and letters, clicking and spinning – gradually slowed. Stimuli were being spun off: sensory compositions and associations formed, recognisable traces emerged stimulating his senses in turn. The first trace was a scent: he was walking in a spring evening, the air ripe with the sweetness of young flowers, their teasing aroma irresistible to a host of insects. A lingering musk from trampled autumn leaves completed the sensual mixture of incense and petals – freshness with a hint of decadence.

Two more traces condensed from the mist of data. He could feel movement, a stirring of the air around him, then a little heat, or was it warmth? Certainly it was radiance of some sort. He heard tones; it was a voice he knew, but had never heard before.

'Thank you. Yes, that's very kind.'

He was on sensory alert, his mind tingling with possibilities. Was this a dream or was it real? Of course he was dreaming, but how can you dream a dream? Surely dream × dream must be reality – easy algebra.

He opened his eyes. He did this with some languor, and without turning his head he could see a girl's face reflected in the soft focus of the darkened window opposite. The image registered as much in his heartbeat as in his eyes. Looking down he could take in finely turned ankles and scantily clad feet that could have been walking on a beach a few moments ago. Two musical-looking hands were resting lightly on a black case. The ticket in her fingers suggested the journey was a novelty – maybe a hint of vulnerability.

Olly resisted a turn of his head to complete the picture, but then reasoned that it would be only natural since before he closed his eyes she had been a large American in clumsy shoes. She mirrored the turn of his sideways glance and their eyes met – for just a fraction of a second longer than is seemly with random strangers. She reddened and looked down at her ticket. Olly was hit; stunned as if he had just witnessed an act of creation, his head filled with surreal thoughts – all uncollected. Matter had materialised. She was by his side, he was by her side; had he bounded, had she bounded, were they bound? 'It's the beauty for the beast,' Olly had heard someone say, as, coming out of his rhapsodic state, he realized that this courteous man had given up his seat to her – to this beautiful girl. The American was now standing above them, aware of and amused by the *frisson* that had passed between the two. He had said this with the best of motives, but unfortunately the words dropped into the well of the young couple's embarrassment, and no one heard the splash.

They sat side by side, confused in the moment, unsure as to action, unsure as to the phenomenon, becoming aware, however, that they had no need to alight the train, were in no hurry to end the journey. Opposite sat a young man, just out of youthdom, though still seemingly comfortable in low-crotched and baggy jeans. With a wispy beard affording only minimal shade to teenage residues on his pale face, his physical appearance was not magnetic – his eyes seemed to say it's ok, I like to be alone, I have no need of interaction. To confound this impression, his companion displayed great affection toward him. She was pretty and chic, and obviously confident in her partner to take care of her – in what was clearly a period of alcohol-induced dependency.

Olly and the girl by his side, together with some of the other passengers, couldn't help noticing the youth's initial reserve to his girlfriend – even her endearments, mumbled as her head lay on his shoulder, seemed not to move him. Maybe he had been here before and knew what foolishness she could exhibit in public. He appeared clearly to disown

4

her, until he discerned that his lack of chivalry was being observed, at which point he gave in to her sweet cooing and relaxed to indulge the delight – after all she was quite a catch, and why should he not bask in his good fortune? It was pretty obvious from their disparate appearances that he must have other powerful fields of attraction, no doubt both cerebral and sexual. Newcomers to the carriage would simply have noted a devoted couple, his arm now around her shoulder, her head dreamingly under his chin, but there was tension in the air lest she believed they were curled up at home and displayed a little too much ardour. This was dispelled, however, by his now confident demeanour – *this is my girl and I know I've charmed her, but I won't let her get out of hand.*

She did, however, get out of hand. The train came to a very active halt at the next station. The sudden arrest jerked the drunken girl back to life, her face twisted with twin realities: she had coiled herself into a perfect stranger's lap, and she had missed her stop. What the ... Oh my God I've missed my stop ... words left in the air as she sprang to her feet, one foot working purely on reflex to the sound of the closing doors, and the other surging forward on the power of mortification. She was gone – or rather she was on the platform striding into welcome anonymity, walking more upright at each step.

There was no such salvation for our hero, or rather our impostor, now trapped with more witnesses to his presumption, to his inglorious reflection, than his deflating ego could bear. He sunk slowly into his seat, his corporeal presence perceptibly shrinking, but his flushed face a beacon to his misery. His eyes, now watering with humiliation, only saw the doors, the doors through which he would soon pass – portals back to a safer level, a lower profile.

Without containment there can be no pressure; without

the containment of some sympathy toward the chief protagonist of this tragicomedy, without the social deterrent of inappropriate laughter, the pressure would not have built. Olly was holding his breath, or at least trying to control his breathing, keeping his shoulders from shaking, not wanting to be unkind – no *schadenfreude* here – but the situation was genuinely comic. It contained all the pith and sap of great humour: the element of surprise, an immediately comprehensible resolution to incongruity, some hubris and pain, all with exquisite timing.

Olly was already tense from the pregnant moment started by the American's light remark. He could also feel tension in the girl on his right, but now, for different reasons, could not make eye contact. Similarly the other witnesses to this scene were all trapped in the same high-pressure zone, with the same compression of their natural instinct to laugh. Eye contact was inadvisable – any acknowledgement of the situation would release a bursting of the banks, a bursting of sides. Composure was holding … only a few more minutes till the next stop … he will get off for sure … oh no don't think of him … don't think of anything … the slightest titter … oh no, it would be so rude … blank your mind … think of something serious … he looks serious … oh no, not yet.

The signs of collapse were there: some faces were vein-popping red, others ashen with concentration – minds searching for emptiness. Was that a stifled giggle? Please, no, we're not quite there. Our man was standing at the doors, fulfilling all expectations, his back now turned to the growing audience, tempting them to let go, but still decorum was maintained. Dark windows became transparent; the next station was there, the train slowing … this was too much … silent giggles spawned more … a contagion was spreading exponentially. At the moment the doors opened, Mr Hubris was blown out by an explosion of pent-up howls and shrieks, the discharge bowling him along the platform, and finally into the soft cradle of oblivion.

In the carriage the recoil was seismic. Olly and the girl were at the epicentre of what became a cerebral event, their neural paths open to endless permutations of comic potential. Laughing subsided only for a chortle to reactivate the synaptic connections, and reduce a dozen people to uncontrollable states. Olly and the girl had found refuge from their awkwardness in the hapless tableau, but now he looked at her and she met his gaze. This time they did not shy away. They had shared a random event, and their residual giggles were becoming somehow more personal. They had known each other now for a long time, long enough to recognise the aura, which seemed to promise a complete and natural fit.

She shed a tear, saying that it was a long time since she had laughed, and that it was a pity it should be at someone else's expense.

'If that chap has any humanity,' Olly grinned, 'he would have a good laugh too when he gets home.'

They were gripped by the mirth again, this time just the two of them, jointly and severally, now it was just them rocking helplessly on their seats, gasping for oxygen. The breathtaking convulsions subsided; they were safe from a side-splitting end – they had survived. They had shared danger. The girl's eyes still brimming with tears of laughter, cleared enough for her to give Olly a look that seemed to say 'Do not ever leave my presence.'

Their mutual feeling was more than attraction; it was as if their every cell was signalling a perfect match, every part complementary, every impulse to be joined at the very soul was requited. Olly was now also thinking 'Do not ever leave my presence.'

She looked down, but Olly could see that the drops that

7

fell onto her hands, and onto the case on her lap, were too big for laughter; their plashes came from a font of sadness. He put his hand on hers, both hands now baptised by her tears.

'Why so sad?'

She held his hand with firmness, with possession. Her head tilted to him, her hair brushing his cheek.

'It's because I'm only dreaming,' she said, 'or if it's real, you will get off and they will then laugh at me.'

'I'm not getting off and I don't have a stop.'

'Neither do I.'

'In any case this is the Circle Line.'

It wasn't, but they chuckled at the fun in Olly's reply.

Nature is elementary … The forces that govern its laws are elemental but nature has learnt to combine the elements in multitudinous chemical reactions. It has worked out which molecules attract and which repel, and followed this by an ever-responsive organic evolution that relies on an infinite combination of factors, not least of which is attraction. Right down to the level of individual human beings, nature has woven intricate strategies that we are powerless to ignore.

Nature is clever. It has programmed us humans to seek out partners by reference to a panoply of attractions – some physical, some social, some more cerebral – but the ingenious bit is to build in a filter of the attainable. It doesn't always work, as some unrequited lovers will testify – misery can lie ahead – but when an attraction is reciprocated, a circuit is switched, a reactor is unchained with limitless power for passion and ultimately fusion. What might have been a simple charm or fancy can turn into a deep and all-consuming desire. Love can be allowed to want; love can be permitted to embrace the risk. Love can offer no resistance to the chemistry.

Our American, still standing a few steps away, despite legs weakened by the considerable weight of mirth, was looking over them with some ownership, some involvement in what had passed between them. He had after all introduced them.

A little after that last chuckle, the girl's face suddenly drained of colour – Olly felt her tense, a catch in her breath. It was confirmed; there was something wrong. The next moments were a blur. Olly was spinning, reeling in the vortex from the speed of events. Matter was unwinding, the reaction was unstable. The train was at a station, the doors had opened, the girl was in a state of utter distraction, complete apprehension. At the click of the door closure, and in one movement, she had pushed her case into his hands, springing from her seat to the now closing doors. The break was not quite clean, the doors closed on her, sensors registered an obstruction, then they opened momentarily just a few inches and she was gone. Those few inches were enough for a pair of strong hands to force a gap, a parting large enough for a man to squeeze through. The gap was sustained by a second pair of hands – those of the American, who was just a stride behind. The American had been quick. He had perceived the look of recognition on the girl's face, and followed the direction of her fear to the same man who had started up the instant she had made her break. He seemed to size up the situation in a split-second, his large shoe jamming against the doors and preventing the closure mechanism completing its cycle on its second attempt. 'I'm on it' – his words directed at Olly as he forced his big frame through the doors in full pursuit.

Olly was on his feet, but the doors were now firmly together and the train was accelerating into the tunnel. His last vision was of two men running pell-mell along the platform, past bemused or frightened commuters. He saw the

American's leading foot swing forward like that of a long-jumper; it was enough to catch the heel of the pursued. He appeared to take a running dive as if into a pool. As the tunnel closed around Olly, he didn't see that the man did indeed finish up in a pool – a pool of his own blood.

The lights of the station were behind, the carriage windows now black again, showing only flickering images of the interior. Olly's world had no aspect, just reflections. For some minutes he existed only as a discarnate puff, a discontinued entity. But he had the girl's case in his hands on top of his own battered satchel. Olly re-condensed; the sight of this tangible evidence returned his sentience. There were no markings on the case, no clues to a name. He remembered her tears – the baptism, we should have got names! He looked down; there were still drops on his hands, the soft dew of her tears. He put them to his lips; salty with emotion, they alerted the last of his senses – taste – and it was the most tender.

The next stop seemed to take hours, valuable time being lost before he could retrace back to the last station. It was fifteen minutes before he was on that same platform. The few people who were waiting were boarding as Olly was alighting. He had to be quick, so asked to no one in particular, 'Did anyone see a man falling?' 'Yeah, think they took him up ... didn't look too ...' – a voice cut off by the departure.

Olly took the elevator to street level. The station exhibited no unusual activity, no climactic end to a great chase. A cleaner was mopping up a spillage – no he hadn't seen no one, though he had washed off some blood from the eastbound down below; probably some drunk this time of night.

Olly descended to the platform. Perhaps they would return – back to the last known location – that's what he was always taught to do if lost. He sat for an hour, studied every poster, looked up at every approaching passenger, read every gem of graffiti, but the writing on the wall said it was all in vain.

On his lap were two bags: her music case and his old satchel. The music was for violin – comprehensive pencil-led notes showed signs of serious study but no indication of ownership. Ownership ... Olly grabbed his own bag, his thoughts seized by a possibility and a little hope. Attached to the handle of his own bag was a label from an exhibition he had been part of last year. The battered card displayed the barely legible inscription 'Mr O. Landing RBS'. Did she notice it, did the American notice it? He seemed so savvy, he had said the words 'I'm on it' with an implicit 'I'll get back to you' hanging in the air. Could someone trace him from that tag? Possibly with some perseverance.

Olly turned for home; he needed to be a fixture – he needed to be contactable. If he had left no tracks, he should make some – he was not entirely without repute in this city.

2

It was quiet in the flat when Olly got home. He had expected to find his father and Phil, his father's oldest friend, waiting for him. Phil was just back from China and they were going out to celebrate his latest victory over poverty and good taste. He was a trader in general merchandise who based his success on simple certainties. He believed that the important thing was money circulating; it didn't matter whether the goods it bought were essential and useful items or ephemeral trifles – after all, he would claim, we had enough stuff anyway. It was good, however, to support production and trade from less developed societies, and if, in so doing, a tiny percentage was added to Phil's account for a rainy day, he would moisten his palm with anybody. Phil was also a treasury of wisdom, some homespun and some worldly.

Olly looked for a note from his dad, gently mocking his lateness – *Where are you? See you in Arthur's, nine-ish* – but there was no note, just two messages on the answerphone. The first was from Phil, chiding both of them for being out – but he would be in Arthur's; the second was from a mobile in what must have been a fast-moving car. The voice was not English but Eastern European or Asian – hard to tell, but the import of the man's words was instantly chilling.

Everything was switched off, the lines were down, no current passed, nothing existed; Olly heard the sounds, and understood them as words; the call ended, no more tyre noise, no more words – possibly no more Dad. Olly's entire physiological entity stopped, his blood no longer circulated, no heartbeat registered, no muscle activity, no breathing, no being. On car journeys when he was young, he would play a game with his dad of holding his breath in a long tunnel – anything approaching a mile would climax in an explosive exhalation, followed by a so-grateful gasp of air. It seemed like some hours before the tyre noise came back – it was of course Olly's mental hard drive assimilating this new input. Simultaneously his mind was reviewing and coordinating this appalling new information – what could be, why it could be, why should it be, why some deep fear made it impossible to accept, would his father survive the trauma? Captivity and helplessness were demons that both father and son had slain; now in one single moment, in one single sinister act, all the monstrous fears had returned.

Olly let out his breath; lungs gasping, heart pumping, he became aware of his own presence again, he became aware that he had a self, that he was a being, he had a head and a mind that was whirring and buzzing with overload, he became aware that he had a musculoskeletal system that offered physical support to the above ... In that moment, however, every muscle in his body gave way and he sank like a marionette suddenly stringless.

Like sleep, a blackout is timeless, but a lot can be done during that suspension of daily chores – the brain is relieved of whole sections of activity, from simple locomotion to high levels of imagination. The subsequent ringing gave Olly just enough time to come to terms with things. He could now think and plan more clearly; he would no longer faint from the sight or thought of the emotional blood that was seeping and soaking into his spirit.

It was Phil on the phone.

'Now then, I didn't come all the way from fucking

Shanghai to sit alone in a Chinese, waiting for two amnesic dreamers to remember the time of day.'

'Oh, Phil, it's you. Listen, don't move. I'll be with you in ten minutes, just don't move.' These were the words, but Olly formed them with barely any sound – he hoped they were understood.

Arthur was the diminutive owner of their local Chinese restaurant. Over the years he had become a stalwart friend to Phil and to Olly's dad, Frank. When Olly arrived, Phil's table was cleared of plates, and he sat sipping coffee with a quizzical look of concern on his leathery face, his traveller's face. He knew that something was up, something was wrong, and that it must concern the missing member of their usually jolly trio. His hands were palm down on the table – large hands that belonged to a world of manual work, but had somehow had a few years to recover a youthful softness. They told of their owner discovering the formula – finessing the cards dealt him, and enjoying a life of dextrous enterprise. He had been curious about Olly's breathless reply to his call, and his present mien suggested that he was prepared either for a trivial excuse requiring a riposte of feigned scorn, or to steel himself for something more serious.

He saw Olly as he came through the door; he saw his face ashen and haunted. Olly was almost not part of this world. Phil pushed the coffee pot toward him.

'Drink some of that and tell me what's occurred.'

He watched Olly gulp down the black liquid and he knew that playful rejoinders were not going to be appropriate – he feared that the one thing in his whole life that could sink him could be imminent. He and Olly's father, Frank, were blood-brothers, not through any shared genes but through a shared boyhood, a childhood without parents or domestic bliss, a childhood where they were the only constants, where they were each other's mum, dad, uncle ... They were never rivals as they were good at different things, and in their institutional world they learnt that life was worth living if you had even only one person to watch over, and be watched by, and that that person would be for life, not just seconded to you.

'Dad has been abducted.' These were the first words that Olly had rendered on that grim message. He heard them for the first time, he voiced them for the first time – it was the final confirmation of what had happened.

Phil was motionless, the agitation showed only in his hands; he fought to prevent them becoming fists, he fought to keep them open – open to compromise, open to negotiation, open to hope. Closed they could be raging fists, fearless but blunt weapons. His faculties had evolved from manual to mental, and now he must listen, listen to the few words to summarise the situation, listen out for any way to use his guile and contacts to promote Frank's freedom. Apart from Frank, there were only two other people in the world who understood what this truly meant – Frank's separation from his son and his separation from his freedom. These were Olly and Phil.

Olly paraphrased the message with what coherence he could find.

'It was left on the answerphone, in a menacing voice. It said we have your father, do not speak to anyone, make no waves, instructions will follow – a call in the morning ... any publicity or official involvement will result in harm ... your father has come to help us in our work, this is not a ransom – your only payment will be utter silence ... we have just crossed the Channel, so there is no hope of your finding him.'

'Utter silence, that's ridiculous – how can you guarantee

that?' Phil breathed through his teeth, and at the same time was rising from the table to catch Arthur's eye.

'I don't know, but whatever else, I need to keep my head down, and not draw any attention to myself. What about Dad's lab? They'll be calling by mid-morning to see if he is coming in. What I really want to do is to shout and scream, call the police, the media. I'd like to catch that bastard and throw him in the Channel – there'd be no hope of finding *him*.'

'Arthur, bring us a bottle of whisky!' Phil shouted.

'Quick as I can,' Arthur was rushing around after a hen party. 'Can't get the staff anymore, all young professionals now.' This was Arthur's stock phrase; of course they were, all those bean sprouts had paid for the next generation's education.

Phil turned back to Olly, 'Sorry, but we both need a stiff one. I have a fear that drugs are at the bottom of this, and it's a world that puts little value on life.' Phil's hands were shaking as the whisky arrived. 'These people will think nothing of cutting their losses if any leads are exposed. They live in a labyrinth of greed and deceit. They exchange fear for huge flows of loot. So much that I can't imagine why the big guys don't just cash in and take off for a quiet life of luxury and debauchery. That doesn't sound so quiet, but you know what I mean.'

'You seem to know a lot about that world,' said Olly, 'and ok, Dad works for a drugs company, but surely they're not after the recipe of a new painkiller or cancer drug.'

'Oh shit, I don't know about it particularly, only that it's lawless and there's nothing to curb how individuals are treated,' Phil said. 'I'm just an old-fashioned trader, still working under laws and customs going back centuries. I'm not saying that the odd camel driver didn't have his throat cut for shrinkage, but basically all those relays of people involved in commerce were sewn into a sort of fabric of mutual performance.'

He cringed slightly hearing himself dressing his theme. Phil had always been Olly's mentor, and had taken it upon himself to instruct him in the ways of the world, at least the world that Phil occupied. This time his world was a little closer to Frank's probable dimension than was Olly's more romantic plane. He continued in a less lofty tone.

'Still kind of works like that: if you get stitched up, no more business with them. Point is, we're now talking about illicit drugs, and those bastards don't give a toss – it's illegal and unregulated, which means that you can sell something for thousands of times more than it's cost you, and you don't have to share it out with a tax man.

'Point is,' he repeated, 'and this is the thorny bit, the only way to find Frank and have any hope of getting him back is to get to the men at the top, nobody else would have any power to do a deal. And then you'll need goods to exchange.'

'Christ, this is so much conjecture, and where the hell do we even begin to start to find your Mr Big? And anyway we have nothing to exchange, and we certainly can't tell them that after a while, in what is basically captivity, he'll be of no use to them anyway, and …'

'Olly, no more ands … unless you can come up with a positive list.'

'Sorry, Phil, but the thought of Dad restrained and subdued … the last time … the last time was enough.'

3

It was winter, somewhere cold anyway; the day was foreshortened, the night brought down. He could remember tension and hardship in his parents' eyes; an enormous event; his mother calling his father's name and his father saying, 'Stay there, I'll be back soon.' Darkness, cold, silence. Light, more silence, still more darkness. His father did not come back, his mother ... just silence.

The car had left the road just above the embankment. A family of oak trees watched helplessly. Three young saplings slowed the descent, but their sacrifice was not enough. The largest member of the group had stood for two hundred years and felt only a slight shudder as it shrugged off the delicate crust of metal. At the bottom, gorse and impenetrable briar engulfed the shattered remains of car and family.

Olly lay for two days. He had no reference point, no ledge for thought to sit on, no reason to think that thought might help. His world was the love and protection of his parents; he had been in their world and he loved it – secure, warm, and stimulating. His new world was cold, unedifying, and lifeless. He ate some chocolate; he felt warmer, but it was an illusion. Some memories came back; they were painful memories but the shock made him impassive, benumbed to the approach of his own death.

Olly was on the verge of death. His father was over the verge, but held on to life by a thread, a lifeline that would lead him to help – he only had to get up to the road, no more than twenty yards. Olly's mother was hurt but felt no pain. She waited for Frank's return – in the meantime she was fine, just a little cold. The coldness reached down, her life slowed down. She called out for Olly and Frank – she would miss them so. But then she felt warm inside; a tear seemed to burn her cheek as, paradoxically, the cold hands of death secured their embrace. In two days Frank traversed just six feet of the muddy ground; the heat from the effort and intense pain denied an otherwise raw and bleak certainty. Frank and Olly were alive when the rescue came – they were lifted away. Deliverance for Bridget, Olly's mother, was in other hands.

Frank was mentally locked away for some months, but physically he was immobilised for nearly a year. He recovered consciousness only to find his body in braces and buckles, his musculoskeletal system held in mechanical equilibrium, all bodily functions abbreviated. He could move his eyes and his hands and feet – no great reward with the main limbs restrained. Adrenaline is produced to help us run or resist; Frank's thwarted production turned to trauma. He was screaming inside to be free or at least make a contribution to his freedom, some therapy, some physio, something to build on, a tangible build-up of activity. His mind now functioned, full movement was being reached, but he did not care to let it wander, to dip into the cold sea of enquiry. There were answers, he supposed, prognoses, estimations, but they gave little comfort. Only time would cure; let time do the work, he heard. But time was not his friend; as it elapsed he was getting further and further away from Biddy and his promise – I'll be back soon … back soon. He would not be back – time had defeated them, separated them into the past and the present.

But eventually he was not alone in the present: there was

Olly, all patched up and full of life. Little Olly – barely six, but now in charge. Olly it was who teased out Frank's will, who fed his spirit. He believed Olly's forecast: that he would be on his feet by the end of the year. Olly had explained that the daily tightening of all the nuts and screws would make him over eight foot tall if he didn't get out of the hospital by Christmas. It hurt to laugh, but he was warmed, happy to find that he wanted to laugh, happy to see that his wife had passed on her gaiety to her son.

For three months Olly was taken care of in a small home for convalescent children. Physically he recovered in a month or so, but his circumstances allowed his stay to be extended. The staff were kind, and while Phil was reorganising his life to provide a settled home for him, Olly found some solace in the company of the other children. He had been in a confused trauma by the sudden stop to his given life – he understood that his mother was gone, but his grief bound him to the past. He could not imagine a replacement life and neither did he want to. Phil's inspiration to help ameliorate Olly's sadness was to give him a cause, that of masterminding his father's recovery. Phil knew that it was a risk, that a great deal of emotional capital would be on the line – he knew that Olly would not only believe that he could make a difference, but that in his innocence he would make all the difference. Knowing nothing about medical administration, Olly would do this purely by his will.

Inseparable during their earlier years, Phil hadn't seen so much of Frank since his marriage to Bridget. Their friendship didn't need much maintenance, and its new context was implicitly understood. Frank and Bridget's devotion was natural and clear, so with his considerable seniority of at least three years Phil turned himself into an avuncular figure, visiting just periodically with exotic presents and tales of adventure. Phil had discovered a talent for business, in his case trading container-loads with the third world: used plant and machinery out, and ragbags of merchandise by return. It required energy and instinct. Phil's instinct was keen rather than sharp, and he was rewarded with an operation run on strictly non-corporate lines, the perfect setting for a rough diamond to sparkle.

He always said that he had a Chinese wife, but no one had seen her. He never brought her back to the UK; probably, Bridget surmised, because there was more than one. He was a charmer, he was life enhancing, but he was impossible to tie down. His life was a game of backgammon – his skill was to make the most of each throw of the dice, any game plan revised accordingly, and continually. He needed freedom to negotiate any changes of fortune, but above all he feared the notion of too much mattering, of positions to cover, the rigour of close dependences. In all those respects he was of course a perfect friend.

Ironically, however, it was his lifestyle that enabled him to take on this responsibility, and his complete devotion to this new commitment. In the time it took Olly to recuperate, Phil had reordered the running of his business, moved in to the family house, and retained a gardener and housekeeper – all intended to provide an, albeit thin, strand of continuity for Olly.

Phil knew, however, that Frank had only a slender chance of a complete recovery; there was also a prospect of no recovery – time in a coma apparently reducing the odds of survival almost exponentially. In any event there was no other course. Phil was the tactician, the navigator of this passage, keeping the ship afloat and the crew alert and willing. Frank must be buoyed up, and the only way to do this was to keep Olly's faith firm and to support his natural volition.

'Now then, my young space hopper, it's time to go and see that father of yours; he's been asleep for weeks and enough is enough.'

It was quiet in Dad's room when Olly came. Phil could see the quiver in his lip and a faltering in his step as Olly approached the still form.

'What you've got to do is wake him up, and I don't mean by jumping on his bed. He got a bit knocked about in that crash, but they've reset his poor body and he'll be fine in no time. He'll need lots of encouragement, though, and that'll be your job. Only you can do it, so you have to be strong.'

'Is he like the children in my room? They all got knocked about, but they're getting better.'

'Just the same,' Phil said lightly. 'Trouble is I think he had a bang on the head – doesn't know what's happened to him yet.'

Olly stood for some moments, taking in the scene. A room, sterile, clinical, and still, yet intense with apparatus and equipment, tubes, wires, monitors, all in attendance on, and connected to, his dad. Phil stood back, the moistening swell of pathos dissolving his composure. He was now six years old as well, and wanted to give way to a dam of grief. He was six when they first met. Frank, a little younger, had fallen from the swing in the orphanage garden; Phil was very frightened but he held Frank's bleeding head till help came.

Olly's trembling lips now pursed, and his brows knitted with responsibility. 'Dad, it's me. I've come to get you better.'

He had been half-awake before, enough, they thought, to be told about Bridget, but he had awoken in the dark, alone in a strange bed, in an uninhabited land – no, go tell someone else, this is not for me. This time he did wake, fully; the call was familiar, it was his son's voice, that was the good news ... but the rest ... where am I?

Phil understood the look of despair in Frank's eyes; he knew that he, too, had to help pull the cart of recovery and he wanted it to be heavy with encouragement.

'Frank, can you hear me? Here's Olly come to see you, and it's time to get up.'

These were early days. Frank was a butterfly held down by pins, an exhibit, a specimen ... what else ... oh yes, an experiment, that's the most terrifying part – this was all for the advancement of science, of medicine, not for any serious belief in his recovery. Initially the presence of Olly and of course the confirmation of his survival gave Frank comfort, but he grew distressed to think of his young son being brought into this desperate and insane place, his little life in suspense, outwardly brave and positive, inwardly dangling between the two loosely retained clasps of hope and despair. Phil was there to calm them both; they were sharing a journey over a great expanse of grey and he needed to be vigilant to any floating doubt, to any wavering of belief that the horizon would eventually yield the shape of land, the shape of substance.

The certain awe in which Olly held the other young patients in his temporary home gave him a qualified measure of his own predicament. Their determination against sometimes grudging progress impressed on him the need for patience and resolve. He was too young to put this into words, but not too young to let the sentiment guide his actions. For many weeks Olly's visits to his father were met with grave sympathy by the staff, and the collection of apparatus, monitor screens, tubes, and contrivances seemed to grow with each visit. The seemingly improvised nature of this repertoire could only induce worries of further decline.

'I see they're making him feel at home,' Phil thought wryly, but said brightly to Olly, 'This place looks more like a laboratory every day.

'How ya doing, Frankenstein? You just keep holding on. As soon as we get a storm and a good bolt of lightning down these wires, you'll be as right as rain.'

There was a flicker of irony in Frank's eyes. 'Which is the button that makes you laugh?' asked Phil.

'You've just pressed it.' These were Frank's first words.

The paraphernalia now seemed justified; Olly grew more confident, unexpressed dread receded. Just being there every few days, reading to his dad, or playing contentedly with some toys, Olly seemed to emit a glow. Frank's countenance, clouded with concern and suppressed hope, began to brighten with a glint of resolve.

Once the time came for physiotherapy, Olly's exhortations made the difference between no progress and an infinitesimal advance. A joint, stiff with non-use like a rusty hinge, can be worked back and forth, any painful resistance and doubts eased by a flow of tangible results. When joints are calcified and seized through prolonged immobility, it's like pushing against a closed door. With Frank's inarticulate body, the mechanical side was mostly closed – the doors were shut. Wasted muscles needed work, but they also needed to remember, to associate cause and effect. Olly, through a combination of encouraging words from Phil, and of course his childish obstinacy, was implacable in his demands for effort.

Advance, recede, progress, regress, pain, belief – Olly experienced these words. He couldn't use them in context but he knew the context; he also knew when progress was gaining more momentum. Doctors were less guarded, their prognoses no longer confined to almost abject caution; their remarkable techniques and care were freeing Frank's imprisoned anatomy. Months of determined effort from Frank, encouragement from Olly, and some subterfuge from Phil were tipping the scales. Gradually Frank's mechanical support was taken back internally, the scaffolding was removed. His organs took on the full management system of his body – his life was self-supporting. The bar was raised; steps became strides, his heart leaping as a discharge date was announced. It takes about twenty years for an embryo to grow into a mature adult; in one year Frank went from a physical and mental foetus to a functioning man. He had observed the metamorphic process with increasing incredulity, watching his life being poured back into the empty vessel which had lain on his bed.

He had been living in the past for the last twelve months – not to say he didn't look forward to a future, but all his experience was before that time, of a time shared in good part with Biddy. Her death caused him sadness but it had a surreal quality: she was just on hold, along with the rest of his life. Subliminal thoughts that she would be waiting on the steps of the hospital, that she would delight and beguile him again, formed an anaesthetic haze around the clearly transparent fact that she had died.

He was ready at the door, the door to the steps, redeveloped, reborn, but this time around it was without Biddy. He had been searching for her in the fog with too powerful a light, his heart burning too brightly to see through the leaden gloom to the truth. A cry formed deep in his chest, the entire span of his long confinement since making that promise – I'll be back – contracted into this one moment. It was a cry of grief, recent and instant and inconsolable grief.

After a while he recovered. He looked back through the door into the busy hospital. The twelve months seemed to expand again in his mind, a thousand memories of discovery, endurance, and humanity. Yes, a year had passed, and he was now here. He left the hospital a hero, an orthopaedic phenomenon, both happy and sad, but relieved to be able to take a turn at life again, and to see his son grow back to a childhood.

4

Phil and Olly returned to the flat. On the fifth and top floor of a typical London mansion block, the original rooms had been adequate when Olly was younger, but the requirements of now two adults increased the demand on space. An elegant solution evolved in the form of vertical expansion. Rights were negotiated and a penthouse commissioned. Connection between the two levels was subtle: stairs that could be prominent or hidden behind a pair of bookshelf doors when two self-contained areas were appropriate. When these doors were closed, a casual visitor would enter a normal single-level apartment. Disclosure of the concealed quarters always produced a *frisson* – a secret door to an unexpected level revealed a glass-topped atrium with stairs suspended from above, as if entry could be withheld by some divine authority, the celestial impression compounded by powerful spotlights amplifying the white walls with domes of intensity. Anticipation was resolved and rewarded by a more temporal setting: a contemporary suite of rooms, lofty but comfortable, all looking onto a large west-facing roof terrace.

The largest of these rooms invited you to browse. Its book-lined walls surrounded a collection of desks, worktables, chairs, chests, and boxes. A sofa and two un-matching armchairs had placed themselves on an old rug; theirs was an invitation to sit and ponder. Half-opened books and papers on the tables spoke of ongoing or forgotten

27

enquiries, models and photographs of Olly's current projects. Carvings and pictures on the floor awaited promotion. It was a room that the two men shared; for each an adjunct to lab or studio; the dynamic was chaos, yet work in progress. Olly and Phil would conduct a thorough search of this room for anything that might be connected, that might give a bearing on Frank's direction. There was a daybook by the phone – jottings, scribbles, numbers, names – they both used it; reminders, notes to each other, the odd cutting, the nearest thing to a diary.

Outside on the terrace, classical statues stood or reclined amongst potted ferns and vines. Imperious and seductive, they invited you to step into their arbour to join them in contemplation. Olly and Phil stood amongst them, each man still absorbing the stubborn actuality of this new status quo. Around them the lights and movement of London were blurred by a layer of mist. At another time it might have been enjoyable to muse over the surreal quality of the scene, but tonight its opaqueness seemed malignant and unyielding. They stepped back into the study.

'Let's start by the front door and work our way up here,' Phil said, overwhelmed by the amount of information just lying around. 'This room will need forensic attention.'

There was no sign of forced entry, no obvious disturbance, no hastily written note or evidence of a hurried exit. Hallway, sitting room, bedrooms, kitchen, bathroom, all composed normally: wash-bag on the shelf, toothbrush in the glass, wardrobe intact, suitcases under the bed, car keys on the hook, newspapers on the table. For two hours they methodically sifted through the spaces. They knew there was no particular reason why they should find anything or indeed recognise a clue. Lateral thought, that's what was needed – imagining what you expect to find.

'Just a minute … Dad never reads an evening paper.'

'Doesn't mean a lot …,' Phil was a little dismissive.

'Dad rarely has visitors in the week. Probably a straightforward explanation – it could have been a mate, or he could have picked it up for some reason. It could have been left here by whoever took him, though, and that means that they were in the flat – he wasn't just snatched off the street.' Olly was turning over the pages as if a ransom note might be encoded.

'If so, presumably he let him or them in willingly,' said Phil, a little less indifferently, at least open to a possible significance. 'He could have known them, or it was some subterfuge, or threat.' That last word hung in Phil's throat; it took force to expel it.

'And Dad would never do the quick crossword anyway.' An imperceptible breath of hope stirred their speculation, both heads now scanning the unfinished puzzle. Actually very few letters were offered up to the empty squares, but the margins were full of jottings, attempts at anagrams, simple synonyms, and misspellings.

'This could be the hand of Dad's captor.' Olly continued, 'doesn't look too bright.'

'Not too bright, or not in his own tongue more like.' Phil had never been good at crosswords or languages, and gave a faint nod of recognition to the attempted answers.

'Pity Dad wasn't here to unravel these clues …' Olly flinched from the irony in this fatuous notion. But then his eyes fell upon some characters at the top of the page, most of them obliterated with heavy lines. He almost crushed the paper as he brought it into focus – the first few characters had not been completely crossed out, and they were figures not letters.

'Christ, look at this. It's a phone number.' He held it up to the light; maybe he could make out the hidden figures. 'Or *was* a phone number, I should say.'

'We may not know whose number it is,' Phil gave Olly a rueful glance, 'but we know where he lives.' Putting his hand on Olly's now rising shoulder, he continued, 'Steady on, I don't mean that literally, but I do know that 0091 is the code for India.'

It was one in the morning, Phil was jet-lagged and Olly drained by an evening which had earlier released and then stemmed a flow of great emotion and enrapture, followed by outrage and anguish at his father's seizure. To ponder this possible clue, its relevance or irrelevance, was just too much at that moment; it could be a momentous lead or just a tease. What were they, anyway, a couple of TV detectives sleuthing their way to some inevitable denouement? No, just two very tired protagonists who had walked on to the wrong set. Phil drew the curtains to block out the glow and some of the hum of London.

'I've gotta sleep. I'll turn this all around as I go.' Phil turned it around pretty quickly: in two minutes he was snoring on the sofa.

Olly flicked off the switch to the stairwell lights; no joyous ascent tonight. He climbed with dark resignation to his room and lay on the bed. He might sleep now but he would not rest until his dad was rescued. This was a man who had devoted himself to his son, who had sacrificed his own fulfilment to repay a debt. No obligation was ever there, no interest accrued, but Frank's gratitude for his recovery appreciated for every year that passed. He had given his son energies, nurtured his talent and self-respect, and if Olly were to let him down, there would not be a puff of respect worth honouring. Olly had to accept a life of limbo until his dad was returned to freedom, and nothing would hinder this vocation.

After some slow drawn-out hours, unable to give himself over to sleep, Olly sat up. Outside, the first grey shadows of dawn were lying flat, the light too weak to prevent a reflection on the still darkened window. But it was not Olly's reflection – it belonged to the girl on the train. Ever since that phone message, his mind had been occupied just with coming to terms with his father's kidnap, any other reveries ground under the heel of this outrageous subjection. Life can present some painful or heartbreaking outcomes, situations which would make an unbeliever turn skywards to ask: why me, why have I been singled out? To see someone else singled out by another human being for some cynical gain jolts the natural angst that we all have. It calls for action, restoration, or retribution. It is exacerbated by helplessness or guilt. Olly certainly felt helpless, but why did his sensibilities wince slightly with a sense of reproach? Why did he flush at the image on the window glass? Had she brought on a sin of omission, some dereliction on his part? Could he have stood up for his dad if he had arrived home earlier, in time?

He distrusted the sleep that was waiting in judgement. Subconsciously it would scan and catalogue the day's events, consider his motives, trim or unfurl his expectations, and reorder his thoughts. Helplessness or guilt – whence the guilt? Anyway the barb of guilt is good if it is a spur for restorative action. Olly did not trust his ego not to re-grade any guilt in the milky white of helplessness, so he would allow only a drowsy rest. Let his subliminal brain do what it must, he would stay awake and do his own review.

He was now back on that platform again; he had sat there for over an hour, the theory being that misplaced persons should return to the last shared position. No avail … perhaps the same time next day, next week, tomorrow? Perhaps a poster, not a missing cat, his own mug-shot … if wanted, please call … He felt the same warm yearning in his heart, but also the cold drip of truth that nothing more would

31

become of it unless the girl could trace him. He must accept that there was really nothing he could do to bring about a reunion except wait for fortune to call. In the meantime he would keep that glorious feeling alive. Was this what was pricking him, maybe a potential lack of constancy, a less than single-minded devotion to his father's return? Would he suffer distraction at a time when he should have only one purpose? Of course not – one quest was active, the other passive. He imagined that there may be a trail to follow to his father; they had one potential lead so far. But what would happen if they found no trace or direction and they were denied action? They would be in a passive state. What if …? But he couldn't examine it further in the deep sleep that finally came and took away all introspection.

The sleep opened the doors to the formal enquiry, but his super-ego stood up to all the legal sophistry. He was allowed the hope that his passion for the girl on the train would not fade, with the whole incident entering the realms of idealized whimsy. His promise – that this would not dilute his energies or resolve in the matter of his father's rescue – was accepted. The court heard that Olly as a child had secured his father's recovery from near-fatal injuries just by the force of his will. It was a will that could entertain no thoughts of the alternative: it had to hold absolutely firm; any preparation for loss would slacken his grip. Olly's earlier experience as a young innocent was that such an act of will could be concentrated on only one object, firm and undivided – only one wish would be granted. It was submitted, however, that to an adult, an act of will was not exclusive and no conflict would arise, provided that any action to support that will would be directed exclusively to the prime objective. The argument was admitted. Olly would be released from sleep with a clear conscience and fixity of purpose.

5

The death of Olly's mother brought him times of great sadness and loss, but later the memories became more bearable, even happy. Later still they became less defined, an amorphous recall of a tender age of nurture. Children grow on a relatively fast track – every day new stimuli flash by, impressions accumulate; like it or not their cells multiply, their bodies enlarge, their brains develop and adapt to their environment.

Characters emerge to respond to the world they are moving along – a linear world where one thing is followed by another, which leads to another. The world they perceive and experience can be warm, secure, and rewarding, or cold, hostile, and impassive. They have no time to mull over their impressions, no time to dwell on the comparative advantage – time is whisking them through the preliminaries.

Canon law prescribes that at seven, children have reached the age of reason; they have travelled through the age of innocence to an age when some moral discernment is expected. Olly's journey had taken him past this milestone somewhat earlier, and when he was given back his young life again aged seven there was a certain momentum about him. But whilst he had moved on from the age of innocence, the legacy of his earlier life was firmly invested in him, those days of the safety and warmth of his mother, a regular father, stimulating and loving. He was ready to branch out from the linear world, the longitudinal path, into latitudes of discovery. Olly's life became a daily pleasure. His journey became a cruise, not in the flannels and blazer sense, but always looking ahead to his next destination or objective – each stop reached after pleasant anticipation and satisfaction from covering ground.

Father and son were inseparable. Frank had a good touch, knowing when to push or pull, subtly arranging situations that led to discovery or testing, all in all piloting his son's passage through childhood and later through fickle currents and tides to manhood. In short, Olly reached his twenties a well-adjusted young man, calm and confident, but not unaware of dangers and pitfalls. He had many faults, but his overall mix was eminently acceptable. He held himself in no great esteem, but never really doubted his ability to get the best out of a situation and to enjoy being.

Scars and stiffness apart, Olly's dad recovered physically from his injuries. Mentally, his capacities were undiminished; if anything his memories were too sharp – Frank's tender age had not really started until he met Bridget. He had bonded with Phil, their mutual dependency a bulwark against loneliness or dejection. It was a bright and rumbustious comradeship, unspoken yet undoubted affection colouring their every mood. The softer hues of female companionship had yet to permeate Frank's temperament, but Bridget's arrival brought a blush of ardour to his cheeks. These were indeed the start of Frank's enchanted years, a period of sublime, almost unsustainable happiness. It was no wonder that Bridget was now embalmed permanently in his memory. Frank was no melancholic, but there was a frailty about him when something caused him to dwell. For the most part, though, he had restarted his life on his previous model. I'll be back … He had transferred that promise to his son and he was back.

The most persistent scar from his ordeal was, however, slow to fade. The sometimes palpable fear of entrapment, the panic from his straightened body being in tight, slow transit, being enveloped in dark scanners, left him with an anxiety of enclosure. The claustrophobia abated, or rather its frequency abated, over the years. The scar grew faint but still visible enough to be a constant reminder, a line not to be crossed. Tube trains, planes, and lifts were avoided, not morbidly, but alternatives held less dread. It was not a life-threatening fear when confronted cognitively, but Frank did not want to endure the involuntary close-down of an attack if it came. He warily occupied even airy buildings, but felt entirely unchallenged in the rooftop haven shared with Olly. Returning home at any time of day, Frank would climb straight to the roof terrace, seemingly to enjoy the view or the fresh air, but actually to re-establish that he could take the lid off the box he was living in, should he wish.

The statues on the terrace were Olly's confirmation of a great gift; they took Frank back to a seminal moment, a shift in Olly's talents. His son's gift of drawing became evident when the typical childish sketch of a potato face evolved into a detailed study of form and expression. His keen eye and his appreciation of the drawn line were a combination that demanded nurture and development, but ultimately it was the third dimension which excited his imagination. Lego or construction kits were not satisfying diversions for Olly; he just needed clay.

'Michelangelo claimed that the job of a sculptor was to liberate the forms that were already inside the stone. The sculpture within would be set free by chipping it out of its confinement.'

Frank related this to Olly just as an interesting maxim and was not expecting a dramatic effect. But Olly was moved; something had touched a chord, maybe a subliminal need to release, going back to the days seeing his imprisoned father. Michelangelo and his notion became his inspiration and stone his only medium. Olly discovered the almost sensual nature of marble, soft and yielding to the carver's chisel and yet capable of being polished to a lustrous finish. The inhabitants of the stone were not rough-hewn creatures but delicate, translucent forms grateful for release. Olly had set free many beautiful figures from their crystalline prison blocks thanks to that chance remark from his father. Whenever Frank entered the roof garden he would wink conspiratorially at the marble figures on the terrace. They acknowledged the confidence with enigmatic silence.

Father and son had moved from the country to London in Olly's teenage years and were now enjoying the life of a couple of bachelors. Whilst not without suitors, Frank had so far never really developed the level of affection that would prompt the desire to re-marry. The same could be said of Olly, although in his case marriage would be an original act. How long their situations would coincide was of no great moment; for the time being they delighted in their partnership.

Phil was a regular visitor to the flat. He had taken a keen interest in certain aspects of Olly's education, making sure, he would tease, that unlike his father he developed some commercial nous. Not to teach him every cut and thrust of business, but to understand affairs enough to survive in the creative world without being constantly prey to what Phil referred to as chancers, schemers, and dreamers. Olly was now in some demand as a stone carver and sculptor, and each commission allowed him to enter a world of joyful artistic distraction. The key to this realm was a coolly com-posed understanding of the brief and the terms of engage-ment. Olly had learnt to steady his hand during these initial proceedings.

Phil's mentoring extended beyond the higgle-haggle of a deal – he had a talent for casting a subject or some of life's concerns into relief. It has to be said that he didn't always throw light onto a particular matter, but even a shadow can bring out the shape of some unexpected angle, can suggest the presence of an unexpressed thought. He was adept at questioning and sharpening Olly's personal perspectives. In a philosophical mood Olly said one day that he was deeply moved by injustice and enslavement in the world. Phil had a legendary ability to tease out a good discussion, to explore misconceptions, his own included, on myriad topics. His travels and trading in the third world had, however, added extra discrimination to his views on this subject. He had sharpened his insight on the cold hard stone of grinding poverty.

'Laudable sentiments, my dear chap, but you are still living in, and being sustained by, a city and a country which to some extent perpetuate their advantage by keeping other peoples in check. I am not saying this in a cynical or indeed a matter-of-fact way, but to challenge the superficial measure we put on our compassion.'

'A laudable qualification, old man, but what does it mean?' Olly always enjoyed these exchanges, partly because of Phil's pocket wisdom and partly because of his inclination to inflate his speech when he warmed to a theme. Phil knew he did it, but, when teased, put it down to his natural erudition. Nevertheless, any hot air in this declamatory habit would soon be released by a deflationary expletive.

'It means that most people have no idea how fucking lucky they are, they do nothing to deserve their easy lives, they have no fucking clue how the world goes round, and how they are kept in their stunted comfort.' The listener is now awake.

'Calm down, but you still haven't told me what it means.'

'It means that to most of us life in the third world is incomprehensible. The accounts we hear of grinding poverty, disease, and daily misery are occurring in another world to another species. We get these images, bites of overpowering wretchedness, but we don't really want to dwell in this vale of sorrows; it's not our world – the real world. Real world, bollocks, we are all living in one world, and if we care to look we might grasp that it is the real world. It's just graded into catchments of wealth and comfort and undreamt riches, counterpoised with areas of abject want. The poor relation is not entirely to be encouraged, not because a little support might not be afforded, but because if he got too close to the family he might realize that he had been swindled out of his inheritance. The family keep their solidarity by preserving and expanding the wealth of the core members. Experience tells them that capital has to be concentrated – capital means investment, investment means potential. When we figure out a way of sharing out the investment we'll let you know, but in the meantime we can do so little to help it's probably better not to squander the benefit.'

'You're losing me.'

'Yeah, sorry, but what I'm trying to say is that it is to our advantage not to have too much competition for resources to protect our own livelihoods. If we all lived as we do in the West, I read somewhere that the earth has enough natural resources to make things with for four years. After that we'd all be in the desert fighting over water again.' Phil was searching for a way to wrap this up.

'Don't get me wrong, a lot of people are working on the imbalance, but for most the gulf is too wide to contemplate and therefore wide enough to ignore.' Phil held up his finger to arrest Olly's reply. 'As Edmund Burke said, "Custom reconciles us to everything." '

Frank and Phil would often recount their time in the orphanage. There was an Irish priest called Father Burke who taught them English. He was full of his famous namesake's aphorisms; there seemed to be one for every occasion. Olly smiled when the association came to him, and still more when Frank, who had been listening in the background, raised his own finger to interject.

' "No one could make a greater mistake than he who did nothing because he could do only a little" … Edmund Burke.'

'*Touché*!' said Olly.

Phil pointed a finger at each of his companions.

'Brilliant and QED.'

6

The compelling sleep that had gripped Olly's attention relaxed its hold. He supposed he had slept as it was now eight o'clock in the morning and he remembered seeing four o'clock the last time he looked ... He awoke slowly; like an efficient p.a., his mind was giving him a brief résumé of the day's priorities, any overnight developments, appointments, and deadlines. Deadlines ... by this time Olly was fully alert, the hollow feeling in his stomach partly hunger but more just emptiness.

Downstairs Phil had found the orange juice, made tea, and was toasting some bread. Olly could hear and smell the activity but was uncomfortable with this degree of normalcy, this unwelcome displacement.

'Are you coming?' Phil called. 'That bastard said he'd call again in the morning, so let's get this over with so we can get down to business.'

Olly accepted the sentiment; acceptance of food implied no acquiescence, just a necessary provision for action. But he was still thinking about overnight developments and which required action and which inaction. In a dream, both his father and the girl on the train were overwhelmed by the same powerful force, a force beyond reason not to be confounded by argument or sanction, but by ... by what? This was not a test of his derring-do; it was a test of his will, his will to accept no other outcome but rescue, not to let time or distance soften the perspective. His father's return required a plan – yet to be conceived, but nonetheless they would find measures … he had no way of tracing the girl, but he did need her to find him, and he could only wait for that.

'I'll have to phone Dad's office by lunchtime at the latest otherwise they'll start looking for him,' Olly said. 'We've got a few hours to sift through upstairs. If there's anything lying around that he's currently working on, it might help me cover for him.'

'What about his computer? Do you have his password?'

'No, but he liked hard copies – *call me old-fashioned*. They didn't like it at work – used to leave the shredder next to his desk as a hint.' A weak smile of recall flitted across Olly's eyes. 'There may be some stuff on his computer, but there'll be no cross-over to the lab IT – absolutely *verboten*.'

'God knows what we're looking for, but you're right, it's got to help to know what Frank was working on.'

'Yeah, he usually had two or three things on the go.' Olly knew that the project required cold detachment and they needed to be as cold and detached as his dad's abductors. But on the other hand his brow was fevered with concern for his father and his fears were stifling any cool assessment.

'Beats me how they dream up all these drugs. Must be like looking for a needle in a haystack,' Olly added – a little idle chat was good for the nerves.

'I suppose,' Phil replied in kind, 'if you flatten the haystack and pass magnets over it you'd soon find your needle. Just about being organised and using your head, sifting through stuff with a theory, to see what sticks.'

Olly looked approvingly at Phil. 'I don't know, I'm just a simple stone carver, nothing cerebral about my job.' They were climbing the stairs, the weight of anticipation lent

41

support by this light banter. Upstairs were answers or no answers. If they couldn't find any they would have to think of some more questions.

'Cerebral?' Phil queried. 'Listen, what goes on inside your head ... how you can get your hands to turn a block of stone into an almost living figure, that's got to be in a kind of cerebral state.'

'Yeah, maybe, but it's just a matter of sorting out the eye's intake, seeing round things, almost through them. That's why we've got two eyes instead of one – that's the 3D bit. Plus I'm just good at copying things... but it's still pretty manual – look at these.' Olly held up his hands, not the horny hands of toil perhaps but nonetheless strengthened by the hammer and chisel, and callused by the rough stone

'Well I use my hands to shake on a deal, but the rest of me is pure intellect.' The glint of raillery in Phil's eye hardened, his countenance greying with menace as he stood at Frank's desk. 'But if I get my hands on these bastards, they'll get more than a piece of my mind.'

Olly, too, was tense again. 'I'll do the tables, you go through the desk.'

Frank was inquisitive by nature; probably why he was a good scientist. His enquiries usually did follow some disciplined line, whether on serious research or just satisfying his curiosity. Often these differing speculations would tap the same source, a tangential association might be brought back into orbit, or rarely sometimes left to peter out, overcome by infinite possibilities. Olly assembled piles of paper on multifarious drug matters: generic drugs; narcotics; psychoactive drugs; methamphetamines; recreational drugs; acetic anhydride; forensic investigations; clandestine laboratories; HIV and AIDS. Any continuities were not at all obvious – plenty of paper, but no discernible trail. Olly knew that his dad's expertise was on chemical compounds – his employers specialised in testing and improving synthetic drugs and also offered forensic services for divining the ingredients or provenance of illicit drugs. There was nothing unexpected in any of these papers, the samplings were unsurprising, and yet the review spoke of a broad sweep of reconnaissance. Some documents required reading beyond the title to put them in the right pile: evergreening; reverse engineering; harm reduction; intellectual monopoly privileges. The more the piles grew, the more Olly knew they were out of their depth. He looked over to Phil who was looking through a pile of letters, bills, and cuttings, marking with a red pen anything that might connect.

'This,' Olly said, pointing to the table, 'is all drug stuff. He seems to have been doing a thorough reading into their illicit production.' As an afterthought he added, 'Dad was always browsing through these journals, scanning academic reports, but this really was a determined enquiry.'

'Know what you mean, and look at this lot,' Phil said with a shrug, flicking through a pile of cuttings all in a similar vein. He knew that they did not have the expertise to make a single intelligent deduction, apart from the obvious fact that Frank had been delving, with some fervour, into myriad drug-related issues. 'He may have been browsing,' he continued, 'but he's cut out this lot. They're all about chemicals and controlled substances. Didn't know there were so many.'

'Anyway,' said Olly, 'now we have laid this all out, we need that magnet to pass over it to find the needle.'

Phil remembered his allusion. 'Quite, if there is one.' But he had an idea about the magnet, someone with the expertise to pull out, not a needle, but the thread that ran through all this research of Frank's.

Just before midday the phone rang, its tone was bright and designed to be heard, but this morning it seemed sharp and insistent like a rapping on the door in the middle of the night. Olly pressed the loudspeaker button – apart from sharing the call with Phil, it seemed right to be hands free, at arm's length from this miserable trafficker.

'Good morning, Mr Landing. I trust you have come to terms with matters, and that you will do all possible to ensure your father's safety.'

Olly cleared his throat to say something, but what to say eluded him – there was nothing. In any event Olly's vocal cords were frozen by the coldness displayed in the caller's matter-of-fact manner.

'I am pleased to say that your father is doing all he can to guarantee your safety.'

There was something impertinent in this remark that returned Olly's voice, and he replied with indignation.

'He doesn't have to worry about *my* safety.'

'Oh, but he does. Naturally we have told him that you are also in confinement.'

Olly met Phil's gaze; they both understood Olly was not in any confinement but it was enough for his father to believe him to be so, and in danger.

'There are certain papers that we are sure will help your father's new research. These are not indispensable, but I'm sure they will make his work here easier. They will make his life also a little more bearable.'

'There are no papers here.' As he said this, Olly realized that the concealed doors to the roof level must have been closed when they had come.

'I know that, we had a good look ourselves. You will

have to go to his lab and obtain them there. I repeat they are not indispensable but your father will be more useful with them and therefore more comfortable. I also repeat my advice to you to maintain utter silence ... the papers are on the subject of "Precursor Chemicals" probably subtitled "new compounds for the prescribed list". I will call you at four o'clock tomorrow to arrange delivery.'

The call ended, its demands made.

'Oh hi, this is Frank Landing's son,' Olly was ringing the lab. This time the phone was in his hand; he hoped its shaking would not travel down the line. 'I'm afraid Dad – Frank's been struck down, with a virus they think. You won't see him for the rest of the week ... Yes, I know ... Oh I see; that's probably why he asked me to pop in and pick up his notes. Presumably it's that precursor stuff ...' Olly was speaking as if he hadn't just heard the word 'precursor'. '... Diversion, oh ok, same thing really ... No, not good at all at the moment, but he hopes he can work on it over the weekend ... Well I can let you know on Monday how he's doing ... In the meantime I'll pick up those notes if that's ok.'

'He's supposed to deliver a paper to the Home Office on Chemical Diversion at the end of next month,' Olly reported to Phil's quizzical expression. 'All about precursors apparently. Sounds like his hosts want a preview.'

'Ok, you pick them up, and anything else lying about. I'm going out to see some people who might know about precursor chemicals, whatever they are.' Phil smiled thinly, adding, 'Plus I have a few favours to call in.'

They left the flat together; Phil hailed a taxi and Olly walked the short distance to the tube. Frank's laboratory was out towards the airport, about ten stops west. Olly

45

found himself on the eastbound train, unseen hands drawing him back to the platform with the bloodstain, just a
small detour, a short reanimation of the previous evening's
rapture, which now flickered between a memory and a
dream.

7

'Can I help you?' Phil asked this with a mixture of suspicion and aggression. It was later in the afternoon when he returned to the flat to find, instead of Olly inside, a large man looking like an overgrown student sat cross-legged at the door. Overall, his dress affected the casual insouciance of an undergraduate, but two incongruities turned Phil's circumspection into caution. His haircut and his shoes both belonged to a different wardrobe, probably a dark suit of a salesman or ... Phil stood over him – his head still alerted by events; he had spent the morning with unpleasant characters; had he overextended his hand? His intuition called for caution, his instinct called for combat.

The stranger assembled his weighty limbs to rise from the floor. The added resistance of Phil's hand prevented further assembly and he slumped back heavily – more heavily than Phil's push intended, but nevertheless the man maintained a benign expression. Holding up his hands, he said, 'It's ok. I've just come to see Arliver.'

Arliver ... Oliver ... no one who knew him called him Oliver. Here was a complete stranger who attempted to present himself other than in his natural guise, claiming familiarity with Olly. He was an American, which on reflection was obvious from his shoes and indeed his haircut, which on further reflection seemed to cast him in some covert role.

'How do you know Oliver?'

'Well, I don't actually know Oliver, but we did sort of meet yesterday. I can assure you he will definitely want to see me,' the American seemed aware of the contradictions in his appearance, 'and it's nothing sinister.'

'Wait there.' Phil opened the door and stepped inside. He would let him in, but not until the bookcase was closed to the roof – no point in sharing that level of information.

'You'd better come in.' Phil returned to offer a conciliatory hand, to help him to his feet, but the American was already up and brushing down his clothes, an action more consistent, Phil thought, with finer apparel.

'Thank you. By the way my name is Gus Hampton, and I'm sorry if I spooked you – you certainly looked spooked.'

'Let's just leave it till "Olly" gets back.'

'That's cool, I'll just sit and read. Ignore me.'

He produced a crumpled newspaper from his back pocket. Phil stiffened at the sight of it; it was the evening paper, an early one presumably, it wasn't yet lunchtime. He called Olly's mobile, out of hearing in the bathroom – blast, also out of signal. Anyway, what's the secret? Back in the sitting room, standing in front of this stranger, he re-dialled.

'I've got a chap here called Gus, says he met you yesterday,' Phil said, and added an aside to Gus, 'he asks – where did you meet?'

'On the subway, yesterday evening.'

'You hear that … yeah, American, large as life … Ok, no I won't … By the way, where are you? … Right.'

Olly had gasped at this development, 'Christ, don't let him out of your sight!' as if Gus might have second thoughts and leave. A stupid notion given that it must have been a determined enquiry that had led the American to him.

*

Olly's detour to the platform had been a test. He had sat on a bench and relived the extraordinary events on the train. Like setting up a dream to be continued in sleep, he steered his fantasy towards a setting where she would suddenly appear and they would resume the fragrant affair. Very little would need to be said – their mutual discovery understood, their senses flushed with sweet intention. But there was no sleep to follow that would take over the narrative – he must be content with reality. He had no doubt that he loved the girl, and his hopes of holding her wanted to float free. The euphoria was, however, buffeted by waves of anguish, tormenting thoughts about her safety, and of the vastness that had engulfed her. Her sudden flight must have been a response to some real or imagined danger. She was gone without a trace, and yet ... and yet.

And yet it was the rogue wave that had swept his father away that ripped through his delusions. He had other priorities; his father was overpowered by something altogether more evil and alarming, that overwhelmed every other consideration. Olly had not been confronted personally by wickedness in his short years. He appreciated the patterns and symmetries of life, the interdependence of everything, but where did this leave evil, this lack of restraint for people to use their minds and inspiration to subdue others for their own means? Or was this just religious claptrap and nothing really mattered in terms of the geological imperative? 'Do no evil' – that was Google's mantra, but what about the sin of omission? That required an understanding of the infinite complexity of forces that produced cause and effect. Olly remembered his dad's apposite quotation from Burke and determined not to let the immensity of the task, or any possibility of limited success, constrain him. He resumed the journey to his father's laboratory. He had had his romantic interlude, and that must remain pending. He was too raw with indignation and fear to be touched by other dilemmas, however balmy the prospects.

Olly's visit went well: he was given full access to his father's workplace and allowed to remove some files and papers. Jocelyn, Frank's assistant, remarked wryly on the fortuitousness of the paper copies as no external connection was possible to the company's computers. The extra level of helpfulness extended to him, Olly admitted to himself shamelessly, was due to an unspoken fact. Jocelyn had always been attracted to Olly, even though he was some years her junior. She liked his athletic gait and his open countenance – no hiding the mischief in his eyes. But today he was extra playful – he did have things to hide. It encouraged her own mischief; she thought of his hands, hands that had caressed every sensuous curve and niche of his female forms – how she would like to be his model. Olly withdrew, a little guilty for the blush in her cheeks.

He was leaving the building when he took the call. Never had he travelled through London more oblivious to the throng. His mind was oscillating between the cold determination essential to deal with the kidnap, and the warmer prospect of the American's report.

Gus had come from New York just a few days before. Originally he was from Montana, brought up in a small town at the foot of the Rockies, but had gone to New York for adventure after graduation. He enjoyed being out of his element, and also the excitement of discovery. Not in the outward-bound sense, as although Gus was a country boy, the adventure he sought was the big city type. Anyway he was a psychologist and he figured he needed psychos. He had become an urban sophisticate, even urbane. He worked for a bank and his job was to 'phase' aspiring executives.

He would confront any entrenched attitude he could detect, challenging the holder into more lateral behaviour. Gus could draw out the improbability of creationism with the mathematical probabilities of chaos theory – he could remove the stabilisers of secure, unchallenged belief and customs, and set people off on their first joyful ride of independent thought. He did, however, need to be phased himself; he had grown stale, the delicious sharp provocations of chance had been blunted by familiarity. He needed to throw his dice elsewhere. A city for sure, a capital city, abroad absolutely, English-speaking for early immersion ... London.

Gus was not interested in physical adversity, or survival, or distant and lonely expeditions in inhospitable regions to find himself – he had already found himself. His adventures were really a series of escapades. He knew from his early days in New York that becoming part of a 'situation' was the best way to get stitched into the fabric of a place. The expression 'be careful what you wish for' haunted him, however, from time to time, especially when the fabric became a sticky web from which escape was difficult. It did happen, it was inescapable, but then Gus was an escapologist. Surely that was what adventure was about. If you didn't regret starting it at some point, then there would be no prize for resolving matters, no pleasure in the final cadence after distant keys and discords – suspense and resolution – the stuff of life, everything from international strife and negotiation, to making up after a tiff.

An energetic quarterback in college, Gus was not averse to physical danger – a typical challenge where most people would probably not have a go would activate an almost involuntary response, not of heroism, more of gameness. He would admit to occasionally running onto the pitch too early. His first day in London saw two such anticipations.

51

He tackled to the ground a man only running for a bus, but much more dramatically he had gone to the rescue of an old lady who had just been mugged. Of course the assailant was a Good Samaritan helping the fallen woman reassemble the contents of her basket. Gus made such a convincing arrest that for a moment the old lady believed that she actually had been mugged.

The scene on the train had provided Gus with a perfect opportunity to participate in a course of events. He had been sitting next to a young man who was clearly absorbed in his own thoughts, oblivious to the boarding of a delightful girl. She stood in front of them, one hand on the grab rail, the other cradling a leather case. Gus guessed she was a musician, not just from the music case, but also from her dress. She presented herself with an enchanting disregard for colour or ornament. She was, however, quite beautiful, if a little too serious in her demeanour. Her sylphlike features were entirely kissable but aroused tender feelings of protection more than possession. Gus observed her downward glances at Olly. She was probably completely unaware of the brightening of her otherwise innocent eyes, but Gus did notice. Recalling an old lecture, he remembered the links between attraction, adrenaline, and dilating pupils. Larger pupils meant darker centres to reflect light – ergo bright eyes.

More with a mixture of mischief and curiosity than chivalry, he stood to offer his seat. She accepted gracefully, becoming aware of some new and novel turbulence as she sat. She was already agitated by their proximity when Olly turned toward her and their eyes had met, but even then none of these stirrings were expressed in words. The length of their gaze, however, produced a pronounced beating, which, she was forced to consider, was either her heart or the wings of a host of butterflies disturbed into sudden flight. Either way, she became aware of the cause of this tender disquiet. Gus stood a few steps away quietly watching this pair – both of them ruffled by warm eddies of potentially mutual attraction. What was the oxygen to enrich this ethereal moment? Gus had considered a diversion to encourage some social interaction, but a far better – and it turned out more effective – amusement was about to engage them, along with half the passengers.

Gus's eyes were wet with the mirth that had rocked the carriage, but through the watery haze he was aware of the sublime hilarity that enveloped the pair, and how it seemed to condense into a pool of shared sentiments. He also became aware, however, of another observer further along the train, an unpleasant-looking man with starey eyes who was craning and adjusting his neck like a bird of prey in flight as the rattling train jostled the intervening passengers. Gus was on a direct line between the searching eyes and the now enamoured couple. By adjusting his body to intercept the malevolent beams, and subtly note the revised position of the sender, Gus was able to extrapolate the object of the man's surveillance. The man's jostling for a clean line of vision had drawn the girl's eye. To Gus it felt that he was standing at the exact spot where their gazes collided; the shock from each seemed to leave a charge in the air, galvanising them for action.

The train had stopped and almost in slow motion Gus saw the girl move, and then the man pushing his way down the train. She had waited till the last moment to jump up and leap through the closing doors. Gus looked at Olly; he could see the recoil of surprise forcing him into the back of his seat. He would never recover in the split-second left, but Gus was already flexed. The doors were confused. The man found enough purchase to force a gap; he was through. The gap almost closed, but with just enough space for Gus's foot, then hands, he was out and on the pitch, taking control of the offensive.

Olly returned to the flat, unsure how he should greet Gus: a formal handshake for a stranger, or a high five to a person who had shared a moment and a little intimacy? Gus was more relaxed – as far as he was concerned they had indeed been part of a great moment, which brought with it a closeness that only an old drinking buddy could equal. Their eyes had met on the train at the moment that Gus's reflex had initiated his headlong pursuit; an understanding had been reached, a tacit contract drawn up. In that split-second Olly knew absolutely that Gus understood the attraction between him and the girl, and that he was doing his bit to help. Seeing Gus standing there in his sitting room, Olly felt no uncertainty.

'Wow, you found me ... what the hell happened?' Suddenly they were old mates, time served – origins forgotten.

8

Before Phil could himself ask what the hell happened, his phone rang. 'Yes ... Oh hi, Sanj ... Yeah, ok, thanks ... Keep your ear to the ground ... Yes I met them this morning, murdering bastards ... No your dad called them and told them I was a dangerous man with powerful contacts ... Yeah, all bollocks, or so your dad thinks,' he winked at Olly and Gus. 'We need as much as he can find out, and don't forget this is just about a trade ...'

Phil put the phone down. Olly was wide-eyed, and Gus impressed with the dangerous and powerful bits. Olly placed his hand on Phil's arm and said, 'Listen, before we go on I've got to explain quickly about this chap ...'

'Gus,' said Gus.

'Gus,' nodded Olly. 'There was an incident on the train yesterday. This girl was running away from some guy; she got off the train but he got out too – looked like she was terrified. Our hero, Gus, jumped out as well, quick as a flash in hot pursuit, looked like he caught up with the guy, but then the train was back in the tunnel. After that I'm in the dark.'

'I told you he would want to see me,' Gus said to Phil. 'The thing is, he and that girl were getting on real well when she upped and bolted.'

Phil raised his eyebrows.

'Anyway I can see that you guys are jittering about something,' Gus continued, 'so I'll give you the short version.' He pulled a mobile phone from his pocket. 'I got this at the airport, pay as you go – they give you a receipt with the phone number on it. I saved the number and stuffed the receipt in my pocket.'

Phil raised his eyebrows further; this didn't sound like a short version.

'Point is, I did catch up with the girl. She'd turned round to see me trip the guy up, so she must have vaguely trusted me.' Gus looked at Olly, 'But she was seriously distressed and wasn't going to stop. I called out – please take this, it's ok I'm a friend of the young man. That made her stop, but only long enough for me to give her that phone receipt. If she wants to make contact, she's got a number.'

'I presume no call so far,' Olly said, 'and by the way, how did you find me? Did you spot the label on my satchel?'

Gus nodded. 'Four or five O. Landings at the Royal Bank of Scotland, but only one at the Royal British Society of Sculptors, the only other RBS on Google. I called them, told them I had a major commission for you.'

Olly's satchel was sitting on the chair just behind them – he drew Phil's attention to the label. 'Some detective, this guy!'

'Yeah, just the man we could use,' Phil looked Gus straight in the eye, 'as long as this is not a set-up.'

Gus returned Phil's challenge with a fixed and steady gaze, and without rancour. 'I don't know what your suspicions are about, but I think your son(?) will bear me out when I say that last night's goings-on could not have been stage-managed.' The interrogative rise on the word 'son' brought a flicker of dissent from Phil. Gus acknowledged this with a nod and continued, 'All I know is that one minute she and Olly were all of a glow and the next she's deathly pale and jumping for the door, with some weirdo on her heels.'

Could it have been a set-up, and what was the point?

Any connection to the kidnap? Someone playing a long and complicated game? Would she reel him in at some vital juncture? Olly had at least to consider the possibility to eliminate it from further enquiry. The consideration was mercifully brief, but it did open the door momentarily to a cold grief, which seemed to freeze any remembered tenderness. Olly almost swooned back to the warm realization that the very idea was nonsense. What more pressure could they put him under, and in any event, why follow him onto the tube with a cast of actors?

Olly signalled his bona fides to Phil. 'No calls then?' he repeated to Gus.

'No calls, no missed calls, no texts,' Gus shrugged, 'but I'm sure she'll make contact.'

'What about the weirdo? Looked like he took a dive.'

'Yeah, he took a dive for sure, straight onto the side of a bench, out cold, blood everywhere. I go back to see about him, he's still on the ground with a crowd around him. Jeez I thought I'd killed him. I go to call some first-aiders, and when I get back he's gone. Apparently staggered onto a train going east, for what it's worth, and that's it.'

Olly let out a sigh from between pursed lips. He was leafing wistfully through the girl's music case. Phil could see that Olly was temporarily lost to them; he said to Gus, 'Who do you think he was? Some sort of stalker? Sounds menacing.'

'Could be, she was like a frightened rabbit ... but you know I'll eat my hat if she doesn't call. She and Olly had a real thing going.'

The three had been standing awkwardly around a low round table, three points of a triangle but only two sides connected. Phil needed to get on. He hadn't found a connection between this newcomer and their predicament, but there was something compelling about him.

Olly looked up from the girl's case. 'Gus you're a bloody marvel. Thanks for getting involved – you're my only link, unless of course she works out the label thing too.'

Involved; that was it, the man got involved – Phil warmed to him. He stepped around the table, offering his hand to Gus, this time in friendship. 'Gus, Phil Donahue, sorry to give you such a welcome earlier. I'm an old friend of Olly's dad ... we had some distressing news last night.'

'Oh, I'm so sorry to hear that,' Gus adopted a pale expression of sympathy.

'No, no, he didn't die,' Phil looked at Olly for assent, 'he was kidnapped.'

Gus's mournful look turned dark. 'Ah, now I get the picture ... no I don't get the picture ... here in London? What is this dad of yours?'

'We'll get to that, but you can see why I was so touchy; those secret agent shoes didn't help either.' Phil had a nice touch – a light dusting of humour can show things in relief.

'I know what you mean, Phil – the haircut as well, someone told me at immigration.' This chap was ok; they were warming to him.

'What are you doing in London?' Olly asked

'Just here for a break – to escape really. No commitments, all the time in the world, sort of sabbatical. Bank gave me half-pay and told me to hang up the suits and get lost for a year.'

Phil looked at Olly. 'Are you thinking what I'm thinking?'

'I think so.'

'Do you think the Lone Ranger here could help?'

Olly turned to Gus. 'How about it Gus?'

'Count me in, or, as they say in the CIA, Roger that!'

It didn't take more than a few minutes to give Gus an

account of the scant details plus some background on Frank and indeed themselves.

'What about that call then?' Gus was pointing at Phil's mobile.

'Right, now we get down to business, or should I say up?' Phil had one hand on Olly's shoulder and the other pointed at the ceiling. Gus followed them along the hallway to the bookshelves with a gasp of admiration at the concealed staircase. He climbed the stairs slowly but lightly for a big man, almost reverently, enjoying the anticipation. They gave him a moment to take it all in. He went straight onto the terrace. 'I'm blown away, seven years in New York I'm used to living up high, but you wouldn't want to stand on the roof.' He came back in. 'Sorry Phil, I'm with you again, that call ...'

'The call was from Sanj, the son of one of my agents in India. I did a favour for him and his father a couple of years ago. His dad owed me one and I think he may have come up trumps.'

'What was the favour?' Olly asked.

'It's a long story, but the gist is that one of my shipments had been sown with a load of heroin. Sanj had been partly tricked by the smugglers, and partly coerced into hiding the stuff – anyway he was responsible. His dad, Ravi, discovered it and went ballistic. Sanj assured him that it was the first and only time. He had tried to back out but he got trapped, not knowing how to escape their tentacles. Morals apart, it would ruin my business if I kept getting turned over, so we came clean with the British drug squad.'

'What about Sanj?'

'They agreed to let the shipment go through intact so it could be discovered somewhere else. Otherwise it would be curtains for Sanj. I got a call offering to buy the container-load of toys and I said it was already spoken for. The guy upped his price, said he was desperate to fulfil a contract. Anyway the police told me to take the money so they could track the stuff – any premium would be reward for risk. We didn't like the risk, especially knowing how these people deal with informers, but there it was. I got a bankers draft for the money and let them pick up the container at the docks.'

'Did they catch anyone?'

'Doubt it, well not directly anyway; they told me it was a long-term sting, they were after the network – more interested in the bankers order than the drugs. £25,000 was the extra and we are using it to get Sanj through medical school in England, so at least he's out of the way. They mustn't have suspected anything because a few months later they came on to Ravi for another dispatch. He told them I was only doing stuff with the Chinese now, so no chance.'

'So you met some people this morning,' Gus prompted, he was now part of the team and eager to be embroiled in the run of play.

'I met two charmless guys in Euston station – on their way up north they said to deliver some goods. I told them I was interested in earning from some import business. Don't know how, but Ravi arranged it, described me as probably evil, but reliable and of course had a good cover. Maybe he's in deep himself ...' Phil's eyes glazed over momentarily. Ravi in deep? A good thing? A bad thing? He became coldly neutral. 'No idea if they're the sort of gang that need to go out and help themselves to a research chemist, but it's a start. I expected them to be cagey, wouldn't talk about drugs. They seemed more interested in how I could launder and move some money around rather than goods.

'Probably a good thing if you think about it,' said Olly, 'it might get us further up the chain ...'

'Yeah, well, anyway they told me one of their treasury

guys would call. Treasury! Christ, who are these people, drug runners or fucking bankers?'

'Definitely both,' Gus interjected.

Phil acknowledged the weary cynicism with a nod, and continued, 'But after I left them I fretted about it for an hour or so then I called Ravi. Told him we didn't have time to work our way up a chain of devious accountants; we needed some serious intelligence from a principal, and we would pay off the favour at some future date. Ravi said the favour was already earned by him and I would get a call. I'm starting to worry about the company he's keeping.'

'But Phil,' Gus gently prodded, 'you're a man of the world, you know basically how the drugs business works, and in any event you can't tell me you've never had a puff or a sniff.'

'Don't get me wrong, I'd be happy if drugs were as legal as booze or tobacco, but whilst the business is being conducted by desperate men outside the law, it's sheer lunacy to present these people with the opportunity to amass such wealth and power.'

'Point taken,' Gus said, 'or as they say here in London … respect!'

Phil noticed Olly roll slightly at the mention of desperate men – he could see it had touched a nerve.

Olly reached over and opened his satchel. 'This is the stuff I picked up from the lab earlier. It appears that Dad was working on a report to the Home Office on precursor chemicals; he's presenting a paper to them end of the month, or he was …'

'What's a precursor chemical?' Gus asked

'Well I can tell you something about them,' Phil reached into his pocket. 'This is the complete list of chemicals that are proscribed … got it off the internet this morning – hardly confidential. Basically it's anything that can convert into some sort of narcotics, or rather be used in their production. Some drugs come from plants but need another agent to extract the essential traces.'

'Yeah I got it,' Gus remembered an old lecture, 'or what they need to go from stage to stage, opium to morphine to heroin.'

'Not just them; a lot of the new drugs are purely chemicals and they need certain other chemicals to synthesise them.' Phil continued, 'The point is some of these substances are irreplaceable, and it's hard to come up with a substitute.'

Olly was leafing through his dad's papers. 'It says here, "if the results prove positive, compounds could be manufactured in relatively unsophisticated environments, using small amounts of genetically altered organic materials, in combination with certain non-proscribed materials readily available in industrial quantities. It is highly likely that these developments could become known to the illicit drug world, so it would be essential to enlarge the list before these chemicals could be stockpiled." '

'That's quite a big deal if you think about it,' said Gus. 'Presumably you can't stop the material going on the list, but you can fill your boots legitimately till it does. And another thing: you know what you said about the bankers – moving money around, getting it laundered and all that. I may be able to help there.'

'How's that?'

'I've worked for banks in New York for the last seven years – resident trick cyclist, had to keep all the young bucks creative. Often wondered whether some of them might be thinking a little too laterally. If someone could give me some names – could be completely legit companies – maybe I could find out who they are trading with.'

Phil gave Gus a look of wonder. How the hell did we find this guy?

'Also we need someone to tell us what particular drug production would benefit from these new compounds,' said Olly.

'No one has mentioned the police here,' said Gus. 'This seems to be amateur day, if I may say.'

'We may come to that,' Olly said, 'but until we get that next call I'd rather keep quiet.'

'Yeah, but I can't believe that they, Interpol or whoever, couldn't give us some of their expertise,' Gus was pointing to Frank's papers. 'There's no way that they wouldn't be able to extrapolate some of this info. Otherwise we're just groping in the dark.'

'I'm sure you're right, but we're terrified of the consequences of Frank being hidden away even more than he is now, if someone gets a whiff of a serious search,' Phil said, giving Olly a knowing look. 'My cynical view is that the only way to get Frank back is by some sort of trade. I may have pushed that down Olly's throat – so Olly, it's your call.'

'I don't need much persuading,' said Olly, 'it's just that Dad's so expendable if things go wrong. I don't like gambling with his chances, but I think they're unlikely to mistreat him whilst he is of use. The biggest danger is if he's locked up in a confined space, or bundled around in the boot of a car; he'll be no good for anything then.'

Phil was turning pages from the pile of Frank's notes and, frowning nervously at his advice being accepted, said, 'Let's just see what we can work between now and tomorrow at four, when our man calls again.' His frown lifted as a text message came through. 'Gents, I think it's time for a Chinese.'

9

Arthur was waiting at the door. 'Ah, Sir Phil and Olly, welcome back so soon!' He bowed slightly to Gus and continued, 'I've kept your usual table free.'

'But the place is . . .' Gus started to say – unnecessarily, he realized, and bowed to Arthur graciously.

'Empty, yes I know, but we've just opened, and it's a Tuesday – why is Tuesday night the quiet one? Why not Monday?' Arthur looked at Phil with a glint of mischief. 'Tonight you have my full attention, no need for the young professionals. Also I have got your order.'

Olly understood some of the references but Gus none of them. He decided to let them have their drollery without a fatuous interjection by him.

Arthur brought over three beers and winked at Phil. 'Be about half an hour.'

Gus leaned over to the next table and picked up a menu.

'You won't need that, it's a quiet night. We'll get whatever Arthur is cooking,' said Phil.

'Sounds like a long wait, what about a starter?' Gus was getting hungry.

'What will "be about half an hour" is not food,' Phil teased. 'Olly, you know how Arthur always says he can't get staff, that they're all young professionals now.'

Olly was starting to catch on, Gus looked blank.

'Well,' Phil continued, evidently pleased with the suspense, 'Arthur's extended family has had four or five restaurants in London over the last forty years. His parents and their brothers and sisters were the first, then Arthur and his generation, and then the next. Except that the next generation are all doctors, accountants, lawyers – they don't want to wait on tables.' Phil paused for effect. 'It occurred to me that at least one of them might have gone into pharmacy.'

Phil watched the penny drop. Arthur, who was already loading the table with steaming dishes, stood back proudly and said, 'Exactly, and you'll have your own tame chemist here in half an hour, young but brilliant ...'

Arthur had cleared the table and was serving coffee when she arrived. Gus was facing the window; the late April sun, flashing its low early evening rays through the swaying branches of the plane trees outside, had a hypnotic quality. Look ... don't look ... now look. It was just a trick of the light that caught Gus as the door opened and for a moment he ducked from a blinding shaft reflected from the glass. 'My God it's Madame Butterfly.' These words from Gus were involuntary – she appeared as if beamed down from the sky.

The other two turned to see the tall silhouette of a lovely oriental girl. 'You may be a big American in a strange port, but Madame Butterfly was Japanese not Chinese,' Phil ribbed Gus, who was still caught in the glare.

She walked toward them gracefully, one foot in front of the other like a dancer.

'Hello, you must be Phil and Olly. I'm Arthur's niece Liu – he tells me you need some chemistry.'

'Chemistry ...' Gus repeated the word as if new to him; she was still surrounded by a corona.

'Yes we do,' said Olly. 'Hi, I'm Olly, this is Phil and this is Gus.'

'Hi Gus.'

Gus found he couldn't speak, but waved a Hi.

Arthur arrived with a bottle and glasses. He said, 'Liu is the daughter of my brother – he and I have known Phil and Frank for many years. We are honoured to be their friends. Liu is keen to help all she can, and knows this is a delicate matter.'

'I'm not a research chemist like Frank,' Liu said, 'I just dispense drugs, but I do speak the language. I hope I can help.' She touched her uncle affectionately on the arm. 'I know that Arthur owes you gratitude for much loyalty over the years.'

Gus was still dazzled, her obvious intelligence adding to the light, the power of a finely presented mind.

'You are very kind,' said Phil, 'and yes it is a little delicate, so forgive us for not telling you everything that has occurred, but we will explain all at a later date. In the meantime suffice to say that Frank is not too well and has gone off to rest for what we hope is just a few weeks. We think it was something he was working on that troubled him, and we'd like to get to the bottom of that. We don't want to tell his colleagues that he has … kind of flipped.'

'I understand totally,' said Liu. 'How do we begin?'

'We need to get you round to the flat to go over a pile of papers.' Olly looked at his watch, it was still early. 'Is tonight ok?'

'I'm better at night.' Unfortunate words in the light of Gus's gaze, and the faintest blush tinted her creamy skin. She wanted to return his look but her modesty had felt the charge in the air; she earthed her own gaze on the safety of her proud uncle.

It was only a second but it was a long one. Relief came when the door opened and six customers entered, buzzing and animated. Three were Chinese and beamed greetings at Arthur.

'Ok you lot, off you go – I've got some accountants to serve.'

As they left, Gus held out his hand to Liu. 'Gus Hampton. Hi, sorry if I embarrassed you. I didn't mean to stare, but when you opened that door the sun hit me straight in the eyes.' That should do it.

'Thank you, Gus. Yes I noticed that.' All square now.

'Open sesame.' Gus couldn't resist it. He opened the bookshelves and stood back to allow Liu through to the staircase. She needed no invitation to ascend.

Olly sat her down at a work-table strewn with Frank's papers and cuttings. 'I just need a clue as to what I'm looking for – some context, or to be more scientific, to define the question,' she said, putting on a pair of half-moon glasses, the same shape, Gus noticed, as her eyes.

'Whatever Dad was working on it seems to have generated interest from external forces – corporate snooping probably. Someone in the generic drug business maybe, or, God forbid, the illicit world. Whatever; something or somebody seems to have put the frighteners on him. Anything you can find that might give us a fix on what kind of operation might be so interested could be useful, where they might...' Olly tailed off. This was the second edited version given to Liu, but she was an intelligent woman who would be hurt, and probably less effective, by a cloak around the truth.

'Liu, before you start you should know the full story, and I apologise for not confiding in you earlier. Dad has not taken himself off on some cure – he has been taken off against his will, by people who need his knowledge. This happened on Monday. I have had two phone calls from his abductors: the first to report his kidnap and the second to demand a report he was working on about chemical diversion. We have till tomorrow afternoon to obtain a copy. I get the impression that whilst this would be a bonus, he would be useful to them anyway.'

'Bloody predators.' Liu's face hardened to contempt. 'One of my lecturers once said that "drugs were made by the human nature that loved money above all things, for the human nature that loved pleasure above all things". He then reminded me of the evil that accompanied the first and the degradation that followed the second.'

'Well said,' Gus declared. He would like to have declared more.

'Olly,' Liu continued, 'thanks for the confidence. I'm so sorry to hear that Frank's been, well, shanghai'd, it sounds like, and I hope I can shed some light on it. I'll sift through this lot for a few hours, but don't expect any early conclusions. I like to circle a problem like a cat with a mouse.' Gus thought of the word he was looking for – feline, that was the one. But more importantly she was intelligent and organised – she would bring some scientific method to the enquiry. If there were clues there she would find them – after all, light only travels in straight lines.

Partly for practical reasons, and partly to remove Gus from Liu's glow, Olly called him over. 'Where are you staying in London?'

'I checked in to a little hotel in Bayswater, just a small bag and a few books.'

'Yeah, I saw the kind of book you read. Was that in English?'

'The one on the tube? Yes, that was English, but I do know what you mean – incomprehensible. I've read a few like it in my time, but that one was totally unnecessary; left it on top of a vending machine.'

'Gus we have plenty of space. Why don't you check out of your hotel? You're welcome to stay here.'

'That would be just great – I might just do that now while the inscrutable Miss Liu stalks her prey.'

'You said that with great admiration.'

'Absolutely, but strictly as one scientist for another ... ok, I'll be an hour or so, and thank you.'

Phil was back at the desk, brows knitted, sifting again through the notes and pads in search of a word, a name, something scribbled absent-mindedly – of no great moment at the time, but some connection in retrospect. But there was no new information to look back from. He looked over at Liu; he, too, with admiration, but, unlike Gus, Phil admired her like a daughter. His own daughter would have been this age – she even looked alike, although she was only half-Chinese. But that was ten years ago. He had had a wife in China. Mother and child had died in the same outbreak of meningitis, leaving Phil emotionally an orphan again. A sad memory but one he tried not to indulge too often. He would cast his mind back further in time to a period before them, inevitably his early life with Frank. And Frank was now his current agenda, but were they really going to find his escape clause amongst all these papers? Perhaps there was more chance shaking a stick over them to divine a direction. But he closed his mind to negative thought; he closed his hands too – you can't be a cynic with tight fists.

He then settled into an armchair to examine the phone number obliterated on the newspaper – every angle; every different light; even the underside of the paper – in the forlorn hope of making out the figures beneath the hard sweeping lines. He lay back and closed his eyes; maybe his subconscious could unravel the shapes now etched into his brain.

Outside the terrace was on fire with the dying rays of the sun. Olly stood by the door; he felt dwarfed by the spectacle. It was impossible to look at such a horizon without being moved to reflection: at simple times just the close of the day, at other times an overwhelming reminder of our mortality. Olly was already dazed by the turn of his day when the call from the sunset drew his attention – the dying of the sun. His father always said that every effort should be made to witness the sun's passing, especially as it was, after sunrise, the only time a naked eye could look at it. Depending on atmospheric conditions it can die in a white and grey bleakness, mournful and cold, or in a blazing fireball, illuminating the atmosphere with brilliant reds and oranges, signalling the end in a glorious departure. It had the power to amplify every emotion: sadden sad things, uplift already soaring ideas, harden resolve for good or even abet evil. That evening, a combination of meteorological phenomena brought about a rare but entirely physical and explicable event.

The green flash lasted less than a second; it was only the third time he had seen it since he was a child, when his father had managed to keep his attention focused on the horizon for just those few moments as the sun went over the edge. They were looking out across the Atlantic from a mountain in Ireland, surrounded by barefoot pilgrims. Most of them missed it, probably, his father had said, because they were too busy looking for some other revelation. You had to hold your gaze so that at the precise moment when the last bending rays of light beamed into the eye, their frequency would register as green on the retina. Nothing supernatural, but nevertheless, to a mind already glowing and almost hypnotised from looking directly at the sun, the final flash is mystical. Tonight it seemed to charge Olly's resolve. His determination had been heated and tempered by the fiery sky, then hardened in the cool that followed. He felt in control of those mental forces that might one day persuade him that his own safety or contentment must rule. He would not cower or hide from them – he would drive them ahead of him like hostages until his dad was released.

Of course this state of mind was just a game brought on by helplessness. Charge his resolve – resolve for what? Resolution required action, a manifest effort to make a difference, but for the moment at least there was nothing Olly could do but wait for a development. He looked out at the darkening sky – the evening star was already shining in the west. The others would follow soon; they had been there all day of course, but outshone by our own sun – the Day Star. But it was Venus, the evening star, that was the first to appear in the celestial vault – Venus, the goddess of love, rising from the horizon. Evocative to most, but to a sculptor, especially of more classical forms, this Aphrodite of the Greeks was an inspiration for perfection. But what stood before him in his mind was not a mythical deity half-draped in marble folds, but a simple figure of a girl in sandals, with light brown hair bobbing over dark and startled eyes.

10

Her name was Lily. It was the evening of a long day, after many months of long days, each one lengthened by an ever-present pull on her spirit – initially a pull of concern, then the drag of unwarranted dependence, and latterly the grip of fear. Her days were slow to close. Her sanity wanted closure.

She was a student at the Royal Academy of Music. She had played the violin ever since she could remember; a permanent love affair with the instrument and the music. There were days when they would fall out, when she would begrudge her constant attention, when she yearned for freedom and wildness, but in the end the beauty of the music would seduce her back. Only in her lowest moments did she have regrets over the sacrifices to her art. She was barely at the beginning of her postgraduate performance degree when she submitted to permanent misgivings – the extreme dedication and single-minded zeal to become a soloist were waning. When the time came for her to accept the probable life of a second or third violin, of just another working musician, she teetered on the brink of a world of insecurity and non-fulfilment, until the wonder of the music, and her ability to reproduce it, reminded her to be thankful for her gifts. It also struck her that she didn't have to be enslaved by the intensity of competitions, and the constant striving for perfection that was needed to reach that pinnacle of virtuoso performance demanded of a solo performer. Lily was rejuvenated by the freedom, and continued her studies with optimism; perversely, too, her playing improved, every performance no longer an audition.

Nature had been kind to Lily, but she did not wear her beauty as a lure. Her presence inspired affection and endearment due more to her effervescence and approachability. What is beauty anyway – proportion, symmetry, function? With Lily the near-perfect assembly of these facets was not the first thing to strike you. She was no oil painting; she was more, but you had to be around her, to see her from all angles, to realize her beauty. Nature had not just sculpted her according to some golden law, but given her a fluidity of motion and a clearness of eye to herald a divine composition. Lily's admirers were restricted to her closed world, but although she had responded quite naturally to them, she enjoyed only fleeting attachments. They had not endured – her real intimacy had been reserved for her music.

But now her reduced and relaxed ambitions brought unexpected dividends. More outgoing, she discovered more friends, more fun; no scuttling back to her parents' house every weekend – she had a life. Take on some pupils, her mum and dad said, pay for the extras. All young, mostly schoolchildren, Lily's students did pay for some extras – they were a sweet and keen bunch, but clearly at the end of their interest. Their instruments would be at the back of their toy cupboards very soon – their owners had more adult strings to pluck.

Claude was the exception. He was exceptional. Thirty-something, he had not had a lesson for ten years, but had played every day alone in his room, nurturing and perfecting his talents for a performance that would never be. He was too disturbed by people. His family kept him safe at home, thankful for his obsession, which brought so much joy and so little harm. His father had found Lily and asked her for lessons, concerned that Claude had reached his limits and was now showing worrying signs of frustration. She heard his playing, and was impressed with his primitive but quite musical interpretations. The passion he clearly felt for the music was locked in by his poor technique – years of bad habits consolidated instead of eradicated. She knew he wasn't well, but could see that the violin was his whole life, his only way of connecting. Maybe she could lead him to some sort of freedom if he could play with more confidence. Claude was pathetically shy at first, but he seemed to know that Lily was the mentor he lacked.

Claude's transformation into a passable musician was remarkable and quite an inspiration for Lily. In a matter of months his personal confidence had grown so much that he would venture out of the house, into the garden, around the block. Lily eventually took her prodigy to a concert with some of her friends. They knew before Lily did that Claude's obsession was Lily and not his music. Mark, a young pianist, returned arm in arm and flirting with Lily after the interval, while Claude had remained fixed to his seat in awe of the occasion. The second half was spoilt by Claude's disgruntled sighs and fidgets – especially in the quieter movements. Lily felt responsible for taking him too soon into a public place, so after the concert she made her apologies; she would see her friends later after she had taken Claude home.

After a dozen steps Claude said, 'I forgot to say goodnight. Hold on.' He turned, and, walking back to the departing group, singled out Mark for a warning.

'Keep your hands off my girl or you'll have me to deal with.' Claude said this out of Lily's hearing; he'd probably heard it on the television. The menace came out quite well, he thought.

'The guy's a schizo,' Mark told her later. 'Steer clear of him'.

But for the moment Lily had no inkling of this as Claude returned to her with a vacant but innocent look. 'Didn't you like the Beethoven?' asked Lily.

'Yes, but all those people ...'

Lily's diagnosis seemed correct – it was being out in public. But it wasn't the general public that bothered Claude, it was Lily's public, and not just one amorous boy but all her friends; they were all complicit. He slipped his arm into hers as they walked to the tube; she didn't resist as she knew he wasn't comfortable down there, though he had managed the six stops earlier. She could feel his discomfort as he sat next to her on the train, but she did not see him glowering at any casual glance that happened to land on her pleasing countenance.

Lily did not take Mark's advice, but, with perhaps just a touch of wariness, continued as Claude's tutor. Her loyalty and compassion blurred the sharp edges of the mindscape he was displaying. His mastery of technique expanded not just his repertoire, but his ability to express himself. Yet his tormented double stopping evoked such maudlin sentimentality that Lily was more disquieted than impressed by the pathos. When Claude's playing became aggressive and strutting, Lily decided it was time to listen to the whispers of her friends and withdraw.

He took it badly. When she had first come, she would enter his refuge and only exist for that time, after the lesson withdrawing into another dimension, her animation held in suspense until the next time. But then she had taken him out into her world, proof that she did have an existence between visits, proof also that she was in danger. He learnt to breathe outside his bubble, for longer and longer periods; it was important that he was there to protect her.

Lily's friends noticed his presence before she did, and

with his shadow casting a pall over their fellowship she found herself increasingly left out. That dreary weirdo would only hover around – best not ask Lily. She became tainted by his interest – what could she be doing to encourage him? Sightings had been reported to Lily before her own first fleeting glimpse. They were always just glimpses, furtive and threatening. But she still felt sorry for him, and a tinge of responsibility coloured her response. She would call his parents to alert them, but for her part would just be more elusive.

She was well into her third term now, and even with her sights slightly lowered needed composure and steady work. Up till recently Lily had never suffered long from lack of flow, that wonderful state of concentration and focus without which life would be just a procrastination … She had moved and performed fluidly in her chosen medium, warm and happy to rise to a challenge without being overwhelmed, with deep reserves of faith in her abilities. Now, however, her calm was being violated by a creeping malevolence, the creeping, seeping obsession of a disturbed mind.

Claude's parents understood. She had exercised tact, but they grasped the problem with perhaps too little prompting, she noted. Had he done this before? Did he have form? These questions Lily found herself unable to touch on.

'Does he know your address?' Claude's mother asked.

'No, but he could have followed me home.'

'Well, yes, that's possible I suppose, but don't worry dear, he's quite harmless. We can't keep him locked up, but we will discourage his outings. He'll soon get over his obsession.'

Lily came away more unsettled than reassured.

Claude followed her; he followed her a lot; he followed her at lunchtime; he followed her to the station in the evening; he followed her daily itinerary. He could be sitting on a bench as she walked past – he had followed her habits. Then he followed her home; she could see him sitting in the little green outside her flat looking up at her windows. Lily no longer saw just glimpses of him; increasingly, Claude presented himself for observation – he wanted her to see the length of his shadow. But now his sunless presence was outside her door, Lily's growing feelings of oppression were hardening into indignation. It was time for confrontation..

'Claude, why are you following me? I want you to stop.'

'I just want to make sure you come to no harm.'

'I am in no danger. You have to go home and stay away, Claude. You know you are disturbing me.'

'Don't worry – I'll be here when you need me,' Claude spoke from the heart, with concern in his eyes, but then with a neutral expression continued, 'when you realize you need me.'

His words were synthetic, their presumption implying an element of control that was intimidating. They hit Lily like an icy gust; she recoiled from the chill realisation of his fixation and that his imagined dangers could be self-fulfilling. She turned away. She still had another full year at the Academy, this and three more terms to elude Claude's maundering attentions; she would move to a new flat, take the bus home or even a taxi, keep a step ahead, vary her routine. She knew the procedures – she had seen the film; probably a journalist or a diplomat in a war zone. She made her plans – it helped in dealing with the mental assault.

Lily did find a new flat, her previous flat-mates sworn to secrecy, her times and means of travel varied and circuitous; she was persuaded that she could keep Claude at bay just long enough to finish her degree and then could disappear. But the stalking continued – not to her home, but most days he would appear outside the Academy, waiting, waiting to be seen, waiting for the intrusion to be recorded.

It was the cumulative effect that caused the trauma. Not all stalkers are predatory, but their very obsession can do no other than build up a level of fear in the victim. The fact that the fear is left to break into the victim's life suggests culpability.

Whatever his motives, the stalker must know that fear is his accomplice – together they exact compensation for rejection or lack of intimacy. At what point does he decide that its causation – the prospect of harm – should be removed, or that the delivery of actual harm should be his rightful redress? These thoughts persisted and gathered weight as the days passed, or rather as the nights passed, fears at those sleepless times that Lily found it harder to make light of.

Sightings of Claude would invoke a revulsion verging on terror. Lily's work declined, overcome by a slump of apathy. Her music, normally a sanctuary from life's wrenches, became wooden, un-spirited and un-soothing. Her beloved violin was tainted by the association with Claude's wallowing laments and strident braying. After months of torment her deterioration was almost complete, when she saw him on the underground. She had started her journey not from the Academy but from home: proof that he had followed her from her flat – he had succeeded in tracing her. This was too hard to bear, and now he was infiltrating her life at the precise moment when matter was disposing itself with miraculous properties. She felt an ineffable bond with the young man on the train and couldn't bear the thought of their kindred spirit being profaned by the neurosis of this detestable prowler.

11

Phil came out onto the terrace, to find Olly in his sunset reverie. The blazing globe had long ago sunk out of sight but somehow Olly could not turn away, could not let it go.

'I was studying that Indian phone number,' Phil said, drawing Olly gently back, 'and finally I put the paper over my head and went to sleep in the armchair. Then something came to me.'

Olly gave Phil a look of faux sympathy, 'Ah the mystic powers.'

'The harsh judgement of an unbeliever, may you eat your words.'

'Are you telling me that you've got the number?'

'Not that mystic, I'm afraid, but I *have* worked out a bit more of it. I kept seeing the letter H, but when I woke up I realized it was actually 11 with some of those crossing-out lines through it.'

Olly still looked askance.

'They were the numbers that followed the code 0091 – that is to say, the area code.'

'Which is?'

'Delhi.'

'Brilliant, may I never doubt you again.'

'I hope we're doing this right – no police and so on.' Phil adopted a sensible air, not to get carried away.

'I hope so too,' said Olly, following the tone. 'We've got from now till tomorrow afternoon to learn what else we can, and work out a response. What about those shady characters you met at Euston – Ravi's contacts?'

'They'll get someone to call me tomorrow morning, but I'll need some sort of lead from Liu as to what Frank was up to and who might like his help, then perhaps I can frame the right question for them.'

'If we draw a blank, then I suppose it must be the police, come clean with the lab, and hope for the best.' Olly looked out over London. He was pressed by the vastness of the scene – too big for individual wishes; he was pressed by the enormity of the situation – too big for best hopes. 'But I don't like it one bit.'

Liu's silhouette appeared at the open door. Gus would have been enraptured by this second back-lit entrance, but Olly and Phil only looked over anxiously, seeing just a scientist with, they hoped, findings to report.

'I've had a good leaf through everything and have some thoughts.' She joined them on the terrace. 'There is no draft of any report on chemical diversion – he obviously hadn't got that far – but piecing together various notes I can see where he was going, or should I say where he thought he was going initially, because he seems to have pulled back from what was probably his main thesis – about an imminent breakthrough in synthetic drug production from unwatched substances. Looks like the tests were not conclusive, so any additions to the watched chemical list would not be proposed.

'A similar thing happened some years ago,' she continued, 'when the term "designer drug" was coined. What they had done was to alter the molecular structure of some chemicals to get around the drug laws; there was quite a bonanza until the laws were changed to outlaw the new drugs which were being openly sold.

'What I can say is that he delved deeply into the world

of ATS – that's amphetamines and methamphetamines and all sorts of synthetic psychotropic drugs. He seems to be an expert especially on purity tests, and even more especially testing new variations of the drugs; supposed to be the biggest drug problem coming, for the twenty-first century. They are so abused by unscrupulous producers, who lace them with additives to cut back the cost or sometimes to increase the effect. Don't forget that regular users are always open for further novelty, and they can be exposed to horrible dangers. A few years ago there was something called PMA that was all the rage, until it became known as Dr Death. For a while it was easier to get hold of the precursor chemicals for PMA than for MDMA, which is ecstasy, so it was sold as ecstasy. Now it appears there is a new ecstasy – I don't know the street name, but Frank refers to it as 2C-I – its full chemical name is much too long to say. There's also reference to something called alpha-methyl-fentanyl – a cheap substitute for heroin which has caused terrible reactions and some deaths in recent years.

'My conclusions are, firstly, that there is no report about to change any proscribed list of chemicals – for what it is worth, you can tell that to Frank's abductors and hope that they believe you; and, secondly, I think you are looking for an illicit manufacturer, large enough to have almost a brand to be guarded. It could have been a distributor – they would be conscious of reliable quality – but the fact of their interest in a potential change in the raw materials points to a manufacturer. If they want Frank, it's not to run some mobile drugs lab but to oversee a large-scale operation with consistent production.'

'All we know is that they could be from India and possibly Delhi. What's the chance of tracking down a particular producer out of hundreds?' asked Olly.

'I'm not an expert on illegal drugs,' Liu continued, 'but

I know that India has a huge generic drug industry, and I suppose some companies could well have a sideline, but my gut feeling is that this is quite a big player in ATS with certain commercial sensitivities or maybe a new operation short on expertise. If you could just find the right circle to ask a few questions in, you may get lucky, and if you're right about Delhi, that could narrow it down.'

'Could you be here tomorrow when they call back?' asked Phil. 'Afternoon at four o'clock?'

'Of course, and if you like I could speak to them with a little technical flim-flam about the so-called "report" that they think exists.'

'Good. Olly, you'll have to say that Liu is your girlfriend and she was with you when they called before.' Phil winked at them both.

'Got you. Then it won't look like we've broken their "utter silence".' Olly looked at Liu, his heart filled with gratitude for her help and also for his father's character, which formed such strong friendships.

It was midnight; Gus had retrieved his possessions from the hotel and was at the main entrance downstairs. 'Come on up.' Olly pressed the entry pad and slipped the latch on the flat door. Liu's body language tried to say she was leaving, that she would just pass Gus at the door, wish him a pleasant goodnight, and leave. Gus was relieved too: it was enough that something had registered between them; he didn't want her company – he would either display or hide his feelings. He would rather she just reflected on their encounter, unclouded by his awkward-ness. If attraction there was, she would acknowledge it in her own way; if not, well he had enjoyed flirting with his own fantasy.

'Good night, everyone. See you tomorrow. I'll be here at

three.' Gus held the door for her; she tripped on the threshold – it must have been, at most, only as thick as a pencil.

Olly smiled at Gus. 'We seem to have reversed roles.'

'Ha, you mean the hasty exit?' replied Gus. 'Well at least she wasn't pursued by a starey-eyed oddball.'

'Maybe she thought she was,' Olly said with a grin

'Is it so obvious?' Gus groaned, knocking his skull with the knuckles of one hand and covering his eyes with the other.

''Fraid so,' said Olly. 'You could get some dark glasses, then she couldn't see in.'

Gus tapped his head. 'God help her if she could see in here.'

They were jousting amiably but Gus could see Olly's brightness fading.

'Olly, I'm sorry I didn't come right out with it, but no, I've still had no calls on my cell – looks like she's gone to ground.'

'Ah well,' said Olly with resignation, 'at least she got away from the weirdo, thanks to you.'

'All I can say is that there is no way she won't call eventually, if only to say thanks.' Gus put one finger on his nose. 'Trust me I'm a shrink.'

'Thanks, Gus.' Olly pointed along the passage. 'There's a couple of bedrooms down there – help yourself.'

'I'll show you, Gus,' said Phil, 'I'm turning in myself. Say, are you really a shrink?'

'Yep, you'll have to keep your dreams real quiet tonight.'

Olly returned to the terrace. He was thinking about his dad. He remembered how as a boy he used to worry about his father's mortality – the absolute and total loss should anything happen to him. Frank had fulfilled the twin roles of parents with such constancy that Olly seemed to invest in him twice the usual love and regard that sons have for their fathers, especially during the early years, when fathers, are after all, the biggest of heroes. As he grew older, the concern abated, partly due to more rational thought, and partly because he knew he was being equipped for independent life. Life without his dad had been unimaginable, but later he could conceive of a time-line with two different schedules. The fear of loss was now replaced by indescribable sadness and poignancy on the occasions when time seemed to pass as discernibly as the second hand on a watch, and the prospect was no longer ever distant.

But time is a fickle master: it always threatens to run out before a task is completed, goading and then frustrating action, or it lacks grip and slips its speed to exaggerate inaction. Olly was at the mercy of events over which he had no control; they were unfolding slowly at someone else's time, and yet his responses had to be immediate when his time came. As he stood there, the permutations of outcomes were yet to be counted – they depended on any further intelligence gleaned tomorrow – but ultimately he had to have a default plan. He'd had enough time to brood over this, and now he was quite resolved.

12

Phil was up first again – five or six hours' sleep was usually enough, especially when he was working on a deal. He was a man who liked action and inaction, and was skilled at both. To Phil, Friday evening was any time when a project was completed, followed by a succession of delicious Saturdays to enjoy the slack water of time between the ebb and flow of the weekly imperatives. Phil's weeks in any event contained no Sundays; they were best avoided – too tinged with sadness and also too frequent.

Phil's sleep had been fitful; tossed around by thoughts of life and death, he was grateful to see the sun rise from the grey morning twilight over East London. This morning he would receive a call from a man with connections. A man whose world was a network of untraceable collusions, rich but guarded, the bonds nurtured and rewarded or severed at the slightest ruffle. Someone who understood the meaning of life and death. Ravi had said he was a dark but curious man from whom a favour was owed.

'Do not under any circumstances acknowledge that you should return the favour if he is of help – the matter is then closed.'

The call came at seven o'clock. 'Mr Donahue, I understand you wish to speak to me on a personal matter.'

'Yes, if you are a colleague of Vinod's.'

'Loosely. Come to my hotel; breakfast is at 8, Grosvenor House, Bordeaux Room – I'll be sitting under the flowers.'

A man who gave little away, not even his name, Phil thought.

'Your friend Ravi has been particularly helpful to us and we are always ready to return a favour.' No preliminaries – just straight to the point.

He was sitting under an enormous art deco jardinière overflowing ostentatiously with fresh flowers – the proximity, Phil dryly noted, appropriate for a man in need of a nosegay. Nevertheless, tainted as his business might be, he exuded wealth, power, and confident disdain. A man of Middle East origins, probably a shadowy figure, yet dressed to be noticed.

'Of course he had little choice, but nonetheless we are grateful.'

'Good morning ... Phil Donahue, Mr ...?'

'Just call me Qasim, that's my name here in London. What is your question? I understand my colleague Vinod was a little too reticent for you yesterday.'

'My question concerns the identity of a drug operation. They have coerced a friend of mine into their employ in the mistaken belief that he could be of use to them.'

'Coffee and a little toast? Good – we must take care of our figures. Figures are important to me, especially the ones on my bank accounts, and of course on my mistresses!'

Why is he even bothering trying to impress me, Phil thought. Maybe just the habit of a man denied public acclamation for his talents.

'My guess,' Phil continued, 'is that the operation is centred on Delhi, and it produces synthetic drugs, amphetamines and so on, and either it has problems with quality control or innovation, or maybe it's a start-up looking for expertise. Whichever, they have need of a good research chemist.'

'Ah the murky world of drugs,' Qasim crossed himself speciously. 'Long may they be illegal. The only trouble is that being outside the law, everybody behaves outside the law – in whatever way is appropriate.'

He chewed slowly on a piece of toast. There was a knowing look to him; he had some knowledge and he would enjoy spending it.

'I believe the people you need to speak to are not in Delhi or even in India ... they are in Hong Kong.'

There was a pause, a pause long enough to prompt Phil's line.

'Why?'

'The Indian pharmaceutical industry is huge, and its offshoots ... shall we say below the line? ... are well provided for with expertise. They would have no need of importing any. What I can tell, however, is that in recent years, the Chinese have been trying to establish bases in India, especially I understand around the Delhi area. They are organised, industrious but ... unwelcome.'

'Why do they persevere?'

'Because of plentiful supplies of raw materials and access to markets, but above all the absence of capital punishment for those caught. That can be a powerful deterrent to recruitment at home. In China, executions are the ultimate penalty for a variety of State displeasures.' Qasim paused to let the chill in the thought encroach.

'I will give you a name and it will be up to you to convince him to take you further. I will of course give you a reference. Do you still have rooms in the China Merchants Tower?'

Phil was impressed – he had done some homework.

'Just the one room and a desk.'

'That's enough. Get there as soon as you can. I will arrange for you to be contacted. One last thing, Mr

Donahue. My assumptions are intelligent, but they are built on the foundations of your own guesswork. If between us we have managed to solve a problem, then I look forward to celebrating that at a later date.'

Before Phil could think up a way to parry that last remark, Qasim's phone buzzed and he held out his hand to him to signal the end of the interview.

Phil left the cultivated opulence of Qasim's setting, hailed a taxi, and called the flat. 'I'll be back in fifteen minutes. Is Olly there and is there any food? I'm starving.'

'Breakfast, yes, but Olly, no,' said Gus. 'He left about eight – didn't say where.'

Phil called his mobile. 'Olly, where are you?'

'I'm in my studio, just tidying up a few things. Did you speak to your contact yet?'

'I've just had a cup of coffee with him – he left me with an interesting notion.'

'Which is?'

'That some Chinese are at the back of it. More later. Make sure you're back by three.'

Olly's tidying up was actually more of a closing down. The unfinished pieces would have to wait some time for final release, but unlike his father, for them time was not of the essence.

'More eggs, Phil?'

'Thanks, Gus, I'm fine. This is my second breakfast, although it's true that my first was just a piece of toast and I didn't eat that.'

'Olly said you had a breakfast date. Doesn't sound like it was up to much.'

'It was all I could wish for – abrupt and to the point. But it wasn't food that was on the table, if you know what I mean.'

'Just so, but what did you learn?'

'I'll give you both a run-down when Olly gets back, but first, as you missed Liu's thoughts last night, I'll fill you in.'

Gus listened attentively, although he did once fade into a reflection on Liu's night thoughts: were they the same as his own? Phil was scant on detail, but the detail was not vital; the profile in essence was very simple.

'Do you mind if I have a couple of hours up there? I might just see something else in those papers.'

'Like what was in his head?' replied Phil, thinking of Gus's speciality. 'Sure, help yourself, but I think Liu's probably told us what he was working on.'

'Absolutely crucial, I agree, but there may have been other things on his mind. I might pick up a nuance here or there.'

In the event, Gus spent the entire morning and half the afternoon sifting and cogitating in the workroom. He looked at the threads of association between Frank's various researches; he could not appreciate the chemical data particularly, but he could see how the overall drift would lead to Liu's appraisal. She had connected all the references to the world of illicit drugs and come up with the best advice for this afternoon's call. There were, however, other lines of enquiry which had nothing to do with recreational drugs. No surprises there, and certainly the drug barons would not be turned on by considerations of global health, drug patents, or a third world AIDS epidemic.

There was a plethora of wordy study papers on the subject of new-generation AIDS drugs and delivery programmes, and, looking at the acerbic margin notes, Gus could see that Frank was quite exercised about this, especially the still prohibitive cost to poor countries, and the lamentable ignorance not just from simple or superstitious people, but from western countries who, Frank had scribbled, spent more money researching hair restorer than antiretroviral drugs. For the moment at least this was more an interesting background to Frank the man than to his present predicament. However, Gus had a compelling feeling that in the blur of so much subject matter there was a substance that events might bring into focus.

'Well, Dr Freud, did we miss anything?' Phil appeared at the door.

'Nothing to unseat the theory proposed.' Gus looked down his nose in mock pedantry.

'Olly's back and Liu's here too.' Phil announced, and, with a wink, added, 'She hasn't changed her position either, having slept on it.' This was pure mischief from Phil. Gus yielded with a sheepish grin.

For what it was worth, the response was agreed. Only Olly would speak, with contributions from Liu where appropriate. The phone would be on loudspeaker so all three could hear. Phil's intelligence about the Chinese gave Olly some courage that there would still be avenues to follow even if the call came to an abrupt end. But that would only pertain if indeed India were the host country. Olly prayed this was so and that he could get an acknowledgement of the fact. He wanted the facts to fit their theory, a theory, it had to be admitted, that turned on the single pivot of a phone code, quite possibly that of just someone's grandmother. Olly began to expect less and less from the awaited call; he realized that his default plan was actually the only plan.

At exactly four o'clock the call came through, the malevolence of the voice amplified by the loudspeaker.

'Good afternoon, Mr Landing. I trust you have had a productive time.'

'How is my father?'

'He is as well as can be expected after his long journey and he is anxious to start work.'

'I very much doubt that; he is a poor traveller.'

'Can we get to the point please ... the report?'

Rather testy, Olly thought. Maybe I have touched a chord here.

'Ah, the famous report.'

Olly was feeling a little unruly, relieved after the anticipation and dread, that the contact was now on the line, and that they might have some interaction, that he may be allowed an appeal on the grounds of his father's obvious incapacity.

'Since we spoke last I have looked into Dad's work and I have to compliment you on your choice.'

'Without the report your father is one of many.'

'I fear that will be the case even with the report.'

No answer.

'You will appreciate that it would be the easiest thing for me to give you the report in the hope of making my father's situation ... as you say... more bearable.'

Silence.

'The fact is the report does not exist. You are misinformed.'

'On the contrary, we have had reliable information for some time that it was in preparation. Please make up your mind. More than your father's comfort is at stake.'

Olly no longer felt wilful; he felt deadened by the caller's easy threat. But what did he expect? This would be written on the man's CV: heartless – yes; mercenary – yes; shameless – certainly; can you close a deal? – yes. Ideal. Don't forget that, Olly. This is just business.

'I understand your threat, and I am sickened that I can do nothing to assuage it. There is, however, someone here who has helped me understand the turn of events. Do not concern yourself that any confidences have been broken – my girlfriend, who is a trained chemist by the way, has been with me for each of your calls.'

Olly, hands on head in anguish, turned to Liu.

'You are correct about the preparation of the report,' Liu started in moderating tones, 'and I can appreciate the great interest it would arouse in the world of synthetic drugs, especially the clandestine world ...' Pausing over these words brought no response; she continued, 'I have inspected all the notes and preliminaries that we could find and I can tell you that the new syntheses depended on unconfirmed experiments. The anticipated results did not materialise and the whole basis for concern on the new structures has evaporated. The report was aborted two weeks ago.'

'Such a pity for Frank, young lady. I hope that your boyfriend trusts your judgement.'

Gus scribbled on a scrap of paper, 'Frank – he called him Frank', and held up two thumbs. Olly thought he understood; the caller was trying to suggest a little empathy between himself and Frank. 'He's wheedling,' Gus's note continued.

'I trust her advice implicitly,' Olly replied. 'She has also told me the kind of organisation you represent, and why they need my father's expertise – testing and quality control, I gather. She has even worked out where he is likely to be.'

'The young lady is very presumptuous, but no matter. Mr Landing I leave you with this comment: should we find the report is eventually published, we will have no hesitation in showing our displeasure. Goodbye.'

'Wait.' Olly almost cried into the phone, followed by a long pause; he hadn't had time to develop the subject of his father's incapacities. He fully imagined that his father's condition after two days of presumably close confinement would be dire, but also that his captors might reasonably assume it to be only a temporary state. There was a fine line between explaining that he would not improve – that his utility was doubtful – and avoiding the corollary that he was expendable. The fineness of this line seemed to taper to breaking point as Olly wrestled with the quandary.

'Wait,' he repeated, 'there is something you must know.'

'There, I knew we would understand each other.'

'It is you who must understand me,' said Olly assertively. Gus, Phil, and Liu all looked uncomfortable – Gus mouthed 'Steady!' 'You may think that my father is suffering from travel sickness,' Olly continued, 'but you need to realise that he will not recover.'

'Again, Mr Landing, that will be a pity, but what will be will be.'

'But I can affect what will be. My father suffers chronically from severe claustrophobia. Any slightest closing in of his environment brings on a completely involuntary collapse. Neither reason nor threat will alleviate the condition. My proposal is to deliver myself into your hands as surety. You can then give my father the degree of freedom he will need to be of use to you. You will have one of the best research chemists in his field to help with your production.'

'A charming suggestion – but completely unworkable.'

Olly felt low. He was playing against someone with a better hand. Actually it was not a better hand – Frank had not been a good choice, and this man might throw in his hand eventually, and with it Frank. Olly had two more cards to play.

'I can be in Delhi in twenty-four hours.'

He was still on the line. Olly held his breath. His second card concerned the Chinese, but of course it was the same suit as the first, only effective if they were already in trumps.

'Very interesting.' There followed a further protracted silence during which Olly turned his back on the other three – they were generally gesticulating at the folly of the enterprise. He did, however, pick up Phil's signal: one finger on pursed lips and another pulling his eye sideways. Ok, say nothing about the Chinese connection. Olly did not have to play that card.

'There's an Air India flight every afternoon at 12:30. I will ring this number at midday for confirmation that you are on tomorrow's flight. You will be met at the airport.'

With that he hung up.

Phil was the most vocal. 'Olly, you are quite mad! You are walking into the lion's den.'

'I had no choice, but anyway just think of it as buying time – time for you lot to come up with a better plan. And incidentally I don't know how you thought we would get confirmation of his location any other way.'

13

'Hello, are you the man on the train?'

Gus was in a map shop. He had rushed out after that phone call, and Olly's reckless promise, to buy some maps of Delhi, topography to commit to memory – Olly would need that. The place was not a library but had the same hush with serious browsers looking through maps of almost unmapped places. A phone was ringing; people were looking at him – it was deep in a pocket. As he finally pulled the phone out and heard these words, he held up his hand, not to apologise for the shrill tone or for taking the call, but for attention and absolute silence.

'Yes, I'm Gus. Are you the girl on the run?'

'Well, yes … my name is Lily. Are you the friend of the young man?'

'Yes, that's Olly, and he's beside himself waiting for a call. Are you ok?'

'A bit shaken, but yes – thank you.'

'Right, where are you? We need to see you right now. Are you in London? I can pick you up, I'm on my way. Where are you …?' Gus ran out of questions.

'I've just got to Paddington Station but …'

'But me no buts, young lady, this is a matter of life and death. I will be there in twenty minutes … and look conspicuous.'

They were all ears: a drama was unfolding; was he the hero? He looked dramatic. Staff and customers alike pressed their help. Is this what you need? How about this? There were so many maps Gus lost his way. He was in a hurry – he bought them all: India road maps; regional maps; state maps; city maps; historical maps; tourist and travel maps; railway maps – anywhere within two hundred miles of Delhi, two large plastic bags, he didn't wait for change.

If he had never seen her before he would still recognise her, standing under the arrivals board looking lost and found. Her eyes were darting at every passing traveller, scanning the hurrying crowd for a man she had only met for a few seconds on a dim underground platform. Gus was just a few yards away when she saw him. With a gasp of recognition her face flushed with a jumble of emotions from embarrassment to relief. It almost brought a tear to Gus's eye and certainly a lump to his throat.

'It's you,' was all Gus could say.

'And you.' Lily held out her hand but withdrew it immediately. A hug was the thing, the only thing.

'Thank you for saving me, and for the lifeline.' She held up the phone receipt.

Gus was choked. 'You precious thing – you sweet, precious girl.

'Good ... right ...' Gus continued, and to help his recovery, 'let's have a quick drink and see what's to be done.'

In the station café Lily told Gus about Claude. The flash of his malignant preying eye on the train at that instant proved that her evasions had been in vain, and tipped her into flight. She could see that Gus had felled him, but for how long would he stay down? Lily ran up and up, out onto the street. She ran and ran, propelled by fear and disgust until there was no fuel left – just gasping, aching, disappointment. She jumped on and off buses until at last she felt no longer a quarry. After a fitful night in a cheap hotel, Lily caught a train out of London to the security of her parents' home. There she slept for twenty hours. That morning she called Claude's parents. He had got home that night covered in blood from a gash on his head. He had refused to emerge from his room since. His parents were quite offhand, suspicious of her involvement in the incident.

This was the final spur to leave the flat she had thought was secure, and to leave London. But first she had to return to pick up her violin and just the few clothes and incidentals that she had moved in only recently; nothing she couldn't carry in one go. Not before she was safely away and disconnected could she ring that number to make contact. If she was ever to see Olly again there must be no possibility of Claude's spectre souring the perfection. But then she was back in London again, if only for a few hours … She trembled over the keypad, her heart beating in her breast like a timorous bird. Every burr of the call tone made her flutter with indecision; Gus had answered just in time.

Gus listened attentively to Lily's story and finally responded with as much assertion as sensitivity would allow.

'Right, the first thing to do is get to your flat and pick up your things. We can take them to Olly's and then you are in the clear. After that … after that, well we don't know, but let's not worry about it.'

'Ok?' Gus pressed gently, with a look of appeal on his face. He had explained how he had traced Olly and how they had become friends; Lily could not deny him her deliverance.

'Ok.'

'Good, now first things first.'

An hour later they were on the pavement outside Lily's latest flat with three suitcases waiting for a taxi. It was a grey, wet evening, the sort of evening in London that only ever brought full taxis. True to form, after nearly twenty minutes along came two empty ones. They both stopped – surely they weren't after the same fare? Gus and Lily boarded the first cab and were away into the gloom with just a moment's idle chat about buses and taxis working in packs. They had no reason to notice who had taken the second taxi.

Gus had a key to the flat but he rang the bell from the street. 'Hi, Olly, I'm sending someone up.' Gus put Lily in the lift. 'There you go, honey. Just press five. I'll be up with the bags later. This is your time.'

Is there a lift up to heaven? With one hand Lily pressed five, and with the other she held out her soul, an offering to the immortals. The ascent was slow, time to compose herself – to prepare for exultation or disappointment. It was not in her gift to choose; it was in the lap of the gods.

A delicate ting of a bell – an angelus maybe? No – just her arrival at the top floor. Nevertheless when the lift doors parted there was an angel. They stood in awe, overpowered by the moment, without words; sight was enough to confirm the undisputed truth. The doors gave a click and commenced their closing cycle.

'Oh no you don't. You're not getting away again.' Olly reached in and pulled Lily out of the lift. The lift's doors shut – a buzz and it was gone. He held her in his arms – it was some time before he spoke.

'I don't even know your name.'

'It's Lily.'

What else, he thought, what else could she be? 'Well, Lily, come in. And where is that magician who went out for maps and came back with the whole world?'

'Ah, my deliverer. He's keeping a safe distance in case he got the wrong girl.'

The lift doors opened and Gus stood surrounded by cases and bags. 'I can explain.'

There were lots of explanations that evening, but all subordinate to the explanation of Frank's abduction and Olly's imminent journey. Lily felt like the great wheel of fate was turning back to crush all it had missed. She wanted to go with Olly, to share his fate, to ...

'While I am away you must stay here, fill this place with music, and keep the faith. That will be my one constant.'

All this time they had just held hands. Their reunion was too charged with almost mythical tones, coupled with a fearful prognosis of their future, for it to be other than spiritual. They were of one soul, but would not be of one body until all this was resolved. As they sat with the others, these two with a rug carelessly thrown over their laps, they were just holding hands, but love was being made.

Left alone, they remained on the sofa consumed by a state of delectable tenderness. It was all they had, hardly yet a relationship. It seemed like love; it had breezed by in a jaunty air, then to be blown away by a sudden gust of panic and derangement. Did the abrupt suspension inflate their emotions? It certainly amplified them. The circumstances of their rediscovery left them content for the moment with just sweet regard. In the early hours Olly let Lily's head fall gently onto the cushion. He covered her with the rug and just knelt beside the sofa for some minutes looking in wonder. Was she breathing? There was no sound – just the slightest rise and fall of the rug confirmed it. Olly touched her cheek with the back of his hand and withdrew to his room.

Lily was not asleep, just holding her breath; she was also holding back a tear, knowing it would exert an unfair pull – she must not fetter Olly's resolve.

Olly had time for a few hours' sleep and to pack a bag. He would do that in the morning – deciding on what to take would induce some sleep. But what do you pack for such a trip ... beach-wear? ... restaurant guides? ... hand-cuffs? What sleep came was dark with foreboding.

Olly and Phil shared a taxi to Heathrow, seats booked to Delhi for Olly, and Hong Kong for Phil to meet Qasim's contact. Travelling counter to London's early morning rush seemed to induce a positive charge to their spirits, and the unity of endeavour they shared. They didn't know how things would end, but Phil took comfort in Olly's fortitude and Olly in Phil's resourcefulness. The final approach to the airport, however, found them in silent contemplation. Phil could see that Olly was fearful – fearful that the stronger current he would be going against might just sweep him, and all he loved, away. Phil's silence was out of respect. It was no good persuading Olly to cancel his undertaking – he knew that Olly had made up his mind and that decisions are easier when you have eliminated all but one choice.

Lily sat in the kitchen with a mug of tea, trying to reorder her thoughts. Like the clothes she had slept in, they were still yesterday's thoughts; she would have to change them to fit an unexpected set of circumstances. For forty-eight hours Lily had been in thrall to just two overriding concerns: that of escaping Claude and that of finding Olly. Providence seemed to have made its inscrutable move: here she was in a refuge from Claude, only to be met by Olly's own flight.

'I've put your bags in Olly's room.' Gus gave her a pater-nal look. 'Why don't you go and catch up on some sleep.' He could see from her blank expression that her mind was railing against further reflection.

'Thanks, Gus, I think I'll do that.' Gus – the hand of providence, but was it one of deliverance? Even Gus was unsure of that.

Lily turned back to Gus. 'You know, I can't believe I am really here.'

'Me either.'

'Poor Olly, what a dreadful thing to happen!'

'Well you're not that bad, but I'm sure he will grow fond of you.'

'I meant his dad!'

'I know – only kidding, especially about the fond bit.'

Lily looked down with modesty, but more, she was shrinking from any conceit that she might want to propel herself into the limelight.

'Sorry, Lily, I was being flippant. It's just my way of dealing with this hideous business. What has happened to Frank is just about the cruellest twist imaginable after all I gather he and Olly went through in Olly's early years. I don't know the half of it, but I'm sure Phil will give us the full history when he gets back.'

As Lily climbed the stairs, she was conscious of a higher plane; she didn't know anything about their pasts, but she did know that she was caught up in a human drama of people with levels of trust and bravery untested in the thin scrapes of everyday life. She lay on Olly's bed, still warm from a man she hardly knew, but had fallen in love with. Lily did not get into the bed – it was too early for such intimacy.

Liu arrived in time for the call. Exactly at the pre-arranged time – twelve o'clock – the phone rang. Gus and Lily stood as still as Olly's statues while Liu took the call.

'Yes,' Liu confirmed, 'Olly is on the flight. He just phoned from the gate.'

'Good, he is in our hands now. I'm curious how he was able to fly so quickly – visas take some days.'

'Olly is a sculptor; he went to Rajasthan recently – you know, white marble, Taj Mahal and all that'.

'I see. Well I hope we can find him a suitable niche here.'

Gus mouthed 'keep him talking' – what we need here is a relationship with this guy, play up to his strengths; he seems to like doing that himself.

'Ha, very good, but where's *here*?'

'I thought you would know. You seem to know a lot.'

'Oh, I just have hunches.'

'You have others?'

'Like, who your bosses are.'

'Oh ...'

Gus zipped his finger over his lips, but it was too late: Liu reddened, and there was a stumble in her voice which failed to cover the slip. 'I mean the sort of people they are.'

'Indeed, well Miss, if you know the sort, then I suggest you take great care not to cast around your silly ideas.'

The line was dead – the conversation was over, no reference to further contact. It was as if the last traces of Olly had been sucked down the line ...

The three of them stood in silence, numbed by the nothingness that the abrupt ending induced.

'Sorry, guys, I didn't think.' Liu looked downcast at Gus, to whom the faintest dip of her head seemed to evoke a glorious oriental bow, supplicant yet proud.

'You recovered well, but he was definitely nettled. Still, it would be better they didn't think you were holding anything back, especially about the Chinese or any other theory. We need Phil to work his magic without hindrance.'

'I suppose if you'd worked out Delhi, they might think you had worked out more.' Lily said this not to state the obvious but to take part. This was the first of the kidnapper's calls she had listened to and she was shaking with the tension and powerlessness it induced. A few minutes before a performance, Lily would tremble, her nerves registering that there was nothing more she could do to prepare, nothing that would change the outcome. Composure would come at the first bar, on the first note of her performance ... She needed a role in this drama; she needed more than her nerves to be strained

'That's what worried me,' said Gus, and, giving Liu a re-assuring nod, he continued, 'but I'm sure it's fine. How could we have worked out the Chinese connection anyway? ... Assuming of course that we have ...'

Outside a bright morning had been doused by a leaden sky, dark and wet with depression. But the rain only registered with Gus as a gentle shower sprinkled with heaven-sent opportunity. He offered to accompany Liu to the tube station – to walk out with her huddled beneath a shared umbrella was the perfect next step for Gus, an ideal way to test for moisture in their otherwise temperate responses to each other.

'I'll be back in half an hour.' Gus walked Liu out, arm in arm even before the umbrella went up.

14

Twenty minutes later a ring at the flat door brought Lily, now alone in the flat, to the spy-hole. At first all she could see was a large bunch of flowers, but the holder stepped back and smiled, always a pleasure to deliver flowers. He looked respectable enough through the distortions of the fish eye.

Lily opened the door to a large man of indeterminate but probably oriental origins.

'Hello, are you Olly's girlfriend?'

'Yes,' Lily replied – she thought she must be – and put out her hand to take the bunch.

In a second the flowers were under her feet and she was being dragged out of the door.

'Scream and I will kill you.'

Lily's slender wrist was being crushed, pinioned in the clamp of his monstrous fist, her arm twisted up her back as he manhandled her into the lift. Her cry for help came regardless of the threat, as much as from pain as from alarm. His free hand sprang to her mouth, stifling further sound. Lily fell silent anyway as they descended; she knew that her life was in his grip, the grip crushing her left wrist, the wrist that contained twenty years of daily practise, the wrist that would manipulate her fingers to produce the pitch and vibrato to attempt the music of the angels on the most devilish of instruments.

He felt her shrug into a limp, quiescent state, overpowered – she would come without a struggle. He relaxed his grasp, but still with his hand over her mouth he wheeled her across the entrance hall and out into a grey cloudburst. The only people still out were scurrying for cover, too busy to notice her being bowled along by her companion; they were just another couple running headlong this way and that. Lily had had a plan, but the possibility of drawing attention to her own peril in the maelstrom that was sweeping the streets clear of people, and of citizenry concern, she now accepted as remote. Nevertheless there were outcomes that impressed her. Never in her life had she inflicted pain purposefully on another human being, but in her feigned resignation she had had time to become indignant, to bare her teeth against any qualms.

As they descended the steps to the street, Lily opened her mouth to let out a high-pitched scream. The thug's hand immediately drew tighter across her mouth – her opening mouth. A small but sudden twist of her head brought two of his fingers within range of her teeth. She closed her jaw with such ferocity that his screech was louder than hers. With his fingers locked in this terrier bite, he had no option but to drop her arm – one blow with his free hand, he supposed, and she would lose her bite and probably the vicious teeth as well. But Lily had felt her release, and before his hammer fist could complete its trajectory, she had let go her bite and was out of reach.

It was a good plan, but ultimately it depended on aid arriving from others; she could never outrun this now wild creature. That afternoon only one person witnessed her distress, the only person not bound up in his own flight. He had been standing in a doorway, fixed to his post, insensible to the storm. A tempest hit him, however, at the moment that Lily appeared, in a life-and-death struggle. His reflexes were fast: in a split-second, he was accelerating toward

Lily's assailant – he caught him from the side, the combination of their two momentums carrying them both out over the edge of the pavement. There was no screech of tyres, just a sickening thud, as the truck hit them.

Lily stopped; she looked back – there were two bodies on the side of the road. The mingling blood from the two shattered skulls was being washed away in the flood with almost undue haste. Nausea and shock stood aside remorsefully for a more confused set of emotions when she recognised Claude. Lily fell to her knees, lashed by waves of sorrow and relief, gratitude and pity, but the wave that engulfed her was guilt. To her present state of mind, her rejection of Claude had been heartless, her antipathy destined to raise his unconditioned passion to uncontrollable levels. What had been no more than a selfish obsession had turned into a selfless sacrifice.

It was sorrow that she clung to, a safe refuge from guilt and self-recrimination. She did not want to hate anyone, certainly now not Claude, probably not even the hapless gorilla who, she reasoned, had been sent to fetch Liu. As for Lily herself – well it was not so easy to withhold the odium she was feeling for her own actions. But she had felt a victim for a long time, and now she did not want to be a victim to guilt, she just wanted to be isolated in her grief. But guilt can follow the lightest of tracks: it can travel along the finest thread, and it can not be washed away by a tear.

More than a minute had passed before anyone came forward. The driver was still in his cab, catatonic with shock. Someone called for an ambulance. An old lady came out of her car with a rug; she tried to pull Lily away – she for one was touched by Lily's tears. How could she dry her tears in the rain? Someone handed the old lady an umbrella – it was Gus. She stood over them as Gus, incredulous at the scene, joined Lily on the road. He had left her less than half an hour ago, inside safe and dry, now she was on her knees in the rain between two lifeless strangers. Seeing Gus next to her, Lily almost buckled with relief. All she could manage was a whisper. 'He tried to take me away.'

'Who? Which one?'

'This one. He came to the door and dragged me out.'

Gus made out her faint reply. He was quick, he worked out the possibilities. He had been a little uneasy since Liu's blunder, and with no particular danger in mind had been happy to get her away, but this eventuality had not occurred to him. He put his hands on each man's chest, wrist, and neck to feel for a heartbeat or a breath. His hands confirmed what their faces were telling him.

The siren signalled the start of a process that Gus realised should not include Lily. He pulled her up from the ground and steered her away from the small canopy of umbrellas that had formed. 'Come, there is nothing we can do here.'

'But we can't just leave him.'

The look on Lily's face suggested an unexpected and pliant disposition to one of the two people ... of course ... Gus now recognised the other man, the man on the train – it was Lily's stalker. There would be an explanation, no doubt, but for the moment Gus accepted it as a matter of fact. He was too concerned with their exemption from any further involvement at the scene.

'We must get away from here. I'll explain later.' The entrance to the flat was only fifty metres to their left, but Gus walked Lily to the right and around the block. Approaching the apartments from the other direction, they could see that the paramedics and the police had arrived with their stretchers and questions. The only clear answer was the confirmation of two pedestrians killed on the road, the cause unknown. The driver of the truck was still in a dissociative stupor, and no one from the now dwindling gathering could claim to be a witness.

As a precaution, Gus and Lily held their heads down to protect their anonymity; there was nothing suspicious about two people diving for an entrance in this weather.

'Right,' said Gus once they were back in the flat, 'a change of clothes, and then let's see if we can work all this out.'

'Ok, you tell first,' Gus prompted. They both now stood in dry clothes but still wet-headed and breathless from the whirlpool of events, and the forces that had been unleashed.

Gus listened to Lily's account, from the innocent bunch of flowers in the spy-hole, to Claude's running tackle. The violence that had burst in on her now seemed like a short-lived trauma compared to the shattering irony of her rescue. Gus could see her whole empathy system snagging on the bitter-sweet conclusion to two quite disparate ordeals.

'It must have been that second taxi,' Lily realized. 'Claude followed us back here last night. My protector, as it turned out.'

'Don't kid yourself. If this hadn't happened he would have needed to protect you from himself. Anyway, that other poor sop must have been sent by our mystery caller to pick up Liu – introduced as Olly's girlfriend, remember – and she did give the impression that she could be a nuisance.'

'So now they will try again' said Lily ...

'Possibly, but here we have a curious situation.' Gus put on the table a thin leather pouch. 'This, and a car key were the only things I found on him.'

'Sounds like you frisked him.' Lily's incredulity faded with Gus's look of confidence.

'Didn't take a second. You can look all over for a heart-beat ... Anyway it was more to prevent the authorities finding his identity than for us to know it. This way the guy just disappears, no report back to whoever sent him, no mention of Liu, just a delicious silence.'

Lily sighed her appreciation. 'Are you sure you're not a secret agent?'

'I think we all are now, not forgetting our two in the field.' Gus was conscious of darkening Lily's light remark. 'By the way, I can take you back to your own flat. They wouldn't have let your room already, and you'll be completely out of danger.'

'I'll be in no danger here, with you as my doorman. Besides, there should always be someone here in case there's a call.'

'Quite right.' Gus bowed with mock deference but actually out of respect. 'I'm sure he will phone – he'll be fishing for an explanation. Presumably he will expect it to be answered by Liu or not at all. So just act innocent. We're only house guests passing through; Olly and Frank are on vacation, and we think Liu must have gone with them.'

Gus opened the pouch. It contained very little: a few coins, some £20 notes, a betting slip, nothing with a name on, nothing of any significance – not surprisingly the man was *'sans papiers'*. He must have a vehicle, however. Maybe an accomplice? Unlikely – surely they would both have arrived at the door. The key was for an undetermined marque, but Gus would look out later for any car gathering tickets in the residents-only parking streets. Lily idly picked up the betting slip; on the back was a phone number – it started 0091 followed by 11 and eight digits. It was complete; both Lily and Gus reeled back. This could be the rest of the number that Olly and Phil had deciphered. They had all of them tried to crack the rest of it, to no avail. It was like being given a secret with a riddle so potent that it could spell life or death, but they could think of no occasion when the number could be used without declaring their hand.

Since his fall on the platform, neither life nor death had meant anything to Claude – the knock on the head had confirmed his attitude to mortality, or rather his own mortality. He was indifferent to his fate, but only as long as it did not compromise his role as Lily's protector. In recognition of this, and oblivious to the possibility that he himself might be a potential malefactor, Claude was even more obsessed with his obligations, and would be ever more vigilant over Lily's care. He had stood outside her flat since leaving his bed, sustained only by a messianic conviction of his vocation. Without the second taxi, Lily would have been lost to him forever and his own life forfeit. Its arrival was a signal that destiny had other plans – that he might devote his life to her safety, or, if necessary, give it up in her service. On reflection the latter was the most elegant outcome.

Lily would one day understand that Claude had died a very happy man, but for the time being she was racked with contrition for her part in his death, for the price she had exacted for her own peace of mind. Neither could she yet contact his parents to share their sorrow and perhaps let them enjoy some pride in their son's valour. Unlike, no doubt, her assailant, Claude would be traced – his parents would learn just of the accident on one of London's wet roads – the statistics usually swelled in weather like that. Lily looked forward to meeting them soon, to share a cathartic narrative that she hoped would lay to rest any feelings of futility which may have surrounded his life and death. In the meantime she would take up her violin, the first time in many months, to see if she could express her respects and perhaps assuage her guilt by playing some of Claude's most melancholic pieces.

15

The flight to Delhi took eight hours or so – time for Olly to come to terms with his situation, to clear his mind of a tangled web of doubts and speculations and thoughts of self. He must relegate his ego – those thoughts would be second thoughts. He still had time for second thoughts: he could refuse to hand himself over on arrival, could make a break, cause a rumpus – who knows? But that would be to allow his self to impose, and he was not the subject at hand; that was his father. Yet Olly must trust what was deepest and best in himself – he must harden his will to the iron necessity of his father's liberation, and accept that whatever happened he, Olly, would be in no worse a position than his father was now in. Olly continued in his brown study, above the clouds, detached temporarily from the earthly business that awaited him. He was flying east, to India, the land of meditation; he must accept his karma, but he would like what good deeds he could muster to be answered in this life, not the next.

Lily was on the plane too. Sweetest Lily, she sat like a bird on a perch in his heart. As long as she ruffled and sang, Olly's fears would be soothed. The sweetest, sweetest thing, she was one of the two prizes Olly must win, but she must not be a consolation prize.

Olly turned to the maps. He had chosen just one from Gus's selection, the only one that showed any degree of topography. It would appear that the authorities allow serious geo-

111

graphical detail only for military eyes. Nevertheless it was just possible to appreciate the nature of the unvaried terrain around Delhi. Might he just be able to recognise the odd bit of rising ground or a road type from under a blindfold? A blindfold, isn't that what they use – so you didn't know where you were, or had been? Maybe it was a good sign, a sign of a two way journey. A single ticket wouldn't require one – it suggested a level of security and incarceration that would transcend any hopes of communication or return. Dark thoughts returned, pricking and taunting Olly's will – what they demanded was timidity and retreat.

Two men stood at the arrivals gate, a card saying LANDING led Olly to them. He did not retreat, but he was timid … he meekly walked to them like a lamb to the slaughter.

Phil landed just after seven in the morning Hong Kong time. He had slept enough to pass the time, flying east into the sun meant an early night anyway. He took the Airport Express to Central, picked up some coffee, and was in his office by nine. It was just a room, shared with a young shirt designer called Yin Sang. Rarely together in the office, they were a good fit.

A letter addressed to *P. Donahue – Urgent By Hand* lay on a pile of correspondence – mostly catalogues, dispatch dockets, pro formas, and junk mail. Phil was impressed – it was less than forty-eight hours since his breakfast meeting in London.

Headed *Quan Wei Transport and Trading*, the note was short and straight to the point. *We have been asked to assist you. Please call Mr Wei on this number…* Phil called the number.

'Ah, Mr Donahue. I understand that you need some assistance or perhaps just advice on a matter.'

'Mr Qasim has explained the situation?'

'It is intriguing, Mr Donahue, but we are a simple trading company; we can't afford intrigues.'

'Of course, but I would still like to meet you. Perhaps we could discuss some simple trade.'

'You come with a good reference, Mr Donahue; I would be pleased to talk over some business. Come here at three o'clock. You have the address.' The same clipped briskness as Qasim in London.

There were two addresses for Quan Wei Trading in the book: one near a Kowloon waterfront and the other as on the note, presumably the corporate HQ. With some hours to spare, Phil decided to have a look at the dockside operation. As he expected, the company was more a shipping than a road transport undertaking. It occupied what looked like a pile of containers, but was actually a building, although architecturally it was too close to the metal hutches that inspired it. The site also housed warehouse buildings, and a large compound littered with real containers, cars, and bicycles. It was a typical shipping firm, in workmanlike surroundings, not unlike its countless neighbours. All their yards were enclosed by tall steel fencing, with varying levels of security equipment, but Mr Wei's railings seemed to be stouter and taller, and his buildings bristled with lights and cameras. Probably meant nothing, and so what? After all, Phil had only been introduced to him, he imagined, because his activities were nefarious. Phil was encouraged, though; he wanted to see signs of shadiness, and all these flood-lights could cast as much shadow as illumination.

The headquarters of the Wei empire were altogether a more polished affair. Occupying two high floors of an opu-lent office building in Queen's Road Central, they spoke of stability and respectability – this was more than a simple trading company. Mr Wei greeted Phil with inscrutable politeness; not the brittle man on the phone.

'Mr Donahue, I am pleased to meet you, and I hope that within the discretions and cautions that confine me, I shall be able to be of some help.'

'Thank you. Mr Wei, I truly am just a simple trader and I would not presume to pry into your own obviously substantial business. My ventures are small and on the whole legitimate – I do not have enough people to look over my shoulder. The problem, which I imagine Mr Qasim has outlined to you, concerns a man with whom I have some ties and …'

'Yes, I have been given the details, and I congratulate you on your perseverance. I have made enquiries, and whilst I have no direct knowledge, I understand that a certain ill-advised … shall we say recruitment? … has taken place.'

Phil felt a shimmer of hope at the words 'ill-advised', but more, the words contained a bigger reward. However loose the connections, this man was at the end of a chain of knowledge, Frank was no longer dangling from a string of conjectures and suppositions; their theories had been correct.

'Such as it is, my information suggests that a further development may turn around this situation.'

'Let's not beat about the bush, Mr Wei,' Phil was now inspirited. 'My friend has been kidnapped; it turns out he is a sick man and of no use. His son has by now handed himself over as hostage for his father's safety. I need someone to intercede for us, or at least point to their whereabouts.'

'I appreciate your frankness, Mr Donahue, and your eagerness. But we are both men of the world. I do not know of the whereabouts of this group, and if I did I would not be able to tell you, as I'm sure my enquiries have been noted. I am meeting you because I owe a debt to your friend Ravi – through Mr Qasim – but we do not hold reserves enough to cover the risks of breaking any confidences.'

114

'Thank you also for your frankness, but might I ask you why you consented to meeting me if plainly there were nothing you could do?' Phil's *frisson* of hope had not quite faded.

'I did not say there was nothing I could do, Mr Donahue, but we do have to be careful and also inventive. These people are ruthless, but the ones on the ground are timorous. They are pioneering an illegal operation in a strange country – panic would be a dangerous result of any disclosure. There is an old Chinese saying: If you stir the long grass you alert the snake ...'

'Then what do you suggest?'

'I suggest you stay in Hong Kong for a few days. I will keep my ears open and by and by I will hear a breath of news. The first thing is to understand the effect of the son's arrival on the health of his father. After that perhaps we can come up with a plan. Under no circumstances, however, must I be compromised.'

'I accept that and thank you for your help, but there may come a time when I need to just jump in with both feet.'

'You will have nowhere to jump without my information. Interceding for you or pointing to their whereabouts is all the same risk for me; we need a plan with winners but no losers.'

'I'll be staying at the Peninsula,' Phil said, a shade disconsolately, handing Mr Wei a card, 'but here are all my numbers.'

Phil was conscious of towering over Mr Wei, but he did not want his large frame and weather-beaten features to suggest just another heavy. He gave him a sagacious look and a parting comment:

'And by the way, you need have no fear of my jumping in alerting the snakes – there is another old Chinese saying: A careful foot can step anywhere.'

'Thank you, Mr Donahue. I will send word.'

Phil left the building, and back down at street level he caught his reflection in some plate glass, looking bowed and demoted. But why? He stopped and looked up at Mr Wei's shiny offices. He reproved himself, a quick review of his meeting up there brought out the extraordinarily positive progress they had made. Not only had he met a man who corroborated their hypothesis, but it was someone who held out a prospect, albeit guarded, of contact. It was nearly nine o'clock in London – time to speak to Gus and Lily.

Gus and Lily were in the flat, half-expecting a call from the man who asked all the questions, and before Phil came through, the man from Delhi did call. He was circumspect and obviously perplexed by the silence from his henchman.

'Hello, is this Mr Landing's apartment?'

'Sure, but I'm afraid he's not here right now.'

'No, but perhaps I could speak to his girlfriend.'

'She's not here either.'

'Can you tell me when she might be back?'

'Well I'm sorry to be so unhelpful, but we only got in the other day – here dossing while Olly's away on a trip – Italy, I think. Liu ... lovely Chinese girl, yeah, she was here, she sort of disappeared. Gone to meet Olly, I suppose.'

'I see.'

Gus couldn't tell whether this was said with suspicion or plain acceptance. He continued in a light and easy manner.

'But listen, we've got Olly's cell number. I'm sure he won't mind you having it if it's urgent. Hey Lil, hand me over Olly's number.'

The irony was delicious as Olly's phone would have been confiscated on arrival and no doubt was now in the pocket of one of his welcoming party.

'That won't be necessary, Mr ...'

'Gus – and you are? ... I can take a message.'

'No message. I'll try some other time.'

He was gone.

'Phew, how did it sound?' said Gus

'Brilliant, completely natural, and if he believed it all, we have a reason to be here whenever the phone goes, either of us – Gus or good ole Lil.'

'Good. He'll call again, but I don't expect any more henchmen to come knocking.' Gus then added with some mystery, 'In case they do, I have to show you our defences.'

Before he could, Phil was on the line.

'Hi, you two – is it you two?'

'Hi, Phil, yes, it's Gus and Lily,' the two of them answered simultaneously into their separate receivers. Gus continued, 'What progress from your Mr Big in Hong Kong?'

'Progress indeed, but I'm not yet sure he's big enough to pull any strings.'

'What have you got so far?'

Phil ran through his meeting with Mr Wei, his operation, and of course the confirmation that their detective work had been on target. The Chinaman clearly wanted to repay the favour or the debt owed to Ravi but was enigmatic about its redemption; the amount of caution implied a level of fear. This Gus, proposed, was a good thing; it suggested that Mr Wei was not a bad, bad guy.

A grunt of acceptance from Phil. 'We are in his hands, and curiously I trust his judgement. Anyway, I have no way of forcing the pace; we'll just have to be patient for a day or so.'

'We may have found a lever.' Lily was speaking; she intended to announce this with an element of triumph, but a fear in her heart took her back to caution. She had just experienced the latent danger that lurks around anyone implicated in this drama and the intimidating power that induces it. She paused, not for a prompt, but for a shudder, and then continued with her account of yesterday's ordeal. It took a few minutes, even though heavily abridged, during which Phil listened in silence. When she had finished, Phil remained silent: all they could hear was a metallic resonance on the line almost like his brain was wiring in all this new testimony. In truth he was lost in wonderment at her extraordinary tale. Where had she come from, where had Gus come from, where had these people come from to arrive in his and his friends' lives at such a time?

'Jesus Christ!' finally summed up Phil's reaction.

'That phone number,' Phil continued, 'are you thinking what I'm thinking – is that your lever?'

'Yes,' Lily assented, 'we couldn't possibly use it without starting a manhunt for the gorilla – Liu, all of us – but you might use it at some point to encourage Mr Wei to take more personal risk. After all,' she said, pursing her lips into a devious pout, 'where else could you claim to have got it but from but him, Mr Wei himself?'

Phil quietly considered this. If it was indeed the number of anyone who mattered, his knowledge of it would be deeply curious.

'Phil,' said Gus, 'while that sinks in, I need you to give me your opinion on some crazy thoughts I have been having about Frank's talents. I'm talking about the possibility of turning these people from a profitable street drugs business to an equally profitable smuggling business.'

'Bless you, Gus – you do talk in riddles, but go ahead, I'm all ears.'

Gus propounded his notions about AIDS drugs in which Frank appeared so very interested. He arranged to email Phil with a selection of papers on the subject. Phil would spend the rest of the day studying the fine detail on a list of related matters, and over the weekend they would see if they could agree on the opportunities Gus saw in the following statement: *You could purchase a reasonable quality ecstasy tablet in Portsmouth or Nottingham for 50p but a single day's often fake AIDS treatment could cost you a pound in Kenya or South Africa.*

16

The two men meeting Olly looked disgruntled. A delay had built up, but no explanations were given. A late departure … headwinds … bungled arrivals procedure, no one was saying. It was nearly half past two in the morning. One young and the other older; they were both local looking, and wore shabby, dusty clothes with scowls to match. The younger one, he was to be Olly's 'host', brightened slightly and feigned a hug of welcome, patting him like a returning friend. It was as efficient a frisk as at any security post. He was led to a small, dusty car. It was battered and worn, not looking in any way fit to travel. The older man, who turned out to be the driver, made no engagement, but picked up Olly's bag and threw it into the boot.

'Phone.' The younger one said this without any of the faux comradeship shown in the airport building but nonetheless without aggression; clearly it was his due. Olly handed it over, still switched off from the flight. He met the man's gaze evenly; it was now impassive, but Olly detected, or perhaps imagined, a hint of respect as the man acknowledged him with the slightest shrug of his lips, a long blink, and a nod of the head.

'How far do we go?' Olly asked, expecting no real answer.

'One hour, two hours depending,' his host replied. 'I'm not supposed to talk to you, but it will depend on roadworks – they are all over Delhi. In some time I must cover your head, but relax for the moment, you have nothing to learn.'

'Thank you – how is my father?'

'I have not seen him.'

'One last question, do you have some water?'

'Yes, but you have to wait. It's in the other car.'

There was a moon in the sky somewhere, but what light came was dimmed and diffused by low cloud. They drove in what, to Olly under the blanket, seemed like figures of eight. Fifteen minutes of caution, stopping, waiting, watching, resuming, and finally arriving on a piece of rough ground. A chill wind from the north was dispersing the cloud, stripping some veils from the moonlight. Olly let the blanket slip to his shoulders and said, 'There is no one to follow me.'

His escorts made no response, but then made no objection to Olly's head craning for information in the now lessening dark ... Stepping out of the car, Olly could see the ground was rough from broken bricks – a brick yard no doubt; the diggings were everywhere round here, wherever they could reach down for the clay.

Behind the silhouette of a large shed they boarded the second car, larger and fitter than the first. Items including Olly's bag were transferred and the journey continued.

'In the box.'

'What?' Olly was distracted, bemused by these precautions, but then what else, what would he do? Well, obviously, something like this, something to shake off any pursuit.

'What?' He repeated.

'Water, it's in the box.'

On the floor next to Olly beneath a bundle of old blankets was a twelve-bottle case of water. Small mercies, Olly thought; it might stave off the day when his gut would be colonised by extra-western bacteria.

Twenty thousand men and twenty years: that's what it took to build the Taj Mahal in the seventeenth century, plus millions of tons of marble. Twenty-thousand men and twenty years: that's what it will take to build the Delhi Metro, plus of course millions of tons of concrete. The car was passing alongside a linear building site stretching twenty miles in either direction, with every thirty yards a monumental pillar growing out of the ground sprouting steel bars like a pollarded tree. Finished columns stood proudly waiting to be given their share of the load. The traffic stopped to allow the night workers space for their cranes to lift one of the fifty-ton overhead railway sections into place.

Both driver and host left the car: the host to watch and admire the operation, the driver to urinate against a hoarding with a gesture of disrespect. He should be grateful, Olly thought. He'll have more room for his taxi when all this new transit system is finished – although more room in it, Olly pondered ruefully, thanks probably to less custom. It was nothing to see twenty people in a three-wheeler.

There was a certain feeling of intimidation in being ignored with the doors left open wide. Where would he run? Why would he run? He was at their disposal, and after all, this was his idea to start with. Olly sat back to watch the engineering feat, just one of thousands for the whole project. He had been to India only once before, and then merely for a few days, and he was left with impression of a people finally pulling together. The Taj Mahal was built as a memorial to one woman; this later construction, however, would improve the daily lives of millions of people, carrying them from home to work or school or even just for a ride. India, Olly sighed, was finally sorting out its priorities.

The road was cleared; the two men returned to the car. The host draped one of the blankets over Olly's head.

'You must lie down now – there is no more to see.'

Olly lay on the back seat under the blanket. Actually there was much to see through the loose weave of the material – only light and dark, but enough to perceive. For the next quarter of an hour Olly traced the flashing lights from the Metro hoardings, confirmed by the sounds from each mini-building site along the way. Over his head, to the right of the car, and slightly ahead of them, a cold but reassuring light came from a waxing, almost full moon which now had a cloudless sky to itself to reflect on the coming sun. Olly had a good idea which road they were on but to pass the time he made a little calculation. A full moon always sets in the west at six on a spring morning. This, he had noticed earlier, was not quite a full moon, so it would set earlier, maybe around four. He hoped they would reach their destination before his celestial beacon had sunk out of sight.

They were travelling slowly south, probably south-west. He knew this anyway since they had turned right out of the airport and were following the metro, but there would come a time when his only coordinate was the moon, so he must lock on to that. He did wonder what good all this would do him, but then no available knowledge must be wasted. They did leave the line of the metro eventually, or rather it seemed to have reached the end of the line. Olly could picture it on the map, the city of Gurgaon, thirty miles from the centre of Delhi, although now almost part of it. The airport was halfway along this road.

They travelled on past Gurgaon, in the same direction for forty-five minutes, and then the moon, still hovering in the sky, became obscured by the driver in front. Olly figured that if he couldn't see it, they were travelling west. He lay quiet as a mouse, a wheeled mouse travelling over the pad, recording every deviation from a given direction, measuring direction and distance to plot the cursor's position.

Another ten minutes and they entered a period of blackness between the moonset and sunrise, and also blackness between the main road and a distant complex. In just a few minutes, however they were passing by lights, illuminated buildings no doubt – industrial Olly surmised, now straining for information.

The car stopped, a large gate rolled open noisily and closed behind them. Two lefts and two rights and they came to rest. Still under the blanket, Olly was guided through a doorway and along a hollow-sounding corridor. The rattle of keys and the metallic creak of a door confirmed this to be no living space. Olly's blanket was removed as he entered a small office, dimly lit by a yard light shining through a barred window.

'Where is my father?' Olly asked of the young man, his host, who stood alone in front of him – still Olly's host, or more probably his guard.

'He is in there,' he replied, opening the door into an adjoining room, shuttered, dark, and airless, a sick room. The host found the switch, and with the light from a dim bulb Olly could make out his father lying under some thin and threadbare blankets on a low bed. In between his shallow breathing he gave a slight start as the door opened and both men approached. A thin chain ran from a ring on the floor to the bed. Olly lifted the rug and found the ankle band. In a second Olly's tender relief at finding his father turned into a dark rage. He turned on his host, one hand on his throat and the other grabbing his hair, forcing the man's head to face the scene on the bed.

'Is he a goat to be tethered?'

For a few moments the young man did not resist, but

seemed to give in to Olly's vehemence. 'I did not know of this,' he said, his hands then firmly prising open Olly's fists, 'Please, you must not struggle. I will do what I can.'

These words, together with the look of humanity that Olly remembered when their eyes met at the airport, caused him to subside. There was something about this man that said he could be trusted, but must not be overtly tested.

'I am free, but I am also a prisoner,' the young man said.

'I understand, and I'm sorry. What is your name?'

'Ashish.'

They released each other and Olly, sitting on the edge of the bed, gently shook his father's shoulder.

'Dad it's me, Olly. I've come to make you better.' Words he had used before.

His father's eyes opened. They were distant and dull like those of an animal in a trap with no fight left ... For a few moments both men were in a different place, in a different time, twenty years ago. Then Frank raised his head and looked up at Olly, his eyes, no longer dull, were shining wet – a tear rolled down each cheek. He opened his mouth to speak but no sound came out.

Olly turned to Ashish. 'Right, I need to see who's in charge here – the man on the phone or whoever.'

'Saleem will be here at eight. Mr Landing, he is a ruthless man and he can be cruel but not stupid. He was told yesterday to make better arrangements for your father. Before that it was assumed that he was just suffering from stomach problems – it is so common for fresh visitors. He was just given pills and left to rest.'

'Ok, glossing over the overriding reason why we are here – that is, my father being kidnapped and dragged over two continents to help some drug lord – let's see how we are going to make the best of it. Are there any quarters that are fit to live in?'

'I can do nothing until Saleem gets here. You still have some hours to sleep, I will go and find some bedding.' He returned with a blanket, a piece of foam, and the case of water from the car.

'What about my bag?' Olly asked.

'I'm instructed that Saleem must see it first,' Ashish replied. He started to exit the room but turned back.

'I must go now,' he said, but, after looking over his shoulder, added quietly, 'There will be times when I have to look right through you, but please know that I am seeing your pain.'

'Thank you.'

He withdrew, back through the office, locking the door to the corridor behind him. In an attempt to sleep for an hour or two before the day restarted, he lay down on a simple truckle bed in another office and tried not to let Olly's arrival raise any of hopes in his head of his own situation. His own father had been caught up in this business a year earlier, hiring out his battered Tata truck for deliveries and collections for what appeared to be a packaging firm with various depots around Delhi. By the time his father had realized the clandestine nature of the operation, his son Ashish had joined him and it was too late for either to withdraw. Both men had witnessed the hard edge of their employers and were frankly traumatised with fear for their own lives and their family's.

In the back room Olly lay on the foam on the floor, and listened to his father's irregular breathing. He was tired from the journey but sleep would not immediately release him from the hiatus of the day. He was not without fear, but he rationalised that it was fear from increased risks not of ultimate doom. To the extent that he was here for a reason, to make a difference, he was calmed by the prospect that he might be allowed an element of control. Also there was one person in the camp who seemed to cast a human eye over their welfare, if not their freedom.

He let go, and for the next few hours Olly was back in a London hospital radiating positive energy over his father's broken body and spirit.

17

Sleep hovered over Olly till the first callow signs of dawn removed the protective blanket of darkness. But still he awoke slowly; he had travelled far in a night of restless sleep, over space and time. The last part of his journey was into the future, and he wanted to remember that. It was now light, half past seven on his watch. The room looked bigger from floor level, but actually was just a small ante-room connected to an office, probably for a security man or a night clerk. A second door led to a lean-to lavatory about a chain's length from the floor ring.

On a hard chair beside the bed were a jug of water, some tablets and a bunch of stunted brown bananas. Olly threw away the water and replaced it with clean safe water from the case Ashish had left. The pills were antibiotics – three gone out of ten. Frank took some waking; he had been lying for days like a sick animal. Lying still was his answer to the nausea, but more importantly it took his mind off his confinement; he must be content to occupy just the few cubic feet of his own personal space, and not to reach out for more. He looked up at Olly and remembered, he remembered a visit in the middle of the night. It was true, Olly was here. How, he didn't know, but he was here. It was over; this would all pass – a sense of a future returned.

'Drink this, Dad,' Olly said, 'and see if you can sit up. I want to see more of you move than just your eyes.'

Still half-asleep and weak, Frank turned slowly under the

blanket, till his knees were over the edge of the bed. Letting his feet fall, Olly helped him sit upright. What length of chain that had been beneath the blanket now wriggled to the floor, link by link like a snake, coiling around Frank's ankle in wait. His blank look at the chain belied the shudder of repulsion that must have started every day.

'Don't worry, we'll have that off in a jiffy.' Olly said it lightly, but inwardly cursed the callous ignorance that justified such a restraint. By eight o'clock Olly had given Frank a crude bed bath and fed him a banana, with water and a tablet – an astronaut's breakfast, he teased. The clothes that Frank had left home in were hanging limply over the chair – they had suffered too.

Footsteps – not strident, but hesitant, almost as in caution – approached. Why caution? Olly thought. Maybe it was guilt. But when Saleem entered the room, he did so confidently, with an imperious air. Olly only saw a slithering reptile.

'This man does not need your chains,' Olly said – no preliminaries were necessary.

'Fetch a key.' Saleem sighed the command to Ashish, who stood behind.

Was this the voice, Olly wondered, was this the man who pulled the strings? He would find out soon enough, but for the moment he was distracted. Ashish had left the room to fetch a key, and as he passed through the adjoining office Olly saw him withdraw a pair of pliers from his pocket. Some moments later he was back with the pliers in his hand; he had thought better of looking already prepared, of presuming anything with Saleem the controller. No one spoke till the link was prised open and the ankle chain removed. Saleem, who might have been watching a ribbon being cut to open a fête, then declared: 'There, now down to business.'

These extra few words were enough to confirm it. The same confident voice on the phone, and now even more assured. Saleem was a man of mixed race, Indian and Chinese certainly, yet not the settled and long-evolved pale mix of the Indo-Chinese of South East Asia. His parent's genes may have met on the Silk Road, but more recently. They had produced a dark man with cold hooded eyes, though with the look of a cultured metropolitan. There was, however, something of a lizard about him, or maybe even a bird of prey, and to Olly his respectable appearance intensified a hidden evil, and added another layer of repugnance born of his activities.

'The business in hand,' Olly rejoined, 'is to get my father out of here, and into proper accommodation so I can nurse him back to health. Then perhaps your 'investment' will show a return.'

'Well said, and I am pleased that you understand the commercial realities. I hope your father recovers soon, as I'm sure you also understand the laws of diminishing returns.'

With that he turned and left, a wave of his hand to Ashish, signalling presumably the commencement of some predetermined arrangement.

'Wait here,' Ashish said, as if there was an option. 'I will be back with help in half an hour.' He looked at the torn and filthy rags on the back of the chair. 'I will bring fresh clothes.'

'Don't antagonise that Saleem,' Frank said quietly, finding his voice for the first time. 'I've seen what he can do.'

It was too soon for Frank to relive the last few days, and Olly knew that this remark was not a gambit for further revelations. He would defer to his father's wisdom, but the most he could offer would be cold neutrality.

'Don't worry, Dad. I think I've got the measure of him, and he needs you better too.'

Olly paced the room and Frank remained in his bed. Mornings in the north of India were cold in April, and Frank, now in a less dormant state, was shivering under the light covers. But the shakes were not just from the cold: Frank was frightened, frightened for Olly. It was not over. Before Olly came, Frank had ebbed into a quiet resignation to oblivion, his mental and physical fortitude destroyed by vicious strains of bacteria, and extreme confinement. But now he was alive again to the danger that he didn't want to share with his son.

Ashish returned with a long white gown, a pair of sandals, and a woollen shawl. He had stuffed them into Olly's confiscated bag, now returned with its harmless contents.

'There is a house a while from here; it is secure and you will be comfortable. I will help you to the car when you are ready.'

The car was a four by four with a separate cabin on the back – no windows, just a canvas flap at the rear. They would not see much en route, but Olly observed enough as they passed along the passage and out to the car to know that they were in a small cluster of industrial buildings, dated and run-down, but in active use. He even caught a glimpse of modern India – vast and modern hi-tech warehouses and offices on adjoining sites, no doubt full of bright young computer scientists, biochemical engineers, and communications wizards.

Frank walked slowly, leaning heavily on Olly's arm, looking in his fresh gown like a holy man deep in some reflection. He attracted no attention from the workforce who cycled and scooted through the gates to the surrounding workshops.

The journey was not physically uncomfortable, but it was a journey further into the unknown. With Frank stretched across the double seat, Olly sat at his feet looking through the rear flap at the receding road, every mile a notch out of his known existence. Two hours' slow driving, more or less due west – maybe sixty miles, not exactly a dead reckoning, but Olly would add these readings to his surmised position of last night's factory. If ever he saw a map he thought he could make a credible stab at their location within, say, twenty miles. But if they could escape beyond their immediate confines, what would it matter where they were; they would be free. It would matter, though, Olly realized, to let others know the locations of this clandestine operation, in order to be free of future and further harassment. In the meantime there might be a way of getting out a message.

In the eighteenth and nineteenth centuries the Marwaris, a hardy and resourceful people from Rajasthan, one state removed from Delhi, prospered from the trade routes that passed through their harsh and arid region. They were adept at collecting and conserving water, which they declared was either too deep in the dry ground or too high in the sky. They became hard-working, canny traders, who learnt how to collect and conserve money as they did water. Commerce, it is said, was taken in with their mother's milk. In addition to trading themselves, they finessed taxes from passing caravans en route from the south and east to the ports of the Arabian Sea, and the mountain passes on the North West Frontier.

The Marwaris dealt astutely with the ruling Mughals and the succeeding British Raj. Their talent for amassing riches, which proved second to none, was celebrated by building in their thousands beautiful *havelis* – ornate and highly decorated court-yarded palaces, sometimes ten or more clustered in a small village, or more in a larger town. But times moved on and the owners followed their businesses to the larger cities and the new trade routes from southern ports.

They left, but never parted with the ownership of their original homes, which stand today, walls and fabric frayed by time, and ownership fragmented by generations of legacies. Descendants of these people, it is said, now account for more than half the industrial wealth of India. Nine out of ten of their old houses are now empty, but no one has the power of sale or a reason to purchase, with just the few leased for institutional or hotel use.

It was to the faded elegance of one of these that Olly and Frank were taken. Occupation had been granted by a distant and disinterested family in return for certain repairs and upkeep. So far as Olly could make out from his restricted view, this *haveli* was set apart from its neighbours on the edge of a small dusty village in the centre of a flat plain, and surrounded by stunted and gnarled acacia trees – firewood and fodder for a struggling rural existence. There were few signs of inhabitants in any of the crumbling village houses, least of all in the other five or six *havelis*, which stood unguarded and unoccupied. Something had dried up the moistening hand of human guardianship, the population shrivelling to just some old, dry sticks too deep-rooted to follow their young. What comings and goings were observed – movements of materials and the general industry of the new occupants – drew no suspicion. The locals had seen attempts at restoration before, but always enthusiasm abated; comforts and display were of no consequence in a land from which the source of all wealth had evaporated. Even if they were interested, no one would notice that this particular project was achieving even less at restoring some former splendour than previous attempts, and that most of the materials and labour were absorbed in a quite different scheme of endeavour.

Steps rose to first floor level, where heavily carved wooden doors announced the main entrance, flanked by lodges with narrow, slitted windows – a drawbridge would not have seemed out of place. A short, cool passage led to a circuit of vast public rooms and spaces overlooking an internal courtyard the size of two or three tennis courts. In one corner narrow steps led down to the courtyard level, onto which issued a series of doors, probably twenty in number, each one serving a cool, lofty apartment. The entire building was inward-looking and what small windows broke through the external walls were barred and shuttered. Life carried on inside the walls as it had done generations ago, screened and secure.

Frank and Olly were taken to one of these apartments, and were probably the first occupants for thirty or forty years to enjoy its grandeur, although its comforts were now somewhat reduced. Two bedrooms, each with adjoining bathroom and shower, led off a large salon. The bathrooms alone faced onto the surrounding country, albeit through small and high windows, but the other rooms looked through a deep colonnade out onto the courtyard, once verdant with lawns and fountains but now dry and neglected. Some fine stone carvings, however, helped maintain its dignity.

Ashish stood by the entrance doors; he observed Olly notice a large bolt that had been moved from inside the door to the outside. 'The doors will not be locked before sunset in normal circumstances,' he said, 'as there is no way out of the courtyard apart from the one staircase, which will be barred or guarded.' This, Olly mused, was the comparative freedom of house arrest, but with the background intimidation of being under the absolute control of one man's dark soul. Saleem, Ashish explained, had gone away for some days, and he had left instructions for his 'guests' to be made comfortable and attended to; Olly could, however, read the implicit urgency in getting his father well again –

well enough to justify his relevance and probably his existence. For the time being, though, he would let things pass. They had a few days' respite, maybe enough for Frank to get better. Olly could then explain to his father how he had come to join him, and the probable reason for his kidnap.

It was less than twenty-four hours since he had left London, but time had been bent around distance and events. Matters now pressing for his attention were outside his normal sphere of existence; he had been transported into a world of darkness and tenuous security. The upheaval of the last few days seemed to be all he had ever known, with all previous life spinning backward into a distant past. Linked to that disruption, however, was the arrival of Gus and Lily; they belonged to this present phase of his life, but even they now seemed to exist in another dimension.

Phil ... Hong Kong – don't forget that combination. Phil would be working on some scheme – this would all be resolved in a businesslike way – but for the time being they needed to play their parts here. It would not be a dramatic rescue – something much more subtle, and it would take time.

18

Phil spent all Friday afternoon and evening reading. Gus's transmissions, supplemented by countless internet references, led Phil into the labyrinth that was the world of clinical drugs, and the advent of the generic drugs that had brought about such challenges to the protection enjoyed by the pharmaceuticals industry. The material that Phil was digesting was both heartening and disturbing. Great progress had been made in the last fifteen years by generic manufacturers, but they had to go through endless hoops and barriers, with the big pharmaceuticals engaging in trench warfare to protect their patents, and the return on their research costs. World health and trade organisations had come up with internationally sanctioned regulations to recognise the intellectual property, on the one hand, but, on the other, to circumvent the patent laws in certain circumstances; either by royalties being negotiated by a generics company under an agreed licence, or by a compulsory licence issued by a country in the case of an emergency.

Gus had no hesitation with his bombardment of information – he had learnt how Phil could get exercised by the iniquities of the world. Indeed Phil did wonder ruefully how many thousands of deaths per week would count to justify an emergency licence. Not surprisingly, it would appear that most sub-Saharan Africa countries had no pharmaceutical capability, so they would look to external suppliers to satisfy their licence quotas – be they agreed or compulsory. India, now recognised as the generic drug producer for the developing world, was the largest player in this supply system.

There were many players actively giving help in sourcing and funding drug supplies for poorer countries, whether for AIDS, malaria, TB, or other debilitating diseases that sap the life-blood out of communities. Wealthy foundations set up by Clinton, Gates, and other benefactors, organisations like Médecins sans Frontières, Oxfam, and countless other aid missions, together with pragmatic rules from the health and trade agencies, had brought the cost of many drugs to a tenth of the 2000 prices. It was claimed, for example, that the annual cost to treat an AIDS patient was now less than $100.

However, these were not necessarily the latest and most effective drugs – an AIDS patient would likely need to change to later, newer, and less toxic treatments as the condition progressed. Even with all the machinations and dispensations of the producers, agencies, missions, commissions, and rule makers, the cost of the right treatment was still out of reach of most people in poor countries.

This was interesting reading for Phil; his previous knowledge now seemed quite superficial, with only a peripheral awareness of all the protests and programmes that surrounded the subject. What brought him up short, however, was the coverage on the subject of fake drugs. These, he learnt, were being produced in industrial quantities, mainly in Asia, for the same diseases he had been reading about. Either the drug was merely some inert substance with perhaps a random chemical added just to provoke a response, or it contained such diluted amounts of the active constituents as to build up a resistance in a patient to the genuine dose if ever it was later administered.

These counterfeit drugs were sold on the streets and

villages or even in large quantities to aid agencies – such was their realistic packaging. Phil read that 30% of the drugs used in the developing world were fake. This was a story of cynical greed and corruption that surpassed any baseness in the illicit world of recreational drugs. He thought of his wife and child dying in China those years ago. A lot of people succumbed with them, regardless of the best efforts of the doctors. A knot was tightening in Phil's stomach as he grasped at a new comprehension, but he told himself that these new fears were probably unfounded; he must not let the acid of bitterness corrode his spirit.

Fake medicine apart, Phil was strongly sympathetic to Frank's cuttings and reviews on the illegal drugs trade and the naïvety of western governments, especially the USA, in effectively supporting the price of illegal drugs by prohibition. Significant sections of world economic activity were being governed by corruption and extortion, with whole countries made craven by the power of infamous criminality. The corruption and extortion were particularly corrosive in a state trying to control a disaffected and disillusioned population, which, by a combination of coercion and manipulation from the underworld, would become ungovernable.

Phil agreed that the drugs issue should be treated as a social and health problem and that we should grow up, and admit where the real harm lay. As well as the pariah states already on the ungovernable list, watching countries like Pakistan or even Mexico falling into chaos convinced Phil of the destructive power of illicit trade, especially drugs. The real harm lay in transferring huge capital to the bad people. To the Afghan grower, the poppy is a cash crop, but he is still living the subsistence existence of an indentured serf. The huge revenues produced further along the line do nothing for his wellbeing. He would be better off growing pomegranates for sale into a legitimate market or – if bans were abolished – even poppy seeds into a legitimate market. Whichever – the rake-off that funded the greed and instability would be curtailed. He recalled Mr Qasim's comment in London – 'Ah the murky world of drugs. Long may they be illegal.'

Phil found himself depressed and angry. He understood trade and how fundamental it was to man's sustenance. He also understood that for every need, somebody would emerge to supply it, wholesome or otherwise, and that was how the world went round. But the world should understand these propensities and deal with them more intelligently and strategically. The richer countries effectively allowed the drug lords to convert their commodities into hard currency for the few. Many of the workers in the country of origin or on a shipment route would not find banknotes in their pay packets, just some white powder, or some other stock in trade. This could only be converted into money and a livelihood by finding or encouraging a further miserable bank of dependency.

It was not difficult for Phil to get troubled about these things on many levels. His strong endorsement of trade generally was being pierced by worries about illicit trade, not because he cared about competition against the makers of a Barbie doll, but because fakery necessitated covert dealings in money and goods – an attractive addition to any portfolio of organised crime. But while he was railing against all this, Phil came back around to Gus's point. Was there as much return to be made in smuggling a genuine drug to be sold at an affordable level to people whose lives depended on it as there was selling ecstasy and the like in the club scenes of western cities?

Clearly it all depended on the cost of production, Phil reasoned, all other logistics being equal, and then he remembered the cabbage. Cabbage was a term used in the clothing industry. Yin Sang, Phil's co-tenant in Hong Kong, castigated the practice, but ironically did very well out of it, since the designer's job was continually to modify style and fabric to keep ahead of plagiarised copies. A manufacturer would fulfil an order for, say, ten thousand branded garments but would then surreptitiously let the production run continue. The extra designer wear would then find itself a market without the label, but with style and quality unchanged. Did they, or could they, do this with AIDS drugs, for example? This would be the sort of cabbage that Frank would savour.

Phil called London – he needed to respond to the insights provoked by Gus's reading list. He also needed to hear himself marshal and present his own thoughts, stripping out the prejudices and fanciful notions, testing the germ of a plan against hard dry actualities. It was just this plan that need concern them immediately, finding a way for him to infiltrate Saleems organisation, and for Frank to serve his purpose and then quietly with his son return unharmed to their previous lives. Then he would see if he had the energy for a broader campaign.

'Gus,' Phil said, 'thanks for the research, and for seeing a side of Frank that we all missed, as well as for knowing it would touch a chord with me. We are so insulated against the lamentable truth in these subjects. We are vaguely aware of progress here or some desperation there; our compassions and sympathies are suspended between the good news and the bad news but really inured against both. Yet ultimately it's not short pangs of conscience or charitable gestures that will change things; it's our ongoing common sense.' Phil was listening to the words as they came out, and pulled back from the philosophical flow. 'Anyway I did follow your drift; you led me through it well, and I think I can see the general idea,' he said, 'but I have no feel for the official or the street prices of any of these drugs, especially the clinical ones. And if the margins are that good, isn't it already happening?'

'Maybe,' said Gus, 'but we'll never know if we don't test the idea. It's just that Frank seemed so bound up in the AIDS subject I can't believe that he doesn't have specialist and valuable knowledge.'

'Our only way in to this is through our Mr Wei. I'm sure he'll understand the arithmetic to see whether or not there is any potential. It may also give him the reason to introduce me to the controllers without appearing to pry into areas that he should know nothing about.'

'Inventive,' Lily interjected, 'that's what he said you have to be.'

'Exactly, Lily, and I still have a card to play – one I have written that phone number on. It may well help stir his imagination.'

'Did all that reading not stir your own imagination?' Gus said, a little disappointed that they were still talking in generalities. 'Did it not stir any reaction to my particular idea?'

'Young man,' Phil said, 'I have been stirred.' He didn't mean it to, but Gus's downheartedness encouraged a certain flourish to Phil's presentation. He announced the magic of cabbage and outlined his idea. If these people could coordinate the delivery of prohibited chemicals, turn them into marketable amphetamines, and follow them right through to their point of sale, then what Gus was suggesting was well within their capabilities.

'Awesome,' Gus said, slapping the table. He was impressed, and felt vindicated.

'Phil,' said Lily, 'I think it's brilliant too, but I think we also need a default plan. So far everything seems to have led inexorably to some overarching great solution, but if we don't get to the next stage at any one time, all is lost.'

141

'I understand,' said Phil, 'and I am not being over-credulous here. I know that any moment we could be left dangling, but until that happens we should keep pushing along. Don't forget that as long as we are not exacerbating the problem we are doing no harm – only time is being spent.'

'I know,' said Lily, more for debate than declamation, 'but surely the police in India are set up to deal with this sort of thing?'

'You would think so,' continued Phil, 'if it were a kidnap for ransom or some negotiation, but there is no negotiation to be had here. Either they are apprehended cleanly due to good intelligence or they disappear leaving no evidence … or victims behind.'

That was the chill of the matter – it hung in the air for some moments before Gus spoke.

'I'm sorry if I got taken up with the thrill of the chase, but I agree we should have contingencies. Phil, if we don't hear from you at the most every twenty-four hours I propose we call the police and go through the whole story. After all, we have some strong leads to start them off.'

'Sounds good to me,' said Phil, 'and the same this end – ok Lily?'

'Fine.'

'Ok, enough said. Goodnight to you both. I'll ring that nice Mr Wei in the morning and suggest we meet.'

Phil's call was put through to Mr Wei's car. 'Good morning, Mr Donahue. We speak again so soon. It's only Saturday – much too early, I'm afraid, to expect any news about your friends, but trust me I will let you know the moment I have anything to report. Then we can consider what steps to take.'

'Thank you. I understand that, but in the meantime it is

important that we meet. I have come up with a few things for you to think about whilst we are waiting.'

There was a pause, which Phil left to run its course, then asides in Chinese to another – it turned out to be his driver. 'Mr Donahue, I have just left for the airport, and shall be away till Monday. However, we can call by your hotel on the way. Come for the ride; my driver will take you back – say twenty minutes?'

'Thank you. I'll be downstairs in fifteen.'

They sat opposite each other in Mr Wei's limousine. 'What are these things that I have to think about?' he said. 'I have been already been thinking about this a great deal, Mr Donahue. Mainly about how I can safely express more than a casual interest in your friend's predicament.'

'I know, and I have not forgotten your remark that we have to be inventive.'

'Quite so.'

'We have come up with a proposal that could make my friend even more productive for them, which may allow me eventually to bargain for his freedom.'

'We?'

'A couple of people who were around when Frank disappeared. They are very discreet.'

'I hope so. I will listen to your suggestion, but I must warn you I am afraid of pressing any causes with these people. I have spent thirty years building my business, and being a transport company there have been certain consignments which, without knowing the exact nature of the goods, I have dealt with in a delicate manner. There have been rewards, of course, but the penalty for exposure exerts a bigger incentive.'

He was hedging – Phil could see that, which made it even better that he should have the means to perhaps tip him

143

into action. He outlined the plan while Mr Wei looked distantly out of the window, thinking, no doubt, was there no other way he could repay his debt to Ravi. He didn't seem to react, one way or the other.

'All I want is for you to find a way of introducing me to the people who count.'

Still no reaction from Mr Wei – he seemed to be struggling with some demons.

'Or,' Phil continued, handing Mr Wei a card with a phone number, 'I will contact them myself.'

Mr Wei sprang forward in his seat, rapping the chauffeur's glass, a few sharp words to his driver and the car pulled off the road. 'Where did you get that number?'

'That's what my friends were wondering,' Phil replied, and, with a most delicate aim, said, 'They assumed I got it from you.'

Mr Wei was flushed and agitated – clearly it was a number he recognised. 'A moment … a moment please to reassess.' He sat back in his seat and closed his eyes. Phil was happy for the pause – he didn't want Mr Wei to feel cornered, just to reflect more actively on his involvement.

After some minutes Mr Wei opened his eyes and looked at his watch. Phil acknowledged the passing of time, yes he had a plane to catch, and gently urged, 'Just put me in the right channels and I will take it from there. I would, however, like your opinion about the trade I am suggesting.'

'I think your plan has merit,' he said after some minutes, 'but please you must give me a few days to engineer an introduction.'

The car resumed its journey; they sat in silence – an understanding had been reached. At the drop-off point the car stopped just long enough for Mr Wei to alight and disappear into the departure lounge, destination unknown.

19

Olly and Frank, Lily and Gus, and Phil, all in awkwardly different time zones and geography, shared the same limbo. Each party to the drama had experienced a whirlwind of action in one form or another, a complete reordering of the pieces that gave pattern to their lives. What further gusts of fate might shape their respective futures were yet to come, and the inactive calm brought a tense disquiet, exacerbated by the heavy punctuation the different time shifts seemed to impose on their contact.

They all understood that there would be a period of slackness before any momentum from their plan could change the direction of events. All should be composed and patient. Olly was content to minister to his father's needs, and watch his recovery – nothing else was possible or required. Lily and Gus, whilst expecting a call from Phil, were resigned to a few days of waiting. Gus had strolled the surrounding streets, but had found no signs of irregular parking, no car chastened with a ticket – so much for the over-zealous wardens he had heard about. He wanted to find the car to match the key – it would confirm that Lily's assailant was alone, and that therefore his disappearance would remain an enigma to his employers. The presence of an accomplice would be unwelcome since it would predicate another call on the flat. Whilst this was unlikely, as surely he would have come looking before, it was a reminder to explain to Lily the workings of the bookshelf door – built for novelty

145

but now a credible line of defence. He would look for the car again in the morning – the warden's zeal might build later in the day.

Phil was the least able to find any temporary repose. Back in his hotel room following the ride with Mr Wei, he planned to spend the rest of the day in quiet contemplation. But the executive responsibility for instigating their plan, with the possibility and consequence of its total rejection as madcap and naïve, weighed on him. The steely calm he usually found in such moments of suspense was also unsettled by the rising bile brought on by the circumstances of his wife and daughter's deaths – his recent cognisance of fakeries even in the world of clinical drugs had dislodged his previous fatalistic acceptance of the tragedy. A realisation that certain inconsistencies, unprobed at the time, could be readily penetrable in the context of counterfeit medicine persuaded him to reopen a painful enquiry. He rang his wife's cousin, who had survived the outbreak of meningitis that had wiped out half her village, and what she told him conspired to fit a theory that sat brooding in his mind. Some antibiotics had been obtained but initially only enough for half the stricken; the others waited for a subsequent supply which arrived mercifully within a few hours. But of the fifty people who contracted the disease, more than half died. It had not gone entirely without notice that the greater proportion of those who died seemed to be the ones who had received the first delivery of medication, but the epidemiology had been scant, and the community accepted that nature had paid a distressing visit, which they bore with a mournful submission. This was rural China, and the fates were accepted at face value as being only slightly worse than other outcomes they had heard attested.

Viral, bacterial – Phil's research was superficial, but enough to learn that of the two main types of meningitis, bacterial was the one that claimed lives. Even with modern antibiotics, mortalities could be 10 or 20%, and, without treatment, double or treble that. To hear that the twenty-five people who perished were mostly from the group that had received the earlier treatment could lead him to only one conclusion: they were victims of a batch of counterfeit drugs. But Phil knew that there was nothing to be done: no authority would carry out a forensic search of the facts; it was too late for clinical suspicion. There was nothing to do but seethe. This was surely one of the most cynical and unconscionable trades a man could live by, and to Phil, an eternally damned soul would not be too high a price to pay for the satisfaction of exacting retribution. At the moment any representative of the trade would do. Perhaps when the time came he might enjoy the power of mercy, but in his present state, thoughts of inflicting execrable punishment were uppermost in his mind. They diverted this fresh bitterness that was souring his grief, which in recent years had softened into a sad but sweet memory.

At four o'clock he called the flat – it was eight o'clock on Saturday morning in London. Yes, he had spoken to Mr Wei, he had met him; yes, he had played the card, the card with the phone number; and yes, it had provoked a reaction. No, their plan had not met with blank incredulity; it actually might have some benefit, but Wei was only a messenger. They would have to wait for the response from a principal.

Gus and Lily could hear that Phil was out of sorts and didn't press him for a more expansive report. He would be calling again in twenty-four hours as arranged, and if he was still diffident they would tease out the reasons for his despondency. They were, however, left a little deflated by the call, as if Phil wanted their expectations lowered. He had made another step forward – indeed he may have found some leverage – but he didn't need to cool their expectations, and in any case all their hopes were tethered to the same hard realities. This notion about HIV drugs providing another conduit for profitable illicit trade was just a notion. It could be dismissed in a second as a lame idea by some solid information about the subject matter – not impossible to learn by patient research maybe, but better to lean it up against the sort of people who would be capable of embracing the trade. They would know if it had economic legs.

Before going out to look again for an abandoned car, Gus took Lily through the procedure for closing the bookcase doors. On reflection, they realized that the man from Delhi was bound to send another operative to investigate – how could he resist in the face of such a conundrum? But if they were to break in to the flat downstairs, they would be unlikely to expect a further level, and should they stumble across the opening lever, Gus had prepared a surprise. The six flood-lights that had produced such a heavenly effect pointing up to the atrium now pointed down. Any unwelcome visitors climbing the stairs would find themselves suddenly blinded, and assailed not just by the lights but by blows from Gus's fists and boots. He would not hesitate in acting the part of an avenging angel.

An old and battered VW seemed to stand out now even without the two tickets curling around its windscreen wiper. Gus felt excited and a little disrespectful as the key turned in the lock of the dead man's car. The interior was devoid of personal effects, though Gus did not expect to find any apart from perhaps a phone. The man was not carrying one, but how could you operate today without a mobile? Gus drove the car west, away from central London, until he found a quiet suburb with no parking restrictions –

it would be weeks before anyone noticed the car was own-
erless, and he could always move it from time to time. He
did find a phone – it was wedged between the seats. It satisfied his curiosity but that was all – security-locked and
disabled, it would divulge no information as to its owner
and permit no other user. Gus wondered idly whether it
would still receive a call; he would listen out but under no
circumstances should he be tempted to answer – the silence
and mystery must be maintained.

Back in the flat Lily took up her violin, but playing some
of her favourite pieces from memory left her head free to
wander in any direction it chose, and the direction was
inevitably India and Olly. Initially warm thoughts abetted
by the lyrical sounds turned eventually to agitated, frightened anguish. Olly's was not an adventure with contained
risks and shortlived discomforts – it was a journey along
a precipice with people to whom his life was worth virtu-
ally nothing. He was a hostage to his own utility, pledged
with no set redemption either in collateral or in time. Time,
Lily mused, was nothing to anybody. All you could do was
let events pull you along, but you must be free to get in
their way, and to pick and chose. That is the problem with
captivity, being restrained from floating in the ever-flowing
wash of time – every moment a new opportunity to make
up for missed chances, to trim your course, adjust strategies
and tactics. This is where Lily saw Olly – in a void, with
a future her imagination must be diverted from. But she
would rather share his fate – be with him as it unfolded –
than be left in her own time without him.

She stopped playing; her hands were trembling, and
her eyes wet with a mixture of pride and grief. She must
find some more positive thoughts or play something that
allowed no other abstractions. She thought of Phil's words,

she heard his mantra that trade is everything, a quid pro quo would be found from an activity with gains for all parties – an event worth latching onto. A perfectly sound principle, but Olly and his father were still just pawns in the game, and Lily must hope that Phil could find some advantage for their protection or even promotion.

A series of very technical studies by Paganini was her salvation, and after some minutes she was subsumed in the absolute concentration it required. You have to approach such absorption carefully, and Gus imagined that he had made enough noise climbing the heavenly stairs, but Lily's oblivion not only shut off all external sensors, it allowed a complete lack of expectation. No stranger to the delicate workings of the mind, Gus had been impressed by Lily's recovery from her recent ordeal. He put it down to her being occupied in the wider engagement in which they had all been enjoined. But as his shadow crossed the page of music, Lily was propelled from her seat by a combination of fear and convulsion, and, turning to avoid the approaching menace, she reeled across the room, violin, music stand, music, pitched to all corners. Fight or flight, her body was preparing her for the choice. But seeing Gus she subsided and her adrenaline ceased its rush. Lily had landed against the side of a sofa and had sunk to the floor, feeling foolish and withered and above all shaken and shaking. She had suffered an aftershock, subsidiary to the main event of two days ago, but still a powerful release of subliminal tension.

'Jeez, I didn't mean to startle you.' Gus gathered up the pieces of her shattered solitude. 'Next time I go out I'll call to announce my return.'

'It's ok. I shouldn't sit with my back to the door – basic feng shui, you know.' She was trying to be light, but Gus could see the signs of shock: cold clammy skin, rapid breathing, and a dazed countenance.

'Listen, Lily. Perhaps you shouldn't stay here, what with me warning of some possible return visit and all.'

'No, I'll be fine. I just got myself in a kind of trance, trying not to think of Olly and his dad in some stinking hole. I wish there was something more we could do rather than all this slowly-slowly thing.'

'We are doing something, but it will take time, and I know it feels ponderous, but for the next few days at least they will be in no danger. Remember Olly's job is to get Frank better; they need his talents.'

'Time ... bloody time. I spend half my life trying to keep up with it, and now I'm sitting around waiting for it.'

'Don't knock it.' Gus pulled her to her feet. 'Time is nature's way of preventing everything happening at once ... Read that on a wall somewhere. Neat, don't you think?'

She had to smile, she looked at her watch: .seconds ... minutes ... hours ... all waiting for each other to let something happen.

20

Phil was still smarting from his newfound comprehension of the circumstances surrounding the death of his wife and daughter. It was ten years ago, but this new insight was only a day or two old, still sharp, and, unchecked, it would bite mordantly into his spirit. He would have to come to terms quietly with the injustice to maintain his presence of mind, but being quiet is not easy when you want to shout and scream. He had called Gus and Lily and apologised for being offhand – just a headache probably. Today was Monday, and he had walked to his office to find Yan Sing sitting on a box just inside the door. He looked pale and alarmed.

'What's up, Yan Sing? You look like an endangered species.'

'I think I'm supposed to – thanks to your visitors.'

'Who were they?'

'No idea, they didn't leave a calling card, apart from this.'

Yan Sing turned his face to show an angry weal on his cheek – the lash of a strap or a belt.

'They were asking about you, your affairs, who you did business with. I told them what I knew – hardly anything really. How long could you talk about my shirts?'

'God, I'm sorry. I've been mixing with some undesirables lately, just trying to get a friend out of trouble. Seems they like to sprinkle around a little intimidation, to spice up any negotiations.'

circumstances. This man was here to enrich his own earthly experience, not humanity's.

'Let me be plain. I am not happy that a good friend has been pressed into some kind of servitude, but there is nothing I can do about that. What I can do, however, is spot an opportunity, one that may make us all some money and coincidently appeal to Frank's scorn of the drugs business. No use to you, but I know he would rather the whole damn thing was legalised and everyone left to sort out their own addicts. He has no objection to what you make – it's just all the graft that goes with it, but more importantly the lack of purity of the output.' There's a fine line between appeasement and blunting points of conflict, but Phil wanted his motives trusted, and the more they shared the same dispassionate goals the better.

'It is just a business,' the man replied confidently, a little less distant, 'and you are right we are pleased to have the value of our commodity supported by witless prohibitions. But while we could never have a global brand, we do still need to watch the quality.'

'Exactly, which is presumably why Frank was co-opted. By the way, was that your idea?'

'No, but I had reports of poor standards affecting street prices. If I express concern, people have to find solutions.'

'Interesting, sounds like your man in Delhi may have been compromising on purity, getting a little greedy perhaps, but with our help he could redeem himself.'

Phil thought he had touched a chord; the reply came too quickly, or maybe they had dallied enough.

'Mr Donahue, please explain your proposal.'

Phil went through the concept from cabbage to consignments of second-line AIDS tablets, sold on the street or to desperate health officials in Africa. It would only work if the right pre-mixed compounds could be obtained and the efficacy assured. The profit would be in repeat orders.

'The next step being?'

'That I would meet with Frank, and your man in Delhi, to see if my idea is practical. It may fail for all sorts of reasons: for example we can't get the constituents, or we can't finish off the process, or we can't sell for the right price. I don't know, but I can't believe, given the resources and skills that your business employs, that this can't be done.'

A lot of 'can'ts' – but ultimately overcome by the 'can do' of the cartel. Phil's intention was not to fawn, more to remove any thorns of censure he might be expected to have. The man remained impassive to flattery, his ego was fully appraised of his own pre-eminence, and Phil realized also that it would be no great thing to these people if it failed. They would not be judged on failure – in fact they were hardly ever judged at all, especially on the lawless outrage that was their corporate governance. Phil thought it best to underline his mercenary side again.

'And by the way, this is a way of me making some money as well as Frank's freedom – let's call it his earn-out.'

'We will not bargain with you, but you will feel our gratitude if results are good. Please do not attempt to outwit us as the result will be immediate – all traces of you and your friends will simply be removed. Is that understood?'

'Understood.'

'I will make the arrangements with our man in Delhi. With our patronage he has become very rich and well connected – he has the resources to take advantage of such an opportunity.'

What the hell am I doing, Phil thought – am I one more to be sucked into the world of the many-headed snake? Only two reserves left – Gus and Lily. He must report back to them before leaving for Delhi, lest the feared Hydra engulf him too.

'I can catch a plane this afternoon and be in Delhi this evening, but I will need a visa.'

'That will be arranged on arrival.'

'I will need to meet on neutral ground. There's no point you having yet another guest to worry about. Besides I am used to shipping consignments all over the world and have a clean record; I can earn my passage, as it were.'

'I won't worry about you, one way or the other. If we take you to our base you won't have any idea where you have been. I will leave that up to Saleem – you might as well have a name. Just get your flight; he will know which one and you will be met. Incidentally, Saleem has contacts in every jurisdiction; he will know if you even only *think* of a betrayal or deception.'

He left. Qasim, Wei, and now him, all polished and assured, but abrupt in their dealings, circumspect and wary of outsiders. Was it traces of paranoia – one slip and they would fall into an abyss – or had they genuinely found heaven and were reluctant to share the secret? Of course it was neither; they just operated in a parallel world of covert dealings, unregulated and unapproved. They all lived in the cold mountains of social apartheid high above the plains and valleys of warm interaction and mutual regard. And they enjoyed only a view.

'Lily – it's Phil. Sorry about the time.'

'Six o'clock, that's fine. I'm having too much sleep anyway. Not much else to do round here.'

'Listen, I'm going to Delhi shortly. They have taken the bait and I'm to meet Frank and their man.'

'Phil, that's brilliant news. Sounds like you've got in the door.'

157

'Yeah, so far so good, but getting out again may not be so easy. I don't know what to expect, but if they do hold on to me for a while, I won't be calling in every day. Point is, I don't think you should send up the balloon if I go quiet.'

'That leaves us in a quandary. At what point do we report you missing?'

'I don't know – a week, two maybe, as long as you can hold your nerve. I may be wrong but I think they will leave me on parole. The consequences of any trickiness on my part have been made quite explicit.'

'So what do you have up your sleeve?'

'Actually I don't know yet, but ironically I think that Frank will be quite tickled to cock a snoop at the big pharmaceuticals for a while. Maybe he'll regard his kidnappers as his new sponsors.'

'Very droll, Phil, and what about Olly? Will they become his patron? Will he become a sculptor in residence?'

'Steady on, Lily. Sorry for being facetious, but remember the best case is for this diverted AIDS medicine to prove profitable. They won't need Frank after it's all set up, and I don't believe they will need him long for the original purpose either. We just have to ensure that Frank is of value to them, and, by association, Olly too. The key figure is their door-keeper in Delhi – his name is Saleem, and I suspect he would answer the phone number you must never call. My hunch is that he has yet to prove his own trustworthiness to the dons in Hong Kong. It may be a weakness we can exploit.'

'I'm terrified for you all. It can all go horribly wrong at any moment.'

'It could, but it will take time whether it goes right or wrong, and now we are in equilibrium, secured by the common interest that holds us. On the other hand the disappearance of that guy who came for you is a loose end, and these people do not like loose ends. You two are the ones in danger. Perhaps you should both move out of the flat for a while.'

'No, we'll stay put. We have our defences and I do believe that Gus is relishing some action if anyone else is sent.'

Phil said his goodbyes and rang off – there was nothing else productive to say. He had heard about the car and the mobile phone; any more talk would just be conjecture that none of them wanted to gnaw at.

Nonetheless Lily was gnawing on the dry bones of her own contribution. All this cloak and dagger stuff – was it really the answer? This contrivance over the AIDS drugs – did it really put Olly and Frank in less danger? Was it just buying time? Time ... back to that game again, waiting for time to move its pieces around the board. Better act before they are all in check. One week, she decided ... if no progress in a week she would ring a number. Whether it was the police or the number from the man's pocket, she would decide at the time.

21

Phil was thinking about Frank, his dear and lifelong friend. This was not a sentimental reflection – it was just a matter of fact that Frank's stress and difficulties were his stress and difficulties. They were not brothers, but the ties were stronger. Passing their early years in the cool transit of institutional life, the two developed a bond, born not only out of compatibility, but also out of interdependence. A child is a very sensitive instrument for measuring warmth and security – later readings will show clearly neglect or indifference in gradations of emotional and social displacement. But these two were not displaced – they both had big hearts that absorbed what warmth was around them and rejected none. Frank was a thinker, Phil a doer – they were a snug fit and were able to deal with life as it came at them without chips or hang-ups.

That he should consider the dangers at any personal level would be to write on water: it would make no impact on the immutable compact that nature had drafted. Whatever he was walking into, he would walk at a steady pace; in fact half of him was already there – his alter ego, Frank.

He walked down the steps from the aeroplane at Delhi. The late afternoon air was cool with a light breeze from the north, a welcome change from the humidity of the Hong Kong morning which he had left hanging over the city. On the other hand he was now to experience a different sort of oppression.

'Mr Donahue?' An airport official waited at the bottom step. Maybe not so clever to know his name – after all, they had traced his flight and seat, and, the only passenger in business class, he was the first off – but it was still a measure of their influence, or more probably that of their local agent, Saleem.

'Please follow me. You have another flight waiting.' A car marked 'Immigration' took them around the perimeter to the domestic terminal. The official stamped Phil's passport, and, with the deference reserved for a VIP, ushered him into a waiting helicopter. With just a pilot, a guard, and Phil on board, a minute later it was on the move, initially vertically, then as if on elastic, whipping over the dusty ground below. The immigration official might have been surprised to see Phil being handed a hood, but, by the same logic as Olly's, Phil was quite content with the precaution.

An hour or so under the hood with the drone and swirl of the machine might have left Phil in a state of discomposure, but he kept hold of his mental balance by collecting his thoughts. They were bleak thoughts that held sway, appropriate to the shroud of darkness over his head. He was fuming with anger and indignation at the world for setting out stalls for the grasping and greedy, the downright murderous, or at the politicians who were led a merry dance, unable to play the long game, or indeed the short one.

Phil knew from his own experiences that global trade had opened the door to a host of illicit activities, from counterfeit brands, music, DVDs, software, and countless other tradable goods. He was aware of the bondage behind much of this output in sweatshops and other kinds of human traffic for effectively forced labour or procured services. He had been content to make an honest trade where it was possible and to reject the sort of business that did not fit

161

his own homespun code, but it was now increasingly difficult to carry on without having to turn a blind eye to the provenance of any merchandise or the circuitous methods of payment. It was a matter of great thankfulness, however, that his personal finances had accrued sufficiently to allow him to sit in the cool, and turn away certain nefarious commerce. He did not have to keep the heat on to satisfy an ever-growing desire for wealth and power.

He wondered, though, about the damage that all this illicit trade would do to the world at a time when there were finally some prospects of wealth and security being shared out more fairly. Was he being haunted by the truth in his own dictum that trade would always fill a vacuum? Was it not better that money circulated, whatever impelled it? No – not if it meant the world resuming a brutish medieval struggle with life dominated by battling warlords, and that seemed to him the likely corollary with illicit drugs. Whatever the profound complexities of these questions, Phil was discovering some simple truths about illicit drugs.

There was a stark contrast between the illicit trade in copied branded goods and drugs. Rather than producing and selling a copy of a branded article for a fraction of the real thing, it seemed to Phil that the manufacture and distribution of illegal narcotics seemed to work in reverse. There was no need to undercut a genuine market, and indeed the value of illicit drugs benefited from a price grossly enhanced precisely due to the attempted ban on their availability. The immense gap between cost in the poorer country of origin and market price in the affluent countries of North America or Europe, whilst partly depleted by the logistics of covert transport and delivery, nevertheless allowed fortunes and power to be amassed of unimaginable size in the hands of a few, with the lives of the great majority in the typical producing country subsisting at no greater levels thanks to the trade.

This drugs business was supported by a consuming minority in the richer countries, and the exaggerated values made for very costly imports, even before the cost of enforcing the prohibition. In the USA alone the government spends $40 billion a year and locks up half a million of its citizens every year to protect a stupid lumpen minority. This was a war that had been waged for a hundred years, that was not only pointless, but was laying waste any hopes of civilized political progress between opposing worlds. It was also a trade with particular propensity to cause abuse. Abuse being the operative word – from the exploitation and abuse of the growers or procurers of the raw materials, through to the indented workers exposed to dangerous processing, to the final users and abusers, and ultimately to the power conferred on the cartel, which would be abused – wielded to spread fear and corruption. Phil remembered leafing through Frank's notes a week ago, skip reading one entitled 'Harm Reduction'. He was beginning to understand the point. It urged for an intelligent debate on the comparative harm from drug prohibition, with the realisation that thanks to the accumulation of wealth and power in malevolent hands, the world had become a more dangerous place, especially since the turn of the century, that short and benign and almost innocent period of celebration. It was now time to examine the arguments in a cold light, unheated by agitation or misplaced emotion.

Where did the least harm lay? Obliging the richer consuming nations, who could afford education and social programmes, to deal with any unlikely increase in drug abuse? Or abetting the breakdown of whole societies in the producing countries, or gateway countries like Mexico, broken and supine before the will of the narco-barons?

163

And here he was, caught in the blades of this relentless machine chewing up anything or anyone that got in its way ... 'Wake up, we've arrived.' It was the guard removing Phil's hood. Whether he had thought the thoughts or dreamt them, he concluded they had been rightly provoking. But now he must not provoke; he must be neutral and businesslike.

They had landed on a piece of scrubby ground in a dry and featureless landscape and transferred from the helicopter to a dusty station wagon. Phil's hood was replaced, although this time for just a couple of minutes – no time for further rumination. But it was of no consequence – Phil had given the subject a good airing, and he was satisfied to get his thoughts in order, but his focus now was not to save the world, but to sell his idea for a little drug rustling as a new venture for Saleem, and, better still, if possible, a joint venture.

Saleem was sitting on a vast, high-backed chair, lined with velvet and silk, just short of a throne. Either side of him was a small Chinese guard, each dressed in a grey Mao suit with soft silent-looking slippers. They seemed quietly ready to satisfy Saleem's every request, be it innocent or sinister. Frank and Olly sat opposite – Frank substantially recovered but Olly looking haggard and drawn. It was as if they had only so much vigour between them and the bloom of health had transferred one to the other. They had been told of a visitor just minutes ago, and guessed it must be Phil, but what sort of horse trading had opened the way for him they could not fathom. He had succeeded in finding them, though, and, it had been hinted, had come with a proposition.

Phil was through the main gate before the hood was removed, the heavy wooden doors thudding behind him as he entered the closed world of the *haveli*. He was shown into a grand salon, at the end of which he could see Frank and Olly, and opposite them a man sitting grandly between two attendants. Not large in physical stature but with a powerful presence projected from an aura of malevolence, he turned to the snap of the door, his birdlike head seeming to hover over a reptilian body, his darting, wary eyes watching Phil's approach.

Phil managed his entrance with theatrical perfection. His very first glance at his two friends told them to keep back any show of jubilation. He did not want to appear as part of a happy team; indeed, he would like them to return his contrariness. They had not seen Phil conduct his business before, but they knew that his demeanour would never have been that of a hostile accountant come to conduct an audit. This he was today, and he received a credit from Saleem, who appreciated his cold priorities.

The transfer of information between Phil and Frank was as between two bridge partners. Frank understood Phil's opening bid and replied in spades.

'Oh God, I might have known it was you. What sort of deal are you cooking up this time?' Frank spoke with some venom; there was obviously no love lost between these two, and perhaps unfinished business.

'My dear chap,' Phil replied coldly, 'It is my business to cook up deals. I am the very knave of invention.' There it was – confirmation, thanks to Father Burke and his namesake Edmund – 'The credulity of dupes is as inexhaustible as the inventions of knaves.' Frank understood the reference: it was one of Father Burke's favourite quotes; he would bring it out whenever he spoke of some political chicanery, or – worse in his mind – Jesuit sophistry. In other words, endless people fooled by clever tricksters.

Poor Olly, partly from relief at seeing Phil and partly out

of the comedy from the interplay, let out an involuntary chuckle. The slightest pressure on his knee from Frank was his prompt. He didn't know the quote but he knew just in time that the objective was to remove any sign of fraternity between Frank and Phil, and dupe Saleem accordingly. Olly adroitly turned his chuckle into a snigger.

'Do I have to be in the same room as this creep?' Olly stood up as he let out this contempt.

'Well I see that we are all the best of friends.' Saleem gestured to Olly to sit down – it was confirmed by both his aides. 'Mr Donahue, are these the two to make our fortunes?'

'If they know what's good for them.' Phil glowered at Frank. 'I know this man, and I know that secretly he is quite a crusader, and whatever our personal animosity I know that my scheme will appeal to his dissident nature. Maybe he'll admit we're not so bad after all.' Phil's attempt to pair himself with Saleem under the context of badness brought no condescension from the latter, but Phil had to be careful – any hint of ingratiation could suspend the credulity his knavery had created. He outlined his scheme in a flat voice: the purloining of anti-retroviral medicine for repackaging. It was a presentation of a skeleton plan that needed input from both Saleem and Frank, although neither wished to deliver the first response. However, Frank knew that he needed to show a temptation to cooperate; he just needed to temper his enthusiasm.

'Technically, this is not an unfeasible proposition,' he said impassively. 'The latest triple-action one-a-day pills are all out of trials and plenty of generic versions are produced here in India. They are also still expensive and not widely affordable in poor countries. As to finishing off production here, I'd need to see your equipment and facilities. Presumably,' Frank continued with resignation, 'I was to make a study of your existing processes to fulfil my originally intended function?'

'We do indeed have work for you in that field,' Saleem replied. 'I mean the field of quality control and testing the deliveries of precursors.' His voice was as flat as Phil's, not from hiding any arousal to this new idea, more the hollowness he felt to the original plan. He had not wanted outside expertise foisted on him, which would inevitably amount to scrutiny, but he knew he could not refuse the suggestion from his backers. The choice of Frank under the pretext of his mooted precursor report and his laboratory skills was masterly, and the terms of his retention – coercion – would leave Saleem in control, with the opportunity for a cover-up. 'This extra work would be quite novel,' he continued, 'but I shall have to review the provision of raw materials with our suppliers.'

'This material will not be raw,' Frank continued. 'It will need to be completely processed, leaving just the final tableting and coating to us. The pharmaceutical process is extremely involved – it requires sensitive apparatus and access to a multitude of excipients and APIs ...'

'Stop there,' Saleem held up his hand– Frank was talking pharmaceutical. 'I shall need one of my apothecaries to hear this.'

The term 'apothecary', it occurred to Frank, had a quaint euphemistic air bearing in mind the work of this clandestine drugs lab. On the other hand, and with deep irony, it did conjure up an old-fashioned mixer of poisons and potions. 'Not much else to say actually,' Frank continued, 'but for your information, excipient is just the inert medium – a vehicle for the API, the active pharmaceutical ingredient. We will need the finished compound in bulk.'

Saleem spoke in Chinese to his revolutionary guards, one of whom escorted Frank away to meet the 'apothecaries' and the other marched Olly to his quarters. 'Come, Mr Donahue, we have mutual business to discuss.' That this was said pointedly, before the others had left the room, seemed to betray Saleem's disposition to Phil. He not only seemed to believe the antipathy of his captives to Phil, but he took pleasure in exacerbating it. It was also proof that the version of Phil's motives given to Saleem's masters had not been passed down to Saleem – to them Phil had admitted a wish to free his friends as well as making some money. More and more he realized that Saleem was on trial.

22

'Mr Donahue, tell me how did you come to know of Mr Landing's disappearance in the first place? You don't seem to be on the best of terms with him and his son.'

Saleem had guided Phil out onto the veranda, overlooking the courtyard. More silent-footed staff, who treated Saleem with more fear than respect, padded about or melded with the frescoes which adorned every inch of the building inside and out: every wall, ceiling, and column bedecked with images of India, from gods in pastoral scenes to more incongruous depictions of aeroplanes, cars, and big city life. The naïve abandon of the decoration was more a display of the multiple successes of the previous owners than an expression of artistic style – it was an affirmation of the wealth not just of their treasury, but of their understanding and experience. Saleem sat vicariously absorbing the reflection of these past glories, insensible to the shades of darkness through which anyone he touched would view him. He appeared at ease in Phil's presence, and Phil hoped his own appearance befitted a man with a similarly cold heart – it was not so difficult to manifest such a mien opposite a serpent.

'That bloody girlfriend of Olly's practically accused me of being behind it. Came at me with all these crazy theories about where Frank was, and who had taken him. It was just after Olly left for here. Anyway, I told her she was demented. She must have convinced those two as well, judging from their reaction just now. Actually we fell out some time ago over some liberties I had taken passing off with some artwork of Olly's – they fucked up a perfectly good deal for want of balls and a little dishonesty. Even then,' Phil added with a scowl, 'they weren't as hostile as just now. I blame that girl.'

'You know, I believe I spoke to her. She sounded extremely bright.'

Yes, you did, you patronising bastard, Phil wanted to say – I heard you.

'I'll give you that,' he said instead. 'She seemed to have it all worked out. Mind you, she was quite wrong about me. As you know, Frank's "extraction" had nothing to do with me, but she inadvertently pointed me in the right direction – all that talk about Frank and his AIDS expertise. Ironic that. Anyway, it got me to thinking of a good ruse myself.'

'Where is the girl now? We don't want her being a nuisance.'

'God knows. Apparently she just disappeared one afternoon. Probably did what I told her – get lost! Couple in their flat told me; they thought it was curious but weren't too bothered.'

All so easy, so plausible, one falsehood after the other; he was weaving a cloak of deceit thread by spurious thread, but he knew that it must be shown to Frank for collusion lest his artfulness be exposed. Just a few seconds, a moment snatched alone with Frank, was all that would be needed. Phil was confident that Frank would be on the same alert; he would see the trip wires too – he would help contrive the moment.

'Yes, it is curious …' Saleem was still thinking about the girl and his bungling henchman who seemed to have got lost himself. He said the words with a little too much curiosity for Phil's comfort. The best that Phil could do to steer him away from this mystery, without arousing suspicion, relied on a typical male dismissal: 'Stupid cow!'

Saleem was lured into a corresponding response and nodded his head sagely. His sagacity was not tested further, however, due to the return of Frank and an intense, nervy man called Dr Chinn, together with three more Chinese men, the stains and acid burns on their white coats a reminder to Phil of the delicate balance these chemicals must achieve before they are fit for consumption. Dr Chinn was Saleem's head alchemist – he oversaw the synthesis of the chemicals into little compressed tablets of mind-altering pleasure and dependency. He ran a large team of technicians all imported from China, whose expertise and willingness ranged from hardened 'cooks' and young chemists taking a year off to pay student debts, to unskilled labour often pressed unwittingly into service with no papers or hope of a passage home.

'Well, gentlemen, what is your conviction? Are you persuaded as to this new enterprise?'

'We will need sanction from Hong Kong before we proceed.' Dr Chinn felt he needed to say this in public, although he knew he would not be heeded and that his situation would never allow more than a token objection to any irregularity. Saleem was irritated but dismissive.

'Let me make this crystal clear,' he said coolly. 'Mr Donahue has come from Hong Kong this afternoon – they have sent him to investigate this very idea.' He turned to Dr Chinn, the crystal now turned to ice. 'I just need to know from you if it is practical.'

Sensing the tension, Frank stepped forward to speak; he would diffuse it, but store the insight it contained. 'We believe that with an investment in some plant, specifically a high-output tableting machine together with new moulds and casts, more sensitive scales, and a spectrometer for testing, we can produce over a quarter of a million tablets a day.'

Dr Chinn watched Saleem's eyes widen; he was grateful for Frank's intervention but needed to disabuse Saleem quickly about the likely output. 'But that figure is of course out of the question in the light of the limited mixed compound we may be able to secure ...' This was the crux: it was one thing diverting chemicals before they entered any chain of production – to some extent less exactly measured and accounted for – but it was another to divert a final batch of a finished compound, the product of infinitesimally exact measurements and record keeping. Saleem and his crew looked uncomfortable – the secrets of procurement were not for outsiders, however bound they were into the rest of the process. The opportunity was heaven-sent.

'Please,' said Phil, 'we do not want to pry into your sources. We will withdraw so you can discuss the matter between yourselves.' Without waiting for any form of assent from Saleem, Phil and Frank turned their backs on the gathering, and walked to the far end of the terrace. For added verisimilitude they also sat some distance apart, ignoring each other. They had walked slowly; it didn't take long for the exchange, Frank was ready for it without preamble: Phil's impertinent and intemperate art dealings last summer; Liu's accusation of Phil's collusion in the kidnap – result, complete enmity. There was even time for Frank to recall the artwork – it was a copy of Rodin's *Hand of God*, made just for a study, but advanced by Phil to some Russians as original. Like all good lies it was grounded in actuality: Olly had produced such a piece, a copy of a sculpture that Rodin had sculpted in three sizes. Phil had joked at the time that maybe the gullible art world was ready for a fourth. A dozen last words each were also enough to confirm their shared suspicions that

Saleem was probably running some scam on his backers' profits.

Saleem's controlling nature would have been to separate these two, not from any overt suspicion – he felt impregnable anyway – but just as his policy of keeping apart all his various disciplines. No one person should understand the entire process – that way there could be no challenges to his authority, or, more importantly, no resistance to his methods. Seeing the two, however, still opposed, across the terrace, out of earshot of both each other and Dr Chinn's assessment, replaced any concern with some satisfaction. Saleem congratulated himself; his pointed remark earlier about a workmanlike mutuality with Phil must have added further rancour to the animus into which their erstwhile friendship had clearly sunk.

'How much could we get?' Saleem asked Dr Chinn. 'I assume from your remark that we could get some?'

'I believe we could obtain a quantity through the offices of our friend Mr Gupta. His company has huge contracts to supply generic versions of these drugs. I'm sure he would cooperate through a mixture of greed and some persuasion, but don't forget that the production is controlled under strict licences and a discrepancy in stock inventories would be quickly noticed. I suppose they could put any initial inconsistencies down to theft.'

'Yes,' Saleem interjected, with a sly solution which was meant to goad Dr Chin as much as cover some tracks, 'and I'm sure we could offer up a culprit if necessary.'

Dr Chinn passed over Saleem's pitiless remark – yes indeed he would get some poor innocent wretch indicted if necessary. He continued, 'After that, reducing levels to avoid suspicion, eventually quite modest amounts.'

'But what do these figures mean in terms of tablets?'

'Eventually a few million – hard to say.'

Saleem's eyes widened again; this could mean unlocking his future. He had sold his soul to the Chinese syndicate, had made them a lot of money and much more for himself than the bargain had sanctioned. But a combination of avarice and brinkmanship had stripped his double dealing of any caution, and he could see now a day when discovery might condemn him. Two lives had been forfeited already to cover up his skulduggery – a small price to pay for his continued enrichment, but he was beginning to understand that his own life had a price too, and he needed that life to enjoy the spoils. To extricate yourself from a contract with the Devil would indeed require a black art, but to leave the deal in deficit would be to taste the sulphur of hell. Saleem needed to balance the books, and this could be his opportunity. He clapped his hands; Frank and Phil were summoned back to the meeting.

'You have two days to confirm the source the equipment and the ingredients. Mr Landing will advise Dr Chinn of the latest AIDS treatments, and what we need from Gupta. I want likely costs and delivery times.'

'Mr Donahue,' Saleem continued, 'I need you to put together a consignment of goods for airfreight to Africa. You can do your work in Delhi – I hope the Oberoi is to your liking. I will drop you off back to the airport – you can find your own way to the hotel. I myself will be back at Delhi airport on Thursday at ten o'clock in the morning, terminal 2 – Air India check-in 1. We will meet there and return here for a further briefing.' This was the chief executive talking, clear instructions and deadlines, results expected.

Ashish sat on a stool outside Frank and Olly's rooms – still the jailer, but also a general wallah to their needs. He had developed a level of intimacy with Olly somewhat short

174

of conspiracy – there was nothing to conspire about; they were both caught in the opposing prehensile grip of Saleem and his masters. He watched as Olly was let through the gate and left to cross the courtyard back into his charge. It was Olly's turn to crawl to a sickbed. Ashish had seen the signs, the exchange of debility from father to son, and now they were endorsed. Olly moved slowly and achingly, his face blotched with the coming fever. Olly also knew he was sinking; he just needed to go where Frank had been, to bed in a darkened room, face to the wall. It would pass, he knew that, and, pleased that his dad was on the rise, he lay down to let nature take its course.

Ashish stayed by his side, provided water, a little dry bread, and what little medical support he could find. There were times, however, when the direction of Olly's delirium seemed irreversible. He lay motionless, almost blind, his entire being recoiling from light and movement. With a mind receded into the confines of his torpor, Olly became unable even to communicate. The two people in his reduced world who were waiting to connect – Frank and Ashish – were both anxious for signs of recovery, signs that what medicines they could find would help. Ashish had seen more than Frank how inflammation can creep up the spine to the brain – these diseases were endemic in India – but he chose not to share his disquiet.

Since their first testing encounter in Frank's fetid cell, a guarded respect had grown between Ashish and Olly. Ashish had told of his own father's gradual subordination into Saleem's will, his attempts to extricate him, and his own subjugation. They were held in check by threats of punishment on each other – violence or cruelty visited on a loved one being a ruthless counter to dissent, not unlike the force that brought Olly here as surety for his father. But the empathy was, however, felt more by Ashish: he was on the inside looking out at these innocent characters, whereas Olly was outside looking in to a nest of people all engaged in activities that, whilst not necessarily evil individually, were complicit in a corrupt and shabby enterprise. His judgement shaded by implication, Olly was yet to entirely reciprocate the sentiment.

Olly had at least seen a plan developing, with a small team of ingenious compatriots engaged on his freedom. A freedom negotiated for him and his father without break-out or reprisal – that was the hope. Ashish had once tried a breakout and had suffered the reprisal: he had seen his father beaten and all resistance crushed by threats being made to watch his son being similarly treated. It can take some time in captivity for hope to fade, but the unrequited longing for freedom from the barbs and binds of oppression eventually abates. And what is left is but sadness – sadness that cannot be read by another, a lonely and personal sadness impossible to show or explain, a sadness that must be hidden from your oppressors lest it gives them succour, and also from fellow oppressed lest it lowers them further into their own misery.

Ashish's sadness was so deep that Olly nearly missed it, but as he lay on his bed, insensible to all around him, his conscious thought returned to the sound of a sob. It was the sob of tormented goodness, and loss of the joy that should accompany it – he had heard it before on that train in London. The plash of Lily's soft tear on his hand that evening had dissolved any doubt about the spontaneity of his affection for her, and likewise this sign of suppressed private grief from Ashish moved Olly on to a higher level of understanding. Ashish did not know that the sound of his sob had been shared, and did not know the power it had on Olly. It was just another of many, although most were saved for his pillow.

Nature did take its course. Olly did recover, weakened in body but mentally hardened by an unbending resolve to smash this syndicate, to expose it to the full opprobrium of the law, to society, and if necessary personal grievance. It was not going to be enough to escape, to become a miserable fugitive from the brutal justice that anyone challenging these criminals would face. Neither would amnesty be enough for people like Ashish; they needed the total obliteration of any association with these thugs so they could lead their lives without fear. In the meantime Ashish deserved that his deep melancholy be lifted with a little hope.

'Ashish,' Olly said this quietly and confidentially, 'if we get out of here, we will not go without you and your father. Stay close, and make sure you keep your job as our guardian, even if it means a cold discharge of your duties in public.'

The young man's usually effacing eyes shone with elation, which was further borne out by the poetry in his reply, 'Thank you, I will be careful. Saleem and his enforcers can sense kind regard on the air,' adding with a glint of newfound brightness, 'I will emit only disdain in their presence.'

23

For some days Olly had lain exhausted from both the fever that had consumed him and the angst that had taken over. Eventually, however, more gentle thoughts soothed his brow – thoughts of Lily. But Olly was scared to recall her face in case the picture had faded, in case a memory test would be a test of his constancy. Yet there was so much else to draw her back: her scent, the sound of her voice, the touch of her hand … and then there she was, refracted in that tear in all her purity, the tear that encapsulated all his feelings. But the association took his reverie into more surreal areas, with images of Lily trapped in a watery droplet unable to sink or swim – a reminder that he had left her dangling, waiting helplessly day by day for news of his return. Their lives were on hold.

For her part, Lily was indeed in suspense. She had been mortally struck by the love for this young man, and only he could save her, only his presence and his love would consummate her recovery. But her suspense was not just of her own plight; it was of the restraints to her capacity to impose her volition on these events.

Her experience of life was that the right amount of work and effort produced results. There was a direct correspondence between the two sides of the equation, and that was the elemental thing about music: you only got out what you put in. No one got through a complicated passage by luck; chance played no part in performance. With her conditioning to connect reward with effort and not reward with risk, her destiny was therefore always in her own hands, figuratively as well as actually. Certainly until Claude her life was simple, not easy, but uncomplicated by contingencies and unknowns. She had even adjusted her aspirations to suit the talents she had; the reward she looked for was to play at her personal best and not be beaten down by struggles for perfection.

Claude had interrupted her studious industry, but the interference was a gradual invasion. Initially she kept her head by taking measures to frustrate his pursuit, always with the hope that he would eventually desist. Whilst latterly she became fearful for her safety, her final deliverance, coming from that blow to Claude's head, was unwished as well as unexpected. She could always have run for help, found sanctuary, re-covered her traces, or even sought protection through legal remedy. The point was that there was always a certain dynamic in her response to the world, and she had now swooned not just into love, but into a state of abeyance. She needed to make a positive effort to save and win the sublime discovery that was Olly, and not just make silent entreaties to providence.

'Gus, I think we should both go and get an Indian visa. One of us may be needed at the drop of a hat in Delhi or wherever.' Lily said this over the weekend when Gus had been spending most of the time harassing ex-banking colleagues in New York to trace the financial dealings of Mr Wei's company or anything associated with him. Not particularly to establish any malfeasance on his part, but rather to find a pattern to any of his corporate dealings, a recurring name or type of transaction, countries of operation and so on – any symmetries would do.

'Good plan. First thing Monday morning then, crack of dawn – I hear they queue in tiers.' Gus's peremptory reply suggested no lack of interest – it was something that should be done. The events of Claude and the failed abduction had left them both withdrawn and literally shut in for the last few days. Lily was right: they needed those visas, they needed to get out, and a trip for visas would be a step in the right direction. It might even enable one or both of them to get out of the country, to India – an urgent imperative might require a quick response.

But Lily was still brooding. Frank and then, in turn, Olly had disappeared behind a vast immovable object. They were working on a plan to get behind it; they had spoken of a lever – some way of getting a purchase on the dead weight that was protecting the enigmatic, uncommunicating, secretive, unscrupulous, and bestial nightmare that was organised crime. It was crime with a structure, with a board of directors and highly paid middle management who kept their morality and humanity in a jar. No code of behaviour could be banked on except that which related to their treatment of each other – draconian rules to enforce allegiance to the collection of villainous predators that was their brotherhood.

The great rock that had been rolled in front of their lair was not to be found in any geological deposit; it was a composite material made up of greed, fear, vested interest, resigned acceptance, and ambivalence to corruption. Much harder to crack than brittle stone, its man-made substrates were the sediment of human nature. Lily was ranting, she knew, but was taking some pleasure from the invective she had discovered. She was not just railing against her personal circumstances, though; she was working up courage to storm the wall herself. How, she did not know, but given the slightest prospect of making an impact she must be ready.

180

Phil called on Monday night. It was a fantastic tale – Lily loved the impromptu standoff between Olly and Frank, and the dastardly knave who was Phil. She hadn't met Frank, but she had seen a little of the drollery that Olly and Phil were capable of, and could well imagine the scene.

'I don't know whether I feel better to hear that the game has started,' she said, suddenly faced with the dangers of their subterfuge, 'or more nervous that there is no way back if they lose.'

Gus had been listening to the account with nods of appreciation. 'You are certainly playing with fire,' he gushed, 'and I must admire your coolness – pardon the wordplay!' He continued less effusively, with a professional air of one who has studied human nature. 'It's interesting that this guy Saleem is so immediately keen on the idea; it's almost like he has his own special reasons to make it work. Also he seems to accept you, Phil, as a man striped with the same narrow self-interest. Mind you, don't expect him ever to trust you – I say that to prevent you from either relaxing or despairing; he just can't afford to trust anyone.'

'Don't doubt it,' said Phil, 'and I agree about Saleem's seizure on this whole idea, but whether his enthusiasm comes from a personal motive or just a desire to give his masters a quick appraisal I don't know. He is clearly a smooth operator, though. Probably just needs answers so he can move on, one way or the other.'

'What you said about the needle between him and this Dr Chinn,' Lily was feeling intuitive, 'sounds like Chinn would like to be a whistleblower for some reason.'

'Yeah, given the chance, but something was holding him in check,' Phil added, warming to the premise. 'Saleem certainly put him back in his box.'

'This is all good stuff,' said Gus. 'We couldn't have hoped for more. Sounds like there's something going on there under the surface. I reckon you can worm your way in, Phil – perhaps not into Saleem's confidence, but somehow to be of service to him.'

'I think I see myself as a mole more than a worm.'

'So do I,' said Lily, affectionately. 'I've seen your hands. And by the way I assume that Frank and Olly are alive to any dissent in the camp?'

'I exchanged only those few furtive words, and yes they spotted it too. Believe me, Frank won't have missed a thing, and don't forget he is going to be working closely with the grumpy Dr Chinn.'

'Phil, on another tack,' said Gus, 'I've been doing some checking on this Mr Wei. I may get some sort of profile on him, you know, bankers' confidences and such. If there is something that can give us a whisper on Saleem, I can run it past my guys. That won't be his real moniker, so keep your eyes peeled for a name, anything, a bit of packaging, a number, whatever.

'And another thing, if you can get to speak to Olly, does he have any idea where he is? He may have picked up some co-ordinates on the way – he went off with enough maps for a major expedition. He was going to learn the local geography on the plane.'

'I'm meeting Saleem on Thursday for a round-up – suppose it'll be the same place, and I hope Frank will be there. If Olly has any information, he or Frank will try to pass it over if they are brought in. Maybe they'll slip me a note – nah, that sounds too dangerous – but don't worry, we'll find a way. And talking of notes, shouldn't someone tell Frank's office that he is still unwell?'

'Ah,' said Lily, 'we got a call this morning from them; they were half-expecting him back in today. Told them Olly had taken him away last night, didn't know where, Maldives maybe, convalescing – Didn't they get the mes-

182

sage? Oh my, aren't those boys hopeless at leaving messages!'

'Nice work, Lily,' said Phil, 'that'll keep them from raising the alarm for a few weeks. Come to think of it, Saleem must be expecting a hue and cry at some point, especially now that Olly can't cover for his father. After all, he knew Frank worked on sensitive material.'

'Maybe that was his scout,' said Gus, 'the guy hit by the truck – his job to report on events.'

'I don't think he was bright enough to relay intelligence; there must be others.' As she said this, Lily thought of the staircase and the lights and just Gus's fists for protection – maybe she'd feel safer in India. Also she realized that she was pining for Olly more now that he had a physical presence somewhere, at a given location, and had not just disappeared into the ether. The location was not of course given to her, but she knew that he was only a plane ride away. If only he would send his new address.

Gus and Phil were having a long and repetitive exchange about bank accounts, labyrinthine subsidiary companies, dirty money, piggybacking lawful transactions to confound laundering regulations, a long list of jargon and activities. Both men had been learning about another country, a vale of intrigue and deceit that 10% of the money circulating around the world visited to be serviced and cleaned up for subsequent respectable ownership. Lily would normally have been enthralled by this dark enlightenment, but she faded out the depressing implications of this insidious under-the-counter realm. Even basically honest citizens were ingloriously abetting these devious mechanisms, without associating the grievous support they gave to the strings of traffickers heedless to the human misery their activities caused, or in some cases relied on.

'Ok, Phil, I'll let you know, but you're right: Ravi may

know about those sort of movements.' Gus was wrapping up the call.

'Bye, Lily. Now you know as much as we do about filthy lucre.'

'Bye, Phil. Actually I drifted off – probably shied away from the disillusionment.'

'I'll send you some notes.'

'Make sure they're nicely laundered. I heard that bit!'

Before the call Lily had spent an hour just playing scales; they were a thread that connected every passing day of her musical life, right back to early girlhood. They were her security. She could remember almost every day, especially times of breakthrough when a difficulty would ease into competence, or connections in her brain would finally start a chain reaction of conceptual thought, bringing elusive points of harmony into focus – a brainwave perhaps. Now she sat cross-legged and barefooted on an old armchair overlooking the roof terrace. In torn jeans and one of Olly's shirts she looked at the same time young, innocent, and girlish, and yet mature and bookish. With a pencil stuck in a short crop of hair stooked together with an elastic band she presented herself artlessly and unfledged, but then, with a furrowed brow and the pencil in her teeth as if to ponder a weighty calculation, her look was one of seasoned and intelligent contemplation. She was calculating, but she didn't need the pencil to record the answer.

It had been a reassuring phone call: great to hear that their plan was being tested, Frank and Olly were unharmed, Gus and Phil working like a couple of old pros from Interpol. All good – in the context of the two men being held against their will, in a place where the law is a dead letter. A detached observer might wager sardonically that their repatriation was unlikely when their usefulness was declared at an end

– their return to sender was only a very slim possibility. But Lily did not want to hedge her bets: she had staked her hopes on a positive outcome; that was what must give her the resolve to wait quietly with a level head, or, if the time came, to risk all to secure Olly's return. It was this balance of hope and uncertainty that defined her nascent state – it amplified her yearning for absolute unity with Olly. Risk all? Yes, she would risk all to bring him back, but equally she would give all, if necessary, just to share his fate.

24

And what of Frank? Frank, the centre of all this – the father of the son, the expert snatched in a clandestine coup, and pressed into service in an upside-down world where good is bad and bad is good. These last words were Frank's first thoughts when he found himself in Saleem's grip, the grip of a wild animal that just followed its instincts. This was no place for rational pleas; the only hope was to play dead, and Frank was well cast for the role.

After eight hours lying low in the back of a car he was in such a state of mental withdrawal that his abductors did consider letting go, but somewhere in Holland he was transferred to a truck to become a secret human consignment in a compartment deep inside a genuine cargo of packing cases. At about eight feet by ten – the size of a garden shed – it contained a few pieces of foam, which could be folded or laid out for chairs or beds, a supply of water in some old jerry cans, and rough provisions consisting of bread, cheese, and salami. Strapped to the wall was a chemical lavatory. There was just enough air from somewhere, and an overhead light which remained on. Frank was the only passenger in this 'wagon-lit', but he could tell from the detritus that many more had travelled the outward journey. Whether they had travelled in hope or despair he did not know, but if it was hope they must have left a bad place to travel this way.

With no track of time or place, Frank did not know that

the fresh air he was carried out to twenty-four hours later was cooled by a mist from the Turkish coast of the Black Sea. He was given a little time to find his feet, then dressed in white overalls on top of his two-day-old, and now beggarly, clothes, and walked up to a small aeroplane by a man who looked part of the crew. It was a private or, more probably, chartered jet. The other nine or ten passengers ignored this spare crewman and technician at the rear. The comparative comfort of the five-hour flight to northern India was just an interlude. With that part of the journey over when he might just be observed, Frank was stripped of the clean overalls and thrown into the back of an old van. Not particularly for concealment, just out of disregard – he was just a payload for delivery, or perhaps the brutality was designed to ensure his arrival in a pliant mood.

But it was not Frank's mood that was pliant, despite the psychological effects of his claustrophobia – his mind had been jolted into a new fear by a warning given to him earlier. It was his body that was limp and exhausted from the physiological trauma brought on by his condition – hour after hour of nausea and heart-racing hyper-ventilation had reduced him to an abject state.

The jolt that had surged through Frank's head, with an electro-convulsive effect, clearing his mind of any torpor that helplessness had induced, was the instruction given to him as he was prepared for the aeroplane – his first and only public appearance. 'Cooperate and we will not harm your son.' Not harm your son ... harm your son ... the words kept repeating, repeating, driving a stake through his heart. There was no way to endure such a thought, and especially no way even to consider its likelihood. He could deal with his own agonies, but this he was not equipped for, no endorphins or neuro-transmitters would ever dispatch or dull this pain.

There was nothing that Frank would not suffer to prevent hurt to his son – the intimidation was absolute. This was a dread that no father could confront, and he shook with a hideous and harrowing fear that he might be a cause of an act of retribution being inflicted on Olly. His cooperation would be total, but somehow, somewhere, there would be a way through all this, and for that he must keep his mental faculties alert.

For some time he did keep his mind awake against its natural propensity to shut down, to let his illness and tiredness take over all activity. He needed especially to control his imagination, which was now haunted by threats on Olly. He thought of the reasons for his kidnap – not too difficult to work out; he had heard of this sort of thing happening in some of the drug regions of South East Asia, but never in the UK. His laboratory was exorbitantly careful with information, but not particularly about its personnel. Precautions were there to counter any competitive advantage – industrial espionage in some eyes – with staff loyalty and discretion continually monitored and tested. No programme, however, had anticipated interference with a person.

With hindsight it was clear to Frank that his field of expertise had been watched by people interested in another kind of competition. People intent on staying ahead of a game that required rules to be subverted and no holds barred. His knowledge was of extraordinary value to the manufacturer of synthetic drugs, in particular the illicit ones that required constant innovation in a highly competitive and responsive market for recreational drugs. This could be the only explanation for his kidnap – he had no personal vendettas, no ransom worth, for either financial or political motives. At least this way he knew he could earn his keep.

Never mind Saleem's audacious and well-executed operation, maybe there should have been a contingency plan in place, some small alert to highlight untoward activity. It seemed to Frank – and this was part musing and part rueing the ease with which he had been extracted from his own country – that a measure to avoid an event is directly proportional to the likelihood of the event, and in this case, this very remote event could have been foiled with the simplest of means. What means he would leave to the spooks or to further contemplation.

Frank tried hard for some hours to withstand the suffocating panic, but eventually his mind caved in to the entrapment and lost all power of cognitive thought. After eight hours in the windowless van he was just a brute cargo again, arriving in one of Saleem's premises to await his inspection. Saleem hoped that he had chosen the subject of this consignment well, but if he proved to be shoddy goods the returns policy was strict – there was no return. It was approaching dusk on Wednesday, nearly forty-eight hours after being bundled out of his flat, that he was dumped in that back office. An old man who had prepared the room lay waiting on the bed, and he rose guiltily when Frank was half-carried and half-dragged in.

'Stay there, old man. He can lie on the floor.'

The old man said nothing, but nodded; he knew not to engage with this man, the driver of the van, one of Saleem's most callous heavies. The old man waited for him to leave and then somehow manhandled Frank's dead weight onto the bed. He was also here under duress, but initially because of his own stupidity and a little easy money. He would pay his own penance, and not inflict it on this fellow human being, who may not even see the morning. But sitting quietly in the corner on a couple of sacks, the old man heard no check to Frank's breathing, just heavy lumbering breaths that belonged more to exertion than rest. Maybe he would last the night; every breath was one of recovery, he reasoned.

But Frank came to, he looked around, his eyes circled the room. The window was open and the shutters folded back; it was as if the old man knew that just light and air were needed. With the threat of suffocation abated, Frank's breathing had eased but the nausea remained – open spaces would not remove the bugs that had hitched a lift in his gut. This was a lull between fighting for air and his resistance being tested by a new illness, and Frank was able to get to his feet and walk to the window, but he felt heavy and ponderous like an astronaut returning from weightlessness. He also had travelled in a capsule . . . Outside the sun was setting in the sky and the air dry with that tangy dust that any movement seemed to raise in this rainless season. Frank observed little activity in the neighbouring buildings, but deduced that they were all part of some industrial estate. In the middle distance, across some empty lots, a hanging sign glinted in the last of the evening light, illuminating each letter – R-a-m-a-c-h-e-m – as it swayed in the breeze. It all appeared eerily normal.

Sharp voices outside the door changed the moment. The door burst open and two men, one the driver from the last leg of Frank's ordeal, and the other a small and lithe creature, well groomed, but with a little too much jewellery. He carried a thin silver-topped cane, more, it turned out, a prop to his authority than his gait.

'Close that window, you cretin!' Saleem struck the old man savagely with the cane, and watched as he painfully slid back the window that he had prised open.

'Now go outside and bolt the shutters and don't come back.' Turning to Frank, he said, 'So you are the famous scientist. I had expected more.'

'You would have got more if I hadn't travelled like an animal.'

'Well you'll get over it, and in the meantime we'll have to keep you in quarantine.'

That was when they chained Frank's ankle, leaving him in a now dark and airless room. The driver returned later with some tablets. Frank recognised the name on the bottle; they would cure the infection he could feel building, but do little for his incarceration.

Olly's coming had sent a shudder through Frank's fevered consciousness – whilst not able to make any coherent exchange with his son, he was overcome with joy to see him at his side. The joy was short-lived, though, as a contra-flow of emotions circulated his head, and the significance of Olly's presence drove home the dark verity. Olly was here, he was unharmed, but it confirmed that he, too, was in their power. But if he was under threat, better that he was here than alone somewhere. Here Frank could see and touch him and know he was safe, provided he gauged his cooperation accordingly. And Frank did understand that actually Olly's arrival had probably saved his life.

To understand later that Olly had come under his own initiative, that he had not been coerced, further aroused Frank's confused and tender feelings – a mixture of grat-itude and inexpressible filial pride being in conflict with personal censure and foreboding. Over the next few days, however, they settled in to a quiet routine, Olly's relaxed front and his unworried manner bringing calm to the pitch and roll of Frank's emotions. Also, Olly had informed him that moves were afoot – Phil and his new assistants were on the case.

In his more fatalistic mood, Frank admitted to a curios-ity about this drug manufactory, for that must be where they were. He had studied accounts of large-scale operations around the world but had only visited small backroom labs at home – these were quite crude, with makeshift equipment easy to move to keep ahead of detection, or indeed leave behind if a more hasty exit was required. How big was Saleem's undertaking? What were their specialities? And, interestingly in view of his abandoned report on precursor chemicals, what were their raw materials? He reasoned that his scholarship in this latter subject would be valuable to people needing ever novel ways to secure their base chemicals, and also his knowledge of almost every pill and tablet that had hit the streets of Britain would be useful in customizing a stock-list of supplies.

As Phil knew and Gus had gleaned from his researches, Frank's views on narcotic drugs were pragmatic – he was bemused by the machinations of the authorities and appalled by the scruples of the providers and pushers. Such an apposite word, 'pusher' – clearly the world's propensity to consume drugs wasn't so large that it didn't need a good push. Catch them young, get them hooked – now that's good business. And really it's pyramid selling with a profitable twist, a pyramid interwoven with dependency, both financial and addictive. Opportunities for advancement, easy entry for the self-employed, fabulous rewards, free samples – you'll never look back.

There would be no going back – you would be just as hooked as some of your customers. A £250 billion a year business third only to oil and arms, much bigger than motor cars and it's all illegal – unbelievable, that's what Frank would tell you; and never mind all the corruption of individuals or institutions. He had seen the results of unregulated production; to him substance abuse was the contamination of drugs, spiked with this and cut with that. That level of adulteration would not be tolerated with

192

foodstuffs – although it occurred to him that a walk down a supermarket cereal aisle might prove otherwise, when you count the packets of sugar branded as a wholesome breakfast.

Frank was warming to his theme, but he wasn't delivering a lecture, just stewing on a few thoughts that he would rage about if asked. The irony of his position was quite exquisite: he was intrigued from a professional point of view in how things were produced, and looked forward now to seeing that, but he found himself in the company and under the power of a damnable iniquity that had mastered this business. In this case, Saleem.

25

'He's got more subsidiaries than you can shake a stick at.' Gus was talking to Phil on Tuesday afternoon about Qasim. 'Minority shareholdings in hundreds of companies; many of them legit and active businesses, and many just shells. Judging from the amount of money flowing in and out of his accounts, I think the main subject of his transport business is money. Lot of presence in Dubai: has at least twenty companies registered there; just the tip of the iceberg – impossible to know about nominee holdings or obscure companies with no obvious connection.'

'Sounds like he's some kind of *hawala* dealer,' said Phil.

'That's what my contacts said – a *hawaladar*.'

'Exactly, and in China *hawala* is called *fei qian* – flying money. Did they tell you how it works?'

'Yeah, don't forget it was my job in the bank to think up alternative ways of looking at things, and I tell you, talk about alternative banking, these guys have got it all sown up – been doing it for centuries, before anyone even heard of a bank. You were on a trip to buy goods, say riding your camel down the Silk Route – you didn't take hard cash, just a coded note for the *hawala* dealer. Nowadays you don't need the note in your saddle-bag – just a call or email between dealers, and your cash is transferred. All based on trust, and God help anyone who breaks that trust – at the very least, it's business suicide. It's legal too, most transfers are quite legitimate ... well some of them.'

'Quite, those are the white ones.' Phil had used them, sometimes indispensable in his business.

It was indeed a brilliant system. If you wanted to send money back home, as many immigrant workers do, it's a much cheaper and faster system than using a bank. And these are the great un-banked – two hundred million of them around the world sending home the equivalent of over £300 billion every year. If £1,000 needs to go back to India or Ethiopia, it's handed over to the *hawaladar*, who calls his opposite number, who then gives the money, less commission, to the recipient in the local currency. The two dealers each keep a book, which just records the balance between them with no record of the other parties. Funds going in the other direction keep the balance within manageable amounts, or else equilibrium is reached by an invoice for goods or services, which is a genuine part of the broker's business. Collectively they'll be selling travel tickets, foreign exchange, phone cards, and a whole gamut of import–export trading, from works of art and antiquities to basic minerals.

'It's the black *hawala* that the traffickers and terrorists use so effectively which worries me,' Phil continued, 'often conducted by the same people – it's easy to imagine what you get when you mix black with white.'

'With you,' said Gus, 'a big grey area.'

'Very shady, and one I didn't want to move around in.'

'So you say,' teased Gus. 'But I think you are a *hawaladar* too, Phil. You certainly tick some of the boxes.'

'Not me, much too frenetic – besides, I keep my business within the bounds of legality; that way I sleep at night. The borderlines of *hawala* are too blurred for comfort.'

'I know just what you mean, about the traffickers and the terrorists. It's the classic example – not of the grey bits; this is pure black. How it was explained to me in the bank, and how I used to pass it on to the new guys, I gotta tell you, it's so fucking neat. You have two parties on one side – one's got a pile of cash from some underground drug activity, and the other party needs cash to fund, say, some terrorism – then two more parties on the other side – one wishes to fund the terrorism covertly, and the other is the drug baron waiting for his profits. Both these two want to deal in legitimate money. The first *hawala* dealer passes the cash from the drug peddler to the terrorist; it never leaves the country, never comes to the surface – leaves no trace. The visible money passes between the donor and the baron, with the second *hawala* broker manufacturing legitimate reasons for them both to pay and be paid. The brokers balance their books, get their commission, and everybody is happy – except, of course,' Gus added sardonically, 'the victims.'

Gus's example was a simple one, but a good illustration. As a way of laundering money it is difficult to detect, especially if the transactions have been layered into a series of smaller deals between different brokers, and the proceeds integrated into normal commerce through a complex international shipping network, with invoice manipulations or forged documents.

'And if those good legitimate reasons for the transfers are hard to find,' Gus continued, 'what do they do? They turn to commodities of high-value gold and diamonds – they fit the bill.'

'That's why Dubai is such a pointer,' returned Phil. 'It must be the biggest centre for this activity, with a banking system that doesn't ask too many questions and one of the largest gold and diamond markets in the world. And it's a huge port. What more do you need? And by the way, that Qasim character I met in London, I bet this is his thing, and I bet he's in Dubai. "Just call me Qasim, that's my name here in London," he'd said. Wonder what his name is in Dubai?'

'May get a tag on him in London. I'll speak to our boys …' Gus tailed off; they both knew why. This had been all very interesting, but the person they needed an edge on was Saleem; he was their main quarry.

'Good, good,' Phil resumed. 'I have a feeling that all this will help us nail Saleem. Not to prove he's bent – no prizes for that, we want something that will compromise him with the Triads. Then we can tip them off and let their natural justice take its course.'

'I've heard about their punishments,' said Gus. 'They sound grim.'

'They are… and they are slow. But on a brighter note, how's Lily? I don't hear her on the line.'

'Gone out for a walk. We found a service door out to next door's car park, figured she was quite safe as long as she didn't walk out the front door. Anyway none of these goons know her face and there are plenty of other women in the block. She could be anyone.'

'Possibly,' Phil said with a tinge of concern, 'but she's the only one who's attractive and young.'

'Point taken, but don't forget they're now looking for someone Chinese called Liu; it's an oriental face that will do the attracting.'

'Point taken here too,' said Phil, with a little mischief in his voice.

'Listen,' Gus replied with a hint of bluster, 'have you spoken to Ravi? How are you going to organise the shipment? What are you going to send? Where …?'

'Steady on, Gus, slow down,' Phil interrupted his flow, 'it's all in hand. Ravi is coming up from Mumbai tomorrow – we've identified some stuff for export. Bearing in mind we might even fit into the budget of some heavy-laden health ministry, we've gone for medical supplies. Could also be an agency looking for direct action with their aid money.' Phil remembered the agency that was sold the fake drugs – it would be nice to deliver the real thing. 'There'll be lots of space for our drugs among surgical instruments, dressings, masks, rubber gloves, maybe even a few hundred boxes of condoms for good measure.'

'Kind of belt and braces,' Gus observed, drolly.

'All forms of medical support.' Phil couldn't resist the pun.

'Ha,' Gus responded, 'but seriously, I don't see why Saleem can't sort this through his normal channels.'

'Maybe he will,' replied Phil, 'maybe this is just a test, or maybe he has other reasons. Whatever the maybe, this is my opportunity to be useful and get involved. If he says go and sell the stuff, I'll do it. In fact, come to think of it, I'm going to suggest it.'

'I bet half of his stuff goes through Nigeria or some-where.'

'Quite likely Nigerians,' Phil agreed, 'from what I've read, but through which countries, no idea.'

'Well, be very careful. If you disappear into the dark heart of Africa, we're all lost.'

'I won't disappear, and,' Phil joshed, 'if you'd read Conrad, you'd know that the dark heart was a white Belgian king.'

'Yeah, yeah, and the rest of Europe – I read *Heart of Darkness* in third grade. Make sure they don't sell you up the river.'

''Til tomorrow.' Phil enjoyed their exchanges – Gus had that innocent wisdom so beguiling in Americans.

Lily's walk was to buy a newspaper, specifically a local one that might just have a report on the fatalities last Thursday.

198

It would probably be a Friday paper – the story might have made it in. It would give her a reason to know of Claude's death and to be able to pay her respects to his long-suffering parents. This would assuage her conscience a little, and it would have to do until she could tell them the whole story. She bought one of the last remaining local newspapers in the shop that covered that part of London, and there was the report, stop press on the back page …

Chased to Their Deaths … Two men died instantly when struck by a lorry in Thursday's storm. Eye-witnesses said that one man appeared to be running from the other. Only the assailant has been named – Claude Herbert White of Barons Court West London. Police are investigating the identity of the other man and are requesting a young lady who was in the vicinity to come forward as a potential witness.

End of story. Most obviously it was also the end of Lily's plan to console Claude's parents. The old lady – Gus had given her his umbrella – she must have mentioned Lily's presence and Lily's anguish. But was her concern any more than that of just a passer-by easily touched by the scene, by that terrible impact? Lily had to admit that in the violence of those moments, she had no thought to hide her genuine personal distress or indeed the self-reproach that induced it – she must hope that the old lady was not a local resident. Now she felt a target again, behind her the soft tread of pursuit. She conceived of no personal threat, but the consequences of her discovery could have unwelcome repercussions. She must return to the flat and lie low, free if necessary to invoke a contingency plan that was forming in her head.

'Ah,' said Gus when Lily showed him the newspaper, 'I was just saying to Phil that you were probably not a marked woman – very pretty looks, of course, but not matching someone with a Chinese name whom Saleem is now after.'

'Pity he couldn't explain that to the ruffian he sent last week,' Lily replied ruefully.

'Anyway,' Gus nodded, 'now that the police are sniffing around, perhaps you should go to the country for a while, spend time with your folks; I'm sure they'd love it. Besides we've all got cell phones; we can just as easily be in touch.'

'I'm staying here. If pressed I could come up with plenty of reasons why Claude might have been chasing that man.'

'Granted, but why then did you not come forward?'

'I know, I know, it's best it all remains obscure, but I am still staying here. I can always hide behind the bookshelves.'

'Good, otherwise I'd get lonely.'

'No you wouldn't, you'd be out looking for a girl with a Chinese name.'

26

A *haveli* traditionally has two courtyards. This was the discovery that Frank made later on Monday evening when he accompanied Dr Chinn back to his production facilities. He understood why the far side of his own courtyard was blank of windows and doors, save one very ornate portal topped by some high-level latticed openings. This once magnificent but now dilapidated doorway would originally have led to a second courtyard reserved for the women – wives and daughters living in purdah, away from prying eyes and external distractions. The women were allowed to observe their menfolk through the latticework, but their known world ended there – the eclectic collection of wall-paintings that continued on this side were probably the only images they had of material life outside.

With the central door now seized, access to the other side was through a small service entrance, into a long corridor leading to some large rooms in the far corner. The decorations to these rooms may never have been applied, or if so they had been obliterated and blackened by the activities within. Originally these rooms would have been kitchens full of ranges and open cooking fires, and it seemed fitting therefore to find the most hazardous part of Dr Chinn's production line there, the black walls now streaked with lighter stains – rivulets of condensate from untold noxious substances and processes. But the plasterwork would no doubt suffer less than the company of Chinese cooks who were now manning the ranges, some of whom bore the scars of acid burns and rattling chests from the corrosive air.

The lab was cramped and overcrowded, and whilst it contained a professional assemblage of glassware and stainless steel, there was something of the mad scientist's lair about it. The most stained of the rooms was clearly the centre of extraction or reduction processes that relied on heat and pressure, where distillation of liquid materials with boiling points much higher than water would, in the regulated sphere, have required such health and safety measures to deal with the escaping vapours as to make them impossible to operate under these conditions. Frank recalled ironically the times he had to accompany police officers to either raided or abandoned 'clan labs', when the dress was full decontamination gear, right down to the boots and breathing apparatus – typically over the top in his view, but even his unconfined approach was tested by the gross laxity of this regime.

The air was more breathable in adjoining rooms, where the product of the long chain of synthesis was left to evaporate over gentle heat, leaving crystalline deposits for milling and pressing into tablets. Further rooms were stocked with raw materials or finished product in various stages of packaging. Frank noted that a large part of the raw material was not so much raw as completely refined – selections of over-the-counter medicines or preparations, with even cleaning fluids and household chemicals. This, he noted dryly, was a sure sign that proper precursors were in short supply, and that the essential chemicals would have to be extracted in an extended process. And yet, in another store, as well as an extensive arsenal of chemicals – concentrated acids, corrosive alkalis, sulphate of this, and chloride of that – he noticed, in industrial quantities, kegs or tubs of safrole, ephedrine, acetone, and other bulk precursors, all ready to go straight into synthesis, instead of having to boil up cold remedies and decongestants, or to make soups of analgesics, antihistamines, and paint solvents.

He counted about twenty people working in the lab, all Chinese and all male. Presumably they slept in the remaining rooms that surrounded their courtyard – the living conditions, in contrast to their working environment, quite acceptable, in a squatter sense. The courtyard, once a verdant garden with flowers and fountains, was now dry and neglected, the only surviving plants untended vines and creepers entangling the surrounding arched cloisters. In the centre, an encampment of canvas awnings kept the sun off a communal eating area. Two or three large woks sat on gas burners among the tables and chairs, a scene redolent of a rural village in China where few people cooked individually at home. Still this was no idyll; the gangers, strolling menacingly amongst the crew, left no doubt as to the work ethic, and neither could it be missed that some of the older workers had injuries and bruises unattributable to dangers of the workplace. These, Frank learnt, were the lifers, their families paid by a combination of a subsistence wage and, as long as the breadwinner stayed, the withholding of harassment – a life of tempered misery.

He noticed two workers taking a break on an upper balcony, their fingers and noses poking through the latticed openings overlooking the main courtyard. Just for the sake of looking out, rather than in, Frank concluded, as there was little activity now to stir interest in the great salons or on the terraces of the men's side. In days gone by the women would have lingered there to enjoy the sights and sounds of the house – banquets and music, the arrival of exotic visitors who rode their camels up a ramp and through the entrance doors, loud meetings of pontificating elders, or negotiations conducted in such gravity that life seemed to be in the balance. It occurred to Frank that Saleem's workers were living as the women had done in a previous age, sequestered and hidden from prying eyes. He had to admit it: he was impressed with Saleem's choice of premises for a clandestine operation.

'You seem to have plenty of supplies,' Frank observed to Dr Chinn. 'I'm surprised you need all the lithium batteries and paint stripper.'

'We had a problem with supplies a while ago, needed some back-up.'

A perfectly reasonable answer, but Dr Chinn looked sheepish. Standing in his white coat, with half-moon glasses grafted onto his nose, a clipboard under his arm, his appearance was that of a respectable and regular scientist brought up on the joys of enquiry and the excitement of small advances from painstaking experiments. It was impossible to say whether the single deep furrow on his forehead was the result of concentration, or a perennial worry, but this was the only enigma his face displayed. The rest of his open countenance would give the lie to any evasion or falsehood. He must have been conscious of this: if challenged on a matter, his habit being to look away as if distracted, or focus intently on the clipboard – his refuge from a measuring gaze.

Frank swept his arm in a wide arc. 'I wouldn't want to let any serious medicinal drugs near this place, even for just the last stage of production.'

'I agree, but don't worry. Nothing will be produced here. Saleem's packaging works – where I understand you spent a couple of nights – that's where it will happen, if it does happen.'

'*If* it happens?' Frank probed. 'You have some doubts?'

'Of course. The main problem I see is the quantity of

the final milled compound that we can get hold of. I think Saleem is seeing too much in all this.'

'I agree that Saleem is a greedy man, but what we get is what we get. The most important thing you have to ensure is that the medication is the latest triple drug – that is what will command the price. I think we will need to see your Mr Gupta together; after all, this is my field'.

'If necessary, it must be arranged,' replied Dr Chinn, 'but then you must expect to be separated from your son. Saleem will want that extra security if you are given some freedoms.'

'I know, it's the way he works,' Frank sighed with some resignation, 'and it's very effective. Is that how he controls Ashish, the lad who watches over us? I gather his father is somewhere.'

Dr Chinn looked down at his clipboard as if the answer was in his notes. 'I don't know about his treatment, but yes, his father is one of a few locals who work for Saleem. They drive the truck or one of the vans. We,' he said, gesturing to his fellow countrymen, 'would be too noticeable.'

'And don't tell me, there's another father and son among them.'

'Maybe,' Dr Chinn answered evasively. 'I don't know. Well they could be – there are just two others.'

Enough said – anyone who may come into contact with the outside and might be a threat or might just want to escape had to provide surety. What better than a filial bond …?

'But they are of no concern to us,' he then declared, with a callousness that he expected Frank to share. 'We have more important things to worry about – this unlikely venture.'

Frank had serious doubts himself about the whole unlikely proposition. The notion of expropriating the mixture for one of the most complex drugs in the world, just to press out in your own dies, was simply far-fetched, not technically impossible, but improbable. But then perhaps Frank was too conditioned by his own controlled and regulated world. This was a huge subcontinent emerging into the world economy by dint of ingenuity and enterprise, and there would be fewer checks and balances to fetter their commercial spirit. And if there were regulations, they came from overseas, imposed to protect not Indian industry but western patents. As a nation it would run all the required programmes for the protection of intellectual property, but how diligently would they be embraced? Frank reviewed these thoughts and concluded that the official line would probably have few champions, and that therefore there would be ways and means.

The following morning, Tuesday, Dr Chinn, with prompting from Frank, outlined his requirements in phone calls to their Mr Gupta and a supplier of equipment. 'I need proposals in person by tomorrow afternoon at the latest and time is of the essence.'

No location mentioned – presumably regular suppliers. Dr Chinn was confident of straight and quick answers from these people. If anything could be arranged, the response would be dynamic; it was very, very good business for them. Arrangements were made for Frank to travel with Dr Chinn back to Saleem's factory to set up this new production. How long Frank and Olly would be parted, whether they could find ways to communicate, how they would individually be treated – these questions were all unanswerable. Olly was still very ill, but they had already swapped what little intelligence they had: Olly's rough triangulation of the position of the factory and the *haveli*; and the words 'Rama Chem' from Frank. If Phil turned up in one location or the other, either Frank or Olly might have an opportunity to invest him with some clues as to their whereabouts.

Frank added protective clothing to the equipment order, including breathing masks and safety glasses, not for full-scale germ warfare but just for the kind of splash or flare-up he could see had occurred. Also some simple testing kits – almost as effective to tell the quality of an ecstasy or amphetamine tablet as more professional laboratory instruments. These might be needed later if Saleem was serious about cleaning up his output, although Frank wasn't so sure he was really welcome in this regard. The largest item on the list – the tableting machine with its attendant hoppers trays and dies – seemed to hold no more concern than an order for a cement mixer or a new fridge. Neither did the sourcing of a selection of spectrometers. Frank was almost enjoying himself – the can-do culture was infectious.

'Keep your eyes peeled, Dad,' Olly said the next morning when his father was leaving. Olly had lost what excess weight he had, and then muscle, and any ability to walk unaided. Some protector he turned out to be – the thought nagged especially now that his father was being taken off again. His mere presence, even lying here on his back, would ensure his father's cooperation, but would it guarantee his protection?

'Don't miss anything,' he continued, 'but don't let them think you've seen anything.'

'Got it,' Frank humoured him gently. He was alive to the fact that now he was Olly's protector as long as he played his part. Olly was the hostage.

Ashish was sitting outside the door as Frank passed through. 'Thank you for your kindness to my son.' Frank said this in low tones, watchful for any signs of third-party observation. He would have liked to shake his hand, but the level of fraternisation it implied would, if noticed, remove Ashish from any future possibility of collusion.

'Your father was also kind to me,' Frank added. He had deduced who he was from Olly's account of Ashish's story. He was the old man who had given up his bed to Frank that first night, and who had suffered lashes both from Saleem's tongue and from his cane.

'Thank you,' Ashish replied quietly, but swelling with pride. 'Please tell him I am well and strong. He must not take any beatings on my account.'

'He looked fine,' Frank assured him,. 'I think they treat him well.'

To say otherwise would have been too unkind.

Frank was given a blindfold for the journey, the sort you take on a long-haul flight, although their journey was not such a long haul as Frank remembered a few days ago – there was plenty of air in the car and occasionally they would stop in some featureless area where Frank was allowed to free his eyes. The driver appeared of local origin, which prompted a question from Frank, to test his theory on the non-Chinese participators, and their malleability.

'Do you enjoy working for Saleem?'

'It's a living,' the man replied with a shrug. Whether the flat response was out of resignation or a disinclination to converse, hung for the moment, in the air.

'Any of your family work here too?' Frank asked innocently after a brief pause.

'Yes.' The reply was final – it invited no supplementaries.

Dr Chinn leaned forward after a pregnant silence and explained. 'Mitesh is Saleem's brother.'

'Half-brother.' Again Mitesh said this with closure – any more questions would be unwelcome.

He had been the driver on Frank's two previous journeys, but apart from the recollection of rough handling, no particular face came to mind. They had all just relieved themselves against a solitary tree beside a single-track road which unfurled across an arid and barren landscape of dusty brown earth. The road ran straight ahead until it disappeared into a shimmering lake, but this was no topographical detail for Frank to study and note, it was just nature's visual dupery in the heat of the day. Instead Frank scanned the driver's face, looking for a similar subset of genes to Saleem's. But it was just his eyes: they had the look of misplacement as if they belonged elsewhere, to another face in a distant and forgotten land. Their oval shape looked incongruous in his otherwise dark Indo-Aryan features. The man's character also seemed to exude displacement, and with his scowling dissatisfaction he was a man of whom to be wary.

No further enlightenment came. The journey resumed in silence, and in darkness for Frank. Two hours later he felt the car turn off the road, wind through some tight corners, and come to a halt. They were at the back entrance to the factory.

'And we can supply desk-top spectrometer for 750,000 rupees,' the dealer was saying, 'hardly used, unwanted by the university, twenty-four-hour delivery.' He proudly confirmed the complete availability of Frank's list, including a rotary tablet press.

'What's the output of the press, and what's the spectrometer, gas or liquid?' Frank asked – he was astounded at this ready market.

'You can have either. They have liquid or gas chromatography – both high-performance mass spectrometers; and the press will do ten to fifteen thousand tablets per hour.'

Dr Chinn looked genuinely pleased to have Frank's expertise – he had risen from the downtrodden tame chemist of Frank's initial acquaintance to a man with a new ally, and, more pertinently, a man with a new strategy.

'Thank you for your timely report,' Dr Chinn said, leading the dealer out of the room. 'I will confirm the order later today – usual payment arrangements.'

Frank had a vague idea where they were from Olly's moonlit triangulations. Strange, he thought. How long could these people keep him hidden away? At some point surely he would come across a reference or a further pointer to their location, or an outside contact. Then he remembered two things: firstly there would come a time when he was expendable; and, secondly, until then, Olly was standing surety. He must ensure his usefulness was not in doubt until whatever devious plan that Phil was hatching could run its course.

Dr Chinn returned with a question which seemed to supply the means to extend Frank's utility.

'The dealer just asked me if you would need any standard tables to go with the chromatography. Obviously we have had no use for them before.'

'A very good point and stupid of me to overlook it,' Frank said, looking very grave. 'I cannot work without them, but the tables they can supply must be cross-referenced. There are so many correlation and deviation factors to be fed in. The calculations would be unworkable without extensive data on absorption coefficients, frequency shifts, and so on.' Frank continued to look grave – it was good to add darkness to all these arcane terms.

Dr Chinn had to admit that the science had moved on since his student days; he was out of his depth. 'Perhaps we don't need to run tests – we won't be altering anything that Gupta sends over.'

'On the contrary, we could be sent worthless or contaminated material. We must run our own tests before our purchasers do. But don't worry, I have my own data – don't forget I have been doing this for years. I can arrange for it to be sent out from London.' Frank looked Dr Chinn squarely in the eye. 'I think we both have reasons to make this work, which are not the same as that snake Saleem's.'

Dr Chinn looked down at his clipboard. 'I will show in Mr Gupta; he will be waiting.'

Mr Gupta looked uncomfortable; this was quite a new challenge for him. Any previous diversions had been easily handled. He was the general manager of a large pharmaceutical plant in Delhi, most of the output of which was generic versions of patent expired drugs. The monitoring of the production process was less intense than for licensed drugs, and in any event the proportion of his stock of raw materials diverted to Saleem was insignificant. He was now being asked to provide the compound for a strictly licensed drug in its penultimate granular form. To intercept the compound before the final stage of its production would require collusion from front-line staff, not just a warehouseman. He just hoped that he could keep Saleem's aspirations to a sensible level. Mr Gupta's fear of Saleem, plus his fondness for life's extra luxuries, would count for nothing if they went over the brink of exposure into discovery.

But Mr Gupta was relieved by Frank's obvious expertise, and his appreciation of the delicate finesse that would be needed to extract the compound. It would help him stand up to Saleem's usual excessive requisitioning.

27

Ravi's sins were of omission rather than commission. He may have acquiesced in an occasional inexactitude on a manifest to overcome a tariff or quota regulation, but at heart he was honest and straightforward. He was a 2% man acting as an agent or broker putting together trans-actions in general goods – anything from toys or cloth-ing to machine tools and paper clips. His speciality was sourcing, driving the bargain, and shipping. His creden-tials were impeccable, and his services in constant demand. Merchandise flowed mostly from east to west under his steerage – cheap imports for Europe and North America. Phil had acted as principal in much of this business, but his abilities to identify the markets and put up the funds were profitless without the smooth transition that Ravi's broker-age skills brought. Recently Phil learnt that Ravi was thriv-ing on a vibrant trade between India and Africa – ethnic carvings and furniture out, and plastic buckets and chairs in. Lo-tech for medium-tech, good, simple barter, and how extraordinarily apposite was this new route to Phil's new venture.

This was the Ravi that Phil had dealt with for years, and apart from that scare with the hidden drugs, Phil believed that all Ravi's business was above board and strictly legal. Insubstantial doubts had only occasionally fluttered across Phil's mind because of Ravi's association with Qasim, the one they had called 'someone from treasury'. But after his long conversations with Gus, Phil's doubts took on more substance – the covert side of the *hawala* system provided a setting for Phil to imagine a role for Ravi behind the drapes of Qasim's counting house. He would confront him when he arrived, not out of censure – fortuitously, in this present dilemma, the delicate art of paperwork manipulation was a perfect endorsement of Ravi's credentials.

Ravi arrived at Phil's Delhi hotel with a large briefcase full of papers, a wash bag, clean shirt, and two mobiles. They met in the cocktail lounge, and but for the great numbers of staff waiting, ushering, or just hovering, it could have been anywhere in the world. With its dark, hushed atmosphere and intimate corners, however, it seemed a fitting place to discuss their business. The clientele were mostly business people – all nationalities, closing a long day, perhaps closing a deal, or just starting an evening. To Phil, it felt like the kind of place where packets were exchanged, conspiracies hatched – conversations were guarded, eyes scanned for unwelcome notice, profiles kept low. Or maybe it was just that he had furtiveness on the mind.

'We're outnumbered two or three to one,' he observed nodding to the workforce suspended around the room.

'This is how we keep full employment,' beamed Ravi. 'Even the staff have staff!'

'I hope they're discreet,' Phil replied, and with added hyperbole, 'there are major treaties being negotiated around here.'

'They don't speak English – except for the ones in livery …' Ravi winked at a passing bar wallah, who returned the collusion with a barely perceptible nod. Ravi put some folders on the table – some admin from recent dealings, and a little housekeeping on their mutual accounts. Business never stopped for him – deals to close, consignments to track, a complicated personal life to support. He put the two mobiles together on the chair beside him – maybe they would talk to each other.

'We look like a couple of *hawala* dealers squaring their books,' said Phil.

'Lot to be said for it,' replied Ravi.

'Yeah, I often think – great, simple enough for the odd transfer, no piles of paperwork – but then I remember all the contortions and sleight of hand, all the offsets and shadowy dealings…' Phil stopped himself waxing on. 'My business is complicated enough. I need a complete audit trail to know where I am.'

'You mean, to know where you have been, not where you are. These guys don't need that. All they want is a daily balance; the rest is history. Anyway, I hope you know where you are going with this lot.' Ravi pulled out the list of medical goods he had lined up for purchase. 'I need to know who's buying, and who's selling, and then the ultimate purchaser. I need names for the shipping documents.'

'Don't know yet; just give me the low-down.'

'I can get all this here in forty eight hours packed in one air freight pallet with room to spare. Also on a plane the next day – you'll have all night to add your extras. The pallet can take 2,000 kg, the last 500 being for you. If it's in your name, your credit's good; otherwise I need three and a half million rupees, or fifty thousand sterling – draft or transfer. That includes all forwarding costs, assuming East Africa.'

'There'll be a lot of paperwork. Are you happy to be inventive with some of the details?' Phil asked.

'I've had to get good at it.' There was the hint of apology in Ravi's reply.

'Now then, you shady character,' Phil said with mock gravity, 'I never thought you would commune with the Devil.'

'If you are referring to Qasim, then you are lucky I do. You would never have found Frank without his help. Actually he is not the Devil. He is certainly selective with his principles, but there are limits to his badness, otherwise I would have been crushed long ago. It's the drug syndicate that's beyond the pale. Qasim just leans on me from time to time when they need to add an extra layer to some devious transfers.

'You may have thought that our scam that time disentangled me,' he continued, 'but it did not. I got roped in. I couldn't pretend that I had not helped them out before, when actually I had gone to the police. I got paranoid about any suspicions they might have and decided not to struggle – they say you should never pull on a knot. In the event all I have to do is to turn a blind eye to some suspicious invoicing.'

'So you come highly recommended for our latest scam.' Phil leaned forward and touched Ravi's arm, signalling his understanding of the predicament. He did not stand in judgement, and even if he did, no sentence would pass his lips.

'Thanks, Phil,' Ravi acknowledged Phil's solidarity, 'but I have no real regrets. We did the right thing at the time, and Sanj got away to medical school. In a few more years he'll be prescribing drugs not hiding them. I am still paying a price, but it's a small price, believe me. Qasim is not such a big man; he gets very little of the Devil's work, and I have to do even less. And by the way he calls himself Qasim generally – not just in London; he was being specious.

Ravi took out a blank piece of paper and wrote the words 'QV Capital Equipment' and 'VJ Resources'. 'The only companies I know of – both registered in Dubai. I've invoiced them both more than once, each time for Qasim. I'm afraid the name Saleem doesn't mean anything to me.'

'Thanks for everything, Ravi. Let's take a stroll and find somewhere for dinner – somewhere these high rollers won't be congregating.'

'I know just the place where you'll never find them.'

'Why's that?'

'No knives or forks.'

'Put those through your scanner.' Phil was calling Gus late Wednesday evening. 'They're both Qasim connections. Nothing yet on Saleem; maybe tomorrow.'

'And they're both Dubai companies,' he added.

'Ah, more from the land of milk and honey, Qasim's land of plenty.' Gus was learning about Dubai's reputation.

'Talking about milk and honey, how's Lily?'

'I'm fine thanks, Phil. All sweet and light.' It was Lily on the extension, gently chiding Phil.

'I was thinking of your colouring – creamy white skin, honey-brown hair. Poor Olly was defenceless against such perfection.' Phil did his best to bow to her gentle reproof with a little chivalry.

'Oh, you old smoothy – still, I can wish.' Lily accepted the compliment with good grace, but she was unused to such eloquences – musical people are not so quick to the visual. Phil could not see her flush at the mention of Olly and his inexplicable but utterly wonderful vulnerability, but Gus stepped back into the banter with his usual light touch.

'This young lady is half-crazed with torment. She's got a visa for India and I don't think I can hold her here much longer. When the hell are you going to bring Olly back?'

'Have faith and be patient, dears. Nerves of steel, that's what you want. Lily, don't do anything daft. I'll report in tomorrow night – could be a big day for us drug traders.'

He was gone. Lily turned to Gus with a cheeky glint. 'Talking about milk and honey, when is Liu back?'

'Now you're talking,' replied Gus. 'There's no point in denying it. I'm half-crazed over her too.' It's always a good feeling to admit the obvious. 'Friday night at Arthur's, eight o'clock, the three of us.'

That Phil could see Saleem hovering by the check-in was no surprise, but that Saleem's eagle eye had picked out Phil's distant approach across the busy airport concourse was a reminder to Phil to be extra-careful in any communication with Frank or Olly. The man kept the entire world under surveillance, watchful for any sign of danger or challenge. He signalled his espial with a wave of his cane and walked toward Phil.

'Good morning, Mr Donahue, so pleased you are early too.' It was 9:30 – half an hour before the appointed time. That's the trouble with Delhi traffic – large margins were allowed for delays, and sometimes no delay; either way you lost time.

'There is a car waiting for us. We are going to a different location today, somewhere I think will be suitable for our new production.' Saleem put his arm through Phil's and guided him away from their rendezvous and through the terminal. 'We can talk as we walk – I trust you have matters in hand regarding a shipment to Africa?'

'Africa's a big place, but I have made the assumption that it will be going to the central belt. We have got together a cargo of medical supplies with space for some extras.'

'I'm impressed, and I like your cover, a perfect choice of goods in the circumstances.'

'Fine, but you need to tell me how you want to play this. I need to give my agent names, addresses, and so on, and of course payment for the goods. We are happy to make all arrangements, but I rather assumed that you would go through your usual channels.' Phil assumed the opposite

– something told him that this was going to be a private enterprise for Saleem.

'I like the way you operate, Mr Donahue. I think we can assume that this will be in your name.'

'What about disposal? I would be happy to run that side – in fact I may have to if all the goods are in my name. Have you some purchasers in mind? I will need as much information as you can give me – I have my agent standing by in Delhi with papers to sign.'

'All in good time, Mr Donahue. I hope our laboratory colleagues will report favourably at our meeting. If so we can get down to details. But yes, I have identified a purchaser for the tablets, and I think it will be appropriate for you to be our link. On the money side, let's just say that you will be part of the chain, and rewarded accordingly.'

'Happy with all that, but let's be clear about my reward. I would normally expect at least 10% of this kind of business. Plus my outlay, which will be around £50,000 or $80,000.'

'Forgive me for my caution, Mr Donahue,' Saleem took away his arm and put it on Phil's shoulder, 'but it is in your interest that you know only what is absolutely essential at any one time. I would prefer therefore to deal only in cash until we have built up a level of trust between us. If we proceed – and, by the way, I prefer to deal in sterling – I will arrange for, say, £75,000 in cash to be given to you – you will need some extra for officials. After that we will arrange your 10% through more regular means – we all of us need our money to have at least a patina of legitimacy.'

Very straightforward, thought Phil; almost a pleasure to do business with you. They had been walking slowly through the terminal all this time and now arrived outside at the waiting car.

'Again in your interest I shall have to ask you shortly to put this on. We are travelling to one of my factories, which, for the sake of my business, I like to keep concealed from outsiders. I'm sure you understand – you would not want the burden of knowing its location. It will only be an hour in this light traffic. Just sit back and relax. I have some phone calls to make.'

As they left the pick-up bay, Phil slipped on the blindfold – no problem with that; anything to make Saleem comfortable. Phil could not understand Hindi but Saleem seemed to speak in the same assured manner – no need for aggressive assertion, just quietly directive. One call was in Chinese – not the Cantonese that Phil had picked up, probably Mandarin. The speech was too fast for Phil to catch any meaning, but Saleem did not sound his usual confident self. Phil could sense him fidgeting in his seat, and thought he detected a petition in his voice, even a little supplication.

The car drove straight into a receiving bay, a roller shutter grated to a close, and Saleem, now sounding confident again, said, 'Well my friend, we have arrived. You can uncover your eyes. Now let's hear what our boffins have to say.' He led the way along a passage to a small meeting room. A man sat outside the door; he looked bored and put upon – it was Mitesh the driver, Saleem's half-brother. He stood as Saleem appeared.

'My dear brother,' Saleem said effusively, 'I'm sorry to confine you here, but you are one I can trust. How are your guests? Keeping out of harm I hope.'

Mitesh muttered a grudging assent.

'Excellent, excellent, this is important work.'

Frank and Dr Chinn were sitting at the table.

'Gentlemen,' Saleem purred, 'I have spoken to Gupta, and I'm convinced our little venture will be viable.'

'Only at a certain level,' cautioned Dr Chinn. 'There's a limit to how much compound can be hived off.'

'Whatever Gupta told you,' Saleem said with an evil smirk, 'I think we can quadruple.'

'He feels confident with 20 to 25 kg a day, for a week or so, and then a review.'

'20 kg is just a small sack of flour, a trifling amount; he will do 100 kg for five days and then we will have our 500 kg for Mr Donahue's shipment. Trust me, I have just agreed his terms, and we have been very generous. First delivery is tomorrow. How many tablets would that make?'

'A million,' Dr Chinn replied. Frank was impressed – he wasn't interested in trifling amounts either.

'A million,' Saleem repeated. 'Good, now tell me about the equipment.'

Saleem was purring again, everything they reported was positive – availability, suitability, affordability. He had the ability to pull this off.

'But why the need to analyse?' he said after Dr Chinn had gone through the inventory and budget. 'We just press out Gupta's stuff, package it up, and ship it out.'

'You won't sell it in any bulk, and certainly not at a good price, without an analysis,' Frank said authoritatively. 'If you line up an agency or ministry to purchase the tablets, they will want tests. We can short-circuit that.'

'And also,' Dr Chinn added, 'we need to be testing the purity of our other output.'

'Isn't this where I come in?' Frank said. 'A little quality assurance for your backers.'

Saleem was nettled by Frank's insinuation, but what the hell. When all this came on-stream he could cover his tracks – no more spiking or cutting his ecstacy, he could stop siphoning off cash.

'Quite so, Mr Landing,' he almost hissed. 'You must have what you need for your testing.'

'What I will need,' Frank continued with some assertion, 'are my correlation tables for the spectroscopy. They include detailed notes and adjustments based on nearly two years' analysis in HIV vaccines, plus forensic standards for other drug tests. Absolutely indispensable. They cannot be transmitted in any way; there is no alternative but to fetch them or have them brought here.'

'Clearly you won't be going to fetch them,' Saleem said coldly. He felt manoeuvred, and he needed to be in control. He continued now warmly, a sweet thought had occurred. 'But of course your son's girlfriend would make the perfect courier ...'

28

Phil had to smile, it was so rich – the way that Saleem brought his pieces into play. But like Olly before him, Phil had to turn the amusement on his face into something more cynical. The very slightest adjustment is all that is needed, but in any event even an open smile can add menace to a scornful word.

'God help me,' he said through his teeth. 'Not that unbearable woman – that is of course if you can find her ...' and then added with feigned resignation, 'Look, it will be far easier for me to jump on a plane.'

Saleem was undeterred by Phil's interjection. The puzzle of his henchman's disappearance and that of Olly's girl-friend still troubled Saleem; it was an unguarded door into his contained and controlled world. Unexpected things could pass through it. Henchmen were controllable and if necessary expendable, but Liu, on the other hand, was still outside his control. She had some knowledge and had alluded to more. Rationally there was nothing she could do to be a serious concern, but still little pricks of unease jabbed at him. He thought of the Triads' favoured method of execution: death by a thousand cuts. But then what was this meddlesome girl to them, apart from being Chinese? ... 'I know who your bosses are' – isn't that what she said? ... He had men watching the apartment. If she did show up, his instructions were clear; he did not like loose ends.

'Surely,' he said, turning back to Frank, 'your son will have a number for his girlfriend. I shall ring and speak with him.'

Olly had explained to Frank Liu's contribution in the pose of being his girlfriend, although neither father nor son knew about the attempt on her. Least of all did they know that it was Lily who had been subjected to the bungled assault. Nonetheless Frank was certain that neither girl should be embroiled. He shrugged the probability of Saleem's assertion and a few minutes later, in the *haveli*, a phone was put into Olly's hand.

'I need the number of your girlfriend, Liu,' Saleem said with no less expectation than a call to enquiries.

'I don't remember it,' Olly replied, perhaps a little too evasively, 'She keeps changing.'

'I don't believe you – it's best that you tell me.'

Frank gestured for the phone; he'd had time to think. 'It's ok. Olly, you can give us a number. There's no problem.'

Frank repeated the number for Saleem, who noted down not Olly's random figures, but the number of a real phone – the spare one beside Frank's bed in London, batteries long dead. Saleem would have to leave a message.

Saleem called the number twice, and then turned to Phil. 'I'll keep trying, but in the meantime I'll leave it to you to get the papers, however you can. What about the couple in the flat?' He was vexed.

'No idea, but my guess is that you are asking for complications. I don't know anything about these people, and I don't want this fucked up,' Phil said this with just enough vehemence to suggest a vested interest in success – an interest shared with Saleem. 'I can be there and back in twenty-four hours.'

Saleem's phone drew his attention, but before answering it he nodded a resigned acceptance to Phil. He took the call by the window, his conversation animated and vital. Phil, Frank, and Dr Chinn remained at the table.

Phil now had a reason to compare notes with Frank on the location of his files, plus, Phil hoped, anything Frank had gleaned about the location of Saleem's operations: a pointer, a name, a shred of material information – geographical, financial, corporate, anything. Perhaps, Phil mused sardonically, even his favourite club. He had a mental picture of Saleem returning everyday to a life of respectability, a thin veneer of gentlemanly repute.

'Could you remind me,' Frank asked, 'which model we were promised for the spectroscopy, and the exact specification?' He knew it would take twenty or thirty distracting seconds for Dr Chinn to refer to his notes.. He needed time to impart some important references of his own to Phil, and he breathed them in between quite ordinary directions to the required paperwork.

'If you go to my workroom ... let me see ... there are two possible locations for my file ... under the computer table *hour and a half south-west of Delhi, Ramachem next door* or ... on the shelf by the clock *sweet auburn another two hours west.* It's a large blue file marked Chromatrophy.' Dr Chinn had found the specification. 'Anyway,' Frank continued, 'it's in one of those places. You'll have to keep looking around till you come across it.'

'Make your mind up,' Phil responded tersely in character. 'You'd better be right. I'll tear the bloody place up if you have me going round in circles.' Phil looked forward to looking around, to drawing some circles on the map. The first would pass through a Ramachem building, and the second would embrace a deserted village. That opening line in Oliver Goldsmith's Deserted Village, the other of Father Burke's favourites – Frank and Phil would never forget his moist-eyed delivery: *Sweet Auburn! loveliest village on the plain.* And later: *Amidst thy bowers the tyrant's hand is seen, And desolation saddens all the green.*

Or lines that perennially haunted and sharpened Phil's spirit, and threatened to moisten his own eye today; *Ill fares the land, to hastening ills a prey, Where wealth accumulates, and men decay.* The good father would recite them from heart, couplet after couplet, each one charged with a poignancy that defied oblivion.

Saleem came back to the table. 'Good, good, good. We have a purchaser, we have our price. Dr Chinn, please confirm the equipment order immediately, I want to start production by the weekend – you will have at least two batches from Gupta by then. We should be ready for our first shipment on Wednesday. Mr Donahue, you will have your cash by this evening. Please confirm all your orders too. Purchaser's details will be with the cash, all other paperwork is for you. You will be given a copy of your own invoice for services rendered. Please give me an account number for transfers. I will arrange payment from the purchaser myself through our own channels.

'There is still no need for you to know anything about my business or our premises,' Saleem continued unnecessarily. 'I hope you feel secure therefore that our relationship cannot be compromised. You have a point of contact with my colleagues in Hong Kong, which should be enough for you to rely on our allegiance.' He raised the hoods over his eyes for assent.

'I feel a lot happier knowing as little as possible,' Phil confirmed with casual worldliness. 'There will come a time when you don't need the likes of us.' Careful, Phil, you're a lone agent; let's have no air of a conspiracy. 'Speaking for myself,' he added, looking at Frank with what he hoped was an uncharitable scowl. 'At that point I'll just take the money and disappear.'

So much easier dealing with adults, Saleem was thinking, people with a proper understanding of the world, and the essential arithmetic of life. Two columns of figures representing success or failure, pleasure or pain, a simple balance sheet, not a complicated spreadsheet of childish codes and ridiculous principles, a whole mosaic of self-defeating and wealth-destroying claptrap just to waft a chimera of fairness across the faces of the great unwashed. A man I can do business with ... as he says, until the time comes ...

'Well said, and I like your candour, Mr Donahue. Now back to logistics. You will need to find your own location to receive your medical supplies, preferably near the airport in Delhi. I will arrange our new "life-savers" to be delivered to you. Book provisional passage and I will confirm by Monday that we are on target for Wednesday. I would suggest a Thursday flight. Please obtain Mr Landing's notes by Sunday morning – they will be picked up from your hotel.

That was it. A quick look at Dr Chinn's equipment tally, and Saleem led Phil back to the car and out into the daylight – that is, until Phil once more entered the darkness of his blindfold.

'I will leave word at your hotel about our next meeting. If you need to speak to me, just leave a note at reception. Any messages will be picked up. I don't believe in our engaging in telephone contact ... as you say, there will come a time when you will wish to disappear. This will ensure that you can do so without a trace.' Saleem slapped Phil's shoulder as he said this – it was the nearest he could get to comradeship and he hoped it would overcome that slip of menace in his last comment.

'My instincts entirely,' Phil responded agreeably. 'Having said that, I have some more ideas up my sleeve. I think I might enjoy joining someone with your sway.' What an ingratiating creep you are, Phil Donahue. The only thing you will enjoy is seeing him sway from a rope.

'We'll see, we'll see, but please, now you must see..., enjoy the view, all the work of your famous Mr Lutyens, I believe.'

Phil took off his blindfold. They were on the outskirts of New Delhi – British-built, wide avenues and circuses lined with government buildings, and solid colonial bungalows for the diplomats and officer class. Saleem ordered his chauffeur to pull over. 'I shall be getting out here – some official business. My driver will drop you off at your hotel.'

It was early afternoon when Phil called Ravi from reception.

'Lunch?'

'Be right down.'

The restaurant was quiet, the deal-makers all out making deals, moving and shaking, making the world go round. A porter brought a package to the table. 'Mr Donahue, this has just been left for you.' The package was full of £50 notes wrapped in a band marked £75,000.

'What are you like with this kind of paperwork?' Phil asked Ravi with a sigh.

'It's a bloody nuisance, all that cash, but I'll just have to work it through.'

Phil pulled out a hand-written note with the name of a medical supplies mission in East Africa. The contact name was Martin Lamumba, Chief Procurement Officer for the Rural Areas. The flight would be to Mombasa.

Ravi nodded sagely when he saw the forwarding address. 'You may ask yourself how they could import drugs from a non-accredited supplier.'

'Well I do ask myself that.' Phil replied. 'I can only assume that this Mr Lamumba has a good budget and he knows how to work the system. We're not talking about some powerful health minister who can keep all the watchdogs on a leash. These smaller agencies are surrounded by networks of onlookers on behalf of the donors – guarding the grant money and checking the provenance of the purchases.'

'You'd be amazed,' Ravi said conspiratorially, 'how little money that goes into the likes of AIDS programmes comes from government coffers – almost none. But there's an election on and the politicians will want to keep their seats secure. What better than doling out drugs? They'll be diverting money into health budgets for the next few months at least. Mr Lamumba's mission will just act as an agent and pass on the drugs and supplies to rural area hospitals or clinics courtesy of the Ministry. No donor money spent; no red tape.'

'For a man who sells plastic chairs and buckets, you seem to know a lot about drug budgets.'

'I know about general budgets in these countries and how hit and miss they are. I'd been trying to sell things to supply ministries for years till I struck lucky with my plastic buckets and stuff. And that was only because I provided an outlet for some rural craftwork.

'But don't forget,' Ravi continued, 'I've just bought you £50,000 worth of medical goods, so I've been learning. Actually,' he admitted with a half-smile, 'I don't really know at all, but I find it hard to believe that corners will not be cut, either by well-meaning officials or by greedy ones out for a bribe.'

'I suppose you're right. Anyway we don't need to understand these dark arts for our purposes, just as long as I know what to say to Mr Lamumba.'

'In the meantime do I assume that this will all be in your name?' Ravi asked. Phil nodded a yes. 'In that case you need to sign some documents after lunch. I'll keep that cash under my bed until we know how this works out.'

'You can't keep all the money – there'll be an extra £25,000 in here for what Saleem called officials. I expect Mr Lamumba will keep most of it – it's not so amazing what people will do for two or three years' salary in the hand.'

It didn't take long to go through all their arrangements – Ravi was a natural problem solver, an ironer out of difficulties. All goods to be dispatched to, and received at a small warehouse owned by a trusted associate in Delhi. This would be on Monday. The associate would help with the repacking of the air pallet. This should be Wednesday. Name and address of recipient supplied by Saleem. Confirm to Ravi the 'extra' goods were on-stream and he would confirm the air freight.

'And Ravi, don't just keep that money under the bed. Haven't you got a safe?'

'That's where I keep my safe; it helps support my wife.'

Ravi left for Mumbai, his parting words 'leave it to me' a reminder of why he needed two phones.

Phil would like to have surprised Gus and Lily – he would be in London tomorrow, Friday evening. But he had another puzzle to set them, this time geographical – one with possible fixes on a location.

Lily answered the call – Gus had gone for lunch with some bankers. She found the file – it was exactly where Frank had said. She swelled with this new information about Olly and Frank's whereabouts.

'I'll need maps and some kind of directory,' she said. 'Probably all I need on the net.'

'There're all those maps that Gus bought,' Phil reminded her.

'Olly took the best one, but I could always pop back for

another.' She could indeed pop back; she was also reminded of that call to Gus in the map shop, the exquisite moment when she knew that she had traced Olly. She could relive that moment, she was not superstitious, but there seemed to be a certain circularity to this; maybe it was a sign to start the cycle again, this time perhaps with a happy ending. She would sneak out the back door – no one would notice her … touch wood.

29

'Hello, dear.'

Lily froze. She was half-way through the service door, the exit that they had discovered safe from watching eyes. It was just a few steps over next door's car park into a back street.

It was the old lady in the rain, the witness, not just to the incident but to Lily's remorse. A material witness, that's how Lily would be described ... Her statement would be required ... Where would she start? ... What consequences would follow? ... It didn't bear thought, she must run.

'Hello, I thought I'd seen you before. Do you live here?'

'Er no, just visiting a friend.'

'Have you spoken to the police yet? They thought you could help them about that ghastly business last week.'

'Yes,' Lily lied, not happily, but in the hope that it would be forgiven, 'I spoke to them the other day. No real help I'm afraid. But it was a ghastly business ... those poor young men ... complete strangers but ... the shock you know.'

'We were worried about you. It looked like you had lost a friend.'

'Well I'm fine now, but I was very shocked at the time. Thank God I didn't know them – that would have been hard, just imagine.'

Whether the old lady's look was one of wise understanding or one of appraisal, Lily knew that she must disappear again, and one more white lie might help create some distance.

'But I'm so sorry, I can't stop. I have to catch a train – off back to the country – goodbye.'

Lily walked around the block, not daring to look behind her until she reached the main entrance – back up to the flat. Gus could revisit the map shop instead. She had not been followed, but her arrival at the door had been noted. With a mandate to monitor all female visitors, two men took turns at surveillance – a white van, a green van, a seat in the gardens opposite ...

There was an almost neurotic concern about Saleem, born of his need for total control, itself a product of managing his own deceptions. He did not believe in coincidences; the root cause of an oddity needed full explanation. But a possible explanation bothered him – the Triads had a jealous way of protecting the faithfulness of the brotherhood. Had they not seeded the original notion of this scientist's abduction? Was the man a mole, the whole thing a test, or just a caution? And what of the others?

How ridiculous, he thought: two hapless people divided by some vendetta from the third, a small-time trader looking for the main chance – an unlikely set-up. Still, he had to be wary, and with deftness he saw no reason that he should not plug the hole both in his returns and in the trust of his ultimate masters. Unwittingly or otherwise they had provided him with the means to alleviate these shortcomings. Nonetheless he must keep everything and everyone on a tight leash. He had evolved a criminal organisation able to deal with the world they encountered, with procedures for enforcing loyalty or discretion. Saleem's word was writ, grievances were not referred to any tribunal, trading irregularities to any commission; his employees and associates were all controlled by a triangulation of their fear, greed, and weaknesses. The only ones who took any pleasure in their work were those who didn't need payment to be cruel; they enjoyed the reflected power of being his enforcers.

'Gus, I need some more of your maps, from that shop – best you can get, showing a hundred miles around west of Delhi. Call me when you get there.' That would do, he'd call her from the shop. In the meantime Lily opened Olly's computer and searched for Ramachem. Quite a few locations in India: Delhi, Mumbai, Gujarat. She narrowed the search down to Delhi – four locations, meaningless addresses. Come on, Gus, finish your lunch. We need maps.

'Lily,' said Gus, a long hour later, 'got your message. I'm back in the map shop. What's up?'

'I've just spent the last hour trying to figure out this map thing, this bloody satellite map thing, bloody computers. I've got some addresses around Delhi ... other locations ... Phil called ... other pointers ... hundred miles west ... hour and a half south-west ... we can pinpoint them ... oh hurry, we need maps.'

'Calm down, I've got the picture – I'll be half an hour.'

Lily had four Delhi addresses for Ramachem: Gurgaon, Okhla, Rewari, and Mayapuri. Tantalisingly, one of them could be next door to Olly and Frank. Oh please hurry, Gus. Christ, had they found them? This was incredible, just four or five words, quietly breathed, under the noses of their captors ... Lily was floating. If one of these addresses was an hour and a half south-west of Delhi she was going straight to the airport. What's an hour and a half – fifty, sixty miles, maybe less. It's a busy place. Gus, where are you? I'll go and pack.

'What did he say, what did he say?' Gus had run from the tube; the exertion had taken his breath away and his calm.

'He's coming back tomorrow, to pick up a file. Must call

him, tell him he doesn't need to. Quick, unfold that Delhi one, and that one, the area one – what's the scale? What's fifty miles? It's ok, I'll explain.'

'There,' Lily breathed out. She felt like she had defused a bomb, 'There they are.'

Gus prised her finger from the map; Lily was holding on. She explained the coordinates, the name of the neighbour, its four addresses – only one fitted … Delhi Road, Rewari. They stood over the map for some moments, Lily awed by the revelation, and Gus sensing the import.

'My God, the place even sounds like "where are we".' Gus found himself caught up in the augury.

'But what did he say?' he repeated. 'What the hell did he say?'

Frank's words, as relayed by Phil, were brief. She repeated them to Gus. 'And he's coming to London tomorrow – oh I told you that. He was taken to this place by Saleem. Frank was there too. He could only whisper a few words.'

'Are they still sworn enemies?'

'Yes, Phil said the charade was still working.'

'What about Olly? You haven't mentioned Olly.'

'I hardly dared ask. Phil said he wasn't there. I'm sure he's ok. Frank would have said something.'

'Then two more hours west … a deserted village.' Gus repeated the second instructions. 'Not so easy to identify. Maybe he's there.'

The land immediately to the west of Delhi is the state of Haryana, and to the west of that, Rajasthan. Gus drew an arc on the map, just into Rajasthan. 'That's two hours, say sixty or seventy miles west of Rewari – a deserted village? Nothing on this map.'

It didn't matter; she was not downhearted. If he was not in one place he would be in the other. If they could find one place they could find the other, even if it meant visiting every un-named village in that circle.

'Lily, why did you say that Phil didn't need to come?'

'Because I can take him the file. I can't sit around here any more like a fugitive.' She recounted her aborted trip out. 'It's just a matter of time till the police come around asking about Claude, and in any event I need to search for a deserted village.'

'That's as may be, but don't stop Phil coming over. I hope by tomorrow night I'll have some more stuff on the banking side. It'll be good to have a complete review. Agreed?'

'Agreed, but I am going back with him.'

Saleem had legitimate businesses, their growth and success underpinned by the free flow of cash from a stable of illicit operations. He was a criminal at heart, a clever one undoubtedly, but his talents and methods crossed over uneasily into the competitive mainstream – trust, merit, and financial acuity lagged behind his ambition. In time his cash converted into less and less value as his visible businesses became wasting assets – his controlling nature stifled what genuine initiatives they should have been making. With more and more funds needed to fend off decline, he worked on his criminality – that was his strength, and diverting more money than was due from his drugs 'franchise' provided the answer. Just a temporary facility was all he needed. Ironically it was his reputed wealth that made his Chinese partners not more trusting, but certainly less expectant that he would cook the books, as well as their drugs.

Two more terms to add to his balance sheet: growth and decline. With growth comes confidence and support, status and influence, and the comfort of inflated values. Decline brings doubt – often self-fulfilling – and the pressure of brinkmanship over an abysmal end. Value deflates, covenants are broken, credit dries, capital evaporates. At all costs he must increase his turnover and cash flow for the next quarter, just enough to renegotiate his loans and mortgages, and leverage out his capital. He would have to manage the plundered revenues on his illicit side, but surely the smoke and mirrors surrounding his book-keeping would overcome that for the time he needed. Every dollar or rupee he could skew into his official accounts would return a hundredfold.

He rued the day when he started to over-legitimise his wealth – all that booty masquerading as sales. But now he must stay cool; a million dollars here or there was all it would take to restore his balances and to save his life. Let no one stand in his way.

Phil arrived back in London on Friday evening – he looked different, maybe older, certainly drawn and less relaxed. Like gravity, failure is a constant force; without luck and determination it is almost the most natural outcome – for every small step a species makes in evolution a hundred million have faltered. For the last week Phil had walked deeper and deeper into a labyrinth, through successive doors, seemingly of his own volition, but were there unseen hands or unseen interests guiding him? Each successful step added to his fears, not just of discovery and failure, but of the certainty of retribution. His objective was clearer than his strategy. The strategy was to insinuate himself into the enemy camp and look for an opportunity to strike a surprise fatal blow to the tyrant leader. The objective was not just the escape of his friends but the expunction of all future recourse.

'You don't look too hot, Phil.' Gus went straight to the point.

'I'm fine. Tea and sympathy – that's all I need.'

Lily handed him a cup of tea. 'There, you poor thing.'

He could see that she had a beam in her eye – he followed it to the table.

'Let me show you where you have just been.' The map had highlighter through the word 'Rewari', and a yellow circle a few inches to the left.

'This is Ramachem, and that's where the deserted village will be. The first one we have an address for, but the second one we'll have to go dowsing for.'

'Shouldn't be too difficult,' Gus threw in. 'A bunch of Chinese squatters in an otherwise empty place.'

'Better than I expected,' Phil said, sitting down heavily on a chair. 'What about those Dubai company names – any good?'

'It gets better,' Gus said. 'One frequently wires money to a packaging firm in Delhi and the other pays rent to a building company downtown – three million rupees every quarter-day – nearly fifty thousand pounds. I'll get more details, but my dollar says it's Saleem on the receiving end.'

Phil looked at them both with admiration. 'Bloody marvellous!'

'All down to you, Phil,' Gus effused. 'You got the names – we're just the bears in the back office.'

That must mean something in Montana, Phil mused, but he got the idea.

'We were lucky,' he replied, not out of modesty, more to keep their hopes in check. 'Actually we've had a run of good luck all along the way, but it worries me how long it will continue.'

'Statistically, luck doesn't come in runs,' Gus chipped in. 'It's a series of random and unconnected occurrences.'

'Exactly,' teased Lily. 'All we are doing is connecting the random, by applying our superior intellect, recognising patterns. Gosh I meant just to be flippant but that sounded intelligent.'

An old-fashioned look was the response from the two men. But they liked the point about patterns; it had symmetry.

'We need local knowledge,' said Phil. They were allowed a little light elation after their successes but feet must be kept on the ground. 'We need the whereabouts of this so-called "deserted village".

'I didn't like to ask in my hotel,' Phil continued, 'or indeed anyone – paranoia probably about Saleem's grapevine. I did ask Ravi, of course, but he comes from Mumbai – another world. But he'll turn up some relations in Delhi. Mark my words.'

'Perfect,' Lily said. 'If he can, he might find a relation to drive me around with my divining rod.'

Gus shook his head, he was waiting for this, but Phil was taken by surprise. 'But you'd stick out like a ...'

'I wouldn't stick out like anything,' Lily interrupted, 'I'd be just another scruffy backpacker in India, plus I can dye my hair black, get a dusky complexion and ditch my western gear. Maybe it wouldn't bear close examination, but I wouldn't stand out in a crowd.

'But ...'

'*You* certainly can't do it, Phil,' Lily insisted, 'and one of us two must stay here. Gus is following the money. I'm the only one without a job.'

'Yes but ...'

'Besides I have to get away from here. I feel like I'm being watched.'

Something subliminal surfaced in Gus's brain. He looked down to the street – a green van was parked on the near corner, next to the entrance to the communal gardens, its one occupant reading a newspaper. Nothing arresting about that picture, any more than a man sitting in a white van on the same spot reading a paper. That was yesterday. And the previous day, unless his imagination was playing tricks, it was the green van.

'On all counts I think it's a good plan,' Gus responded, his imaginings adding to his own measure of where least danger lay, 'provided Lily can get a trusted guide, and,' he added with a gentle admonition, 'she promises no lovelorn heroics.'

Phil took out his flight details and handed them to Lily. 'Might as well fly out together if you can get a seat.' He could not resist the inevitable.

30

'I'm saving it for a celebration,' Phil said, declining the trip to Arthur's. 'I've got calls to make and it's well after bedtime in India. Then I'll turn in myself.' It was true, his next visit to Arthur's should be for a reunion, but it was also true that he was dog tired. Not from the time change, but from bottling up all his anger and worry. In deference to Gus and Lily's fears, and in reaction to Saleem's suspicious and viperous nature, he had become a closed vessel. His fermenting emotions were building up a dangerous pressure.

Phil managed the tensions and vicissitudes of his business life well, he was always able to walk away from a deal, but now the stakes were high and personal. His hands had been just a lunge away from Saleem's scraggy neck on many occasions, but that was not the answer. He knew that Saleem's inner circle would close around a desperate attempt to find a new leader, and then collapse into a vengeful anarchy. He had to find a way to hang Saleem out to dry, to let others pick over his fate. He would be his nemesis.

'And I have to wash my hair,' Lily said, winking at Phil. 'Has anyone got any black dye?'

Gus was happy either way; two different evenings but both would be agreeable. On the other hand perhaps they should save it for a homecoming, a thanksgiving. His date with Liu would stand, although he approached it with almost teenage trepidation.

'I'll stroll out and get some hair dye,' he offered. 'You've got tickets and stuff to organise.' He had time to kill, and curiosity was compelling him to walk past that van before dark.

'It's all organised.' Ravi was back on the phone – Phil wondered if the man ever slept. Ever reliable, he had come up with a relation with a lock-up near the airport, and another to be Lily's guide.

'We are all cousins; they are plentiful in India.' Ravi gave Phil an address and phone number for Bishen, he of the lock-up, and the name of Mahinder, who would be Lily's driver and mentor.

'He is an ex-teacher, very knowledgeable, hates crooks, and is excited about the adventure. He will look out for her at the airport, or rather he'll hold up a card with his name. She will be expected to stay with the family. Bish will be awaiting a delivery on Monday – he will help you intermingle the real payload. Any problems, call me.'

He was gone. Ravi was short on words and long on action.

Phil put Frank's file in his holdall; in the morning he would be back on a plane to Delhi, this time with Lily. He felt better; they were on a good run, good enough to get a night's sleep.

Gus left through the rear door, with a street map in his hand; he was about to get lost.

'Excuse me sir,' he knocked on the van's window. 'Can you tell me where the heck I am?'

He held up the map. 'I'm trying to get to Olympia.'

Very few people can resist giving directions – it can give an empty moment a purpose. The man in the white van had spent many empty moments. 'Round the corner, down to the traffic lights, you'll get a bus from there. Cheers, mate.'

Young, English, Londoner, almost local, quite chilling really. Perhaps Gus would have felt better if the man were an alien.

Three hours later Gus returned, light-headed and enchanted from an evening of gentle courtship, a temporary respite from the pressure and frustration of his new team's predicament. He was not a man of high, high principles but believed that human society should work within certain checks and balances of empathy. However, his philosophy was being crushed beneath the dead weight of dispassion from a misanthropic and predatory layer.

His steps slowed as he neared Olly's block; they grew heavy as he saw in the distance a van, a green van this time, parked under the trees. He still carried the street map, but some intuitive caution ruled out a repeat of his earlier boldness, and under cover of the gardens he approached the vehicle. It was the same man, different van, the same likely lad – must be doing a double shift. There was no doubt about it now, and Gus felt depressed as well as oppressed at the thought of this person being the organ of a distant evil, just a paid apprentice who would carry out any work without compunction. Work experience for later promotion in some cancerous league.

He was pleased that Lily was leaving. She was in danger from any initiative by the boys in the van, if only out of frustration; and a police interview would surely compromise the security of silence surrounding Claude's fatal chase. But she was also in danger of giving in to her inclination just to dive in, but it was only her indignation that was raging; her teeth and nails were no threat to Saleem, she was no shecat. She now had a positive mission, a strategic role in the great game, which Gus suspected she would cherish more than her own safety. If he believed that the future outcomes were in any way written, he would say she was following her destiny. He did not believe that, but hoped that in some way she would shape it.

'From the moment we check in,' Phil insisted as they approached the airport, 'we're strangers. You've got everyone's numbers, but don't call mine unless it's an absolute emergency. Call Ravi's first every time.'

Lily was already a stranger, dark-skinned with black hair swept back under a silk scarf worn as a hijab.

'Got it. Shall we synchronise watches? ... Sorry, Phil, just a nervous quip.'

'That's ok, but don't forget: feed every bit of info to Ravi. All we need is their whereabouts. Don't go scaling any walls. Take this, there's enough money to pay for any number of excursions.' He gave Lily a hug. If she were as delicate mentally as she felt in his arms, he would have succeeded in preventing her trip. He had considerable qualms about her ability to moderate her eagerness – her passions could easily be stirred into some quixotic tilt at Olly's confines.

'Lily,' he said, 'I know you want to get Olly out as soon as possible, but you must give me time to neutralise Saleem, otherwise we'll never get them completely off our backs – understood?'

'How much time?'

'Don't know – a week, two, maybe more. Just get the addresses and sit tight.'

It was midnight when Phil arrived back at his hotel. He had kept his room, and smiled as he fished out Saleem's package – he had always wanted to find a large bundle of banknotes under his mattress. Tomorrow he would leave Frank's file at reception with a note: *All in hand, our delivery arriving Monday to this address ... Please confirm your own delivery and I will book flight. PS: I could take your Mr Lamumba samples for testing before the main batch. Let me know. PD.*

Mahinder and his extended family lived in adjoining apartments in a Delhi suburb. He was an intelligent, educated man, with that disarming gentleness that soothed the traditional western culture shock of new visitors to his country. The shock was not of poverty – so heavily presaged – but of sheer numbers of people. They had learnt to live in such close proximity by adopting codes of behaviour at first sight seemingly rude to western sensibilities, but actually that were just a series of filters between one person and the essential world they had to focus on. Lily quickly felt at home with the four generations who took refuge in the apartments, and who had all stayed up to greet her.

'There have been thousands of towns and villages in India deserted over the centuries from either climatic or political upheavals.' Mahinder thought a little historical perspective would be a good starting point. He also thought it might give a measure to the size of the challenge – not to overwhelm Lily's obvious ardour for the chase, but to pace her patience, to keep a rein on her expectations.

'My family came from the Punjab – they had to join the march eastwards after the partition in 1947. Millions of people were wrenched from their lands and it's taken three or four generations to get any real feeling of resettlement.

'The only truly deserted places left are either uninhabitable ruins, or perhaps an abandoned medieval city, now a tourist site. It will not be easy to find your deserted village in the areas you have marked unless you can think of any other clues.'

They were standing over Lily's map; she had drawn a series of arcs fifty, sixty, and seventy miles west of Rewari.

Perhaps he had overdone his review; Lily looked downcast.

'Is there any more information other than a deserted village?' Mahinder repeated gently.

'The building that Phil visited sounded like a large house around a courtyard, dilapidated but quite ornate.'

Mahinder looked up from the map, and, nodding his head in that Indian way, said, 'That my dear is a *haveli* – there are thousands in the region, it's known as Shekhawati. But you have marked its eastern outposts, where these palaces are thinner on the ground – possibly only a hundred or so.' Mahinder let some enthusiasm show, no more leavened by the prospect of a futile search.

'It's the properties that are deserted,' he explained, 'although it is true to say that they make up the bulk of the buildings in many towns and villages where they are found. The villages would indeed feel deserted and forlorn with nine out of ten of the largest houses empty and gathering dust.'

'Then,' Lily said with a determined frown, 'we should visit every village, and look for a *haveli* that is occupied.'

'Splendid logic,' Mahinder replied enthusiastically. 'It will be done. We start in the morning.'

'Of course these lines are approximate,' Lily cautioned. 'They're just me guessing how far you would get in two hours.'

'Then,' Mahinder said, copying her own determined frown, 'we will drive for two hours and see where we get to.'

'Splendid logic!' Lily declared, returning Mahinder's enthusiasm.

Lily knew it would take many days, even weeks, but she was fired up for the search, although not knowing how they would conduct it without asking around in each place, which in itself posed a threat. But that would come after their first stop, which was the address in Rewari – the Ramachem building. How close they dared go depended on the lie of the land; it was daunting to think that one of its neighbours belonged to Saleem.

Saleem's note of reply came back surprisingly quickly. The file was in the hands of his 'chemists'. They were ahead of schedule: delivery on Tuesday evening; book freight and flight to Mombasa for Wednesday; until then stay put in Delhi. No need for pre-testing; samples would be taken from full delivery, after that no further tests for same batch numbers. Presumably dictated to someone at the porter's desk – still only mid-morning. He called Ravi – freight to arrange – he would leave it to him. A report from Lily – arrived safely – now a little Indian girl just off to search the plains of Shekhawati with her Uncle Mahinder; first stop, Rewari.

By midday Phil had booked a seat to Mombasa, a hotel, and a car. His work was complete until Tuesday night. Pity he had to 'stay put', as Saleem had directed, in Delhi; he would love to join Lily on her search. But the consequences of his being spotted would be bleak – he would have to be content with the twenty-four-hour cricket channel.

Gus called.

'The boys have more time over the weekend for some lateral work. They've come up with some stuff. Still early days, but there's one thing you can check out for me. Seems that the packaging firm is based in Gurgaon – according to my map that's not far from Rewari. It's called Haryana Box and Packaging. The building company is called Connaught Holdings and they have found two more quarterly rental payments of seven million rupees each. If this is Saleem, he's getting nearly a million pounds a year from rent alone.'

'Can't check the rents,' Phil said, 'but we'll see if Haryana Box has got premises in Rewari. What we also need is someone sending money back to Qasim; it usually goes in circles.'

'Gotta have a name,' Gus replied. 'Can't run a check without a name. So far they've only been able to check payments not receipts – all very delicate.'

'Also, Phil, I can tell you that the flat is definitely being watched: couple of guys probably, taking turns. I could go out and break their necks just like that.'

'Interesting. This Saleem is really jumpy about something. But keep your hands off. Best to let them die of boredom.'

It was late on Sunday morning when they left Delhi. 'My daughter will take you out and find some more suitable clothes,' Mahinder had said to Lily. 'The jeans and top would not stand out in the city, but in the country you must blend in.' Sound advice for any western girl, but even more apposite in their situation – to keep a veil over their expedition.

They had driven around the edge of New Delhi, along wide boulevards where road sweepers waited for leaves to fall, and out to the ring road and beyond where, in contrast, chaos ruled and detritus accumulated. The traffic, a challenging mix of every conceivable wheeled conveyance, seemed to move like a flock of birds, each driver attendant on the vehicle immediately on each wing, nose, and tail. The formation was held together by lightning reactions to sight and sound.

'You see everything in front of you and to the side,' Mahinder explained, noticing Lily's amazement at the continual, seemingly pointless hooting. 'You use your ears to know what's behind. The hooting is not rude, it is a requirement.' The speed of the traffic was not great, so most of the time people fulfilled the ideal, which was eventually to get somewhere without hurting anybody. A three wheeled tuk-tuk with a soft and fragile cargo of a dozen people would be given a wide berth.

An hour and a half later they left the main highway for the road to Rewari. They had started the journey with Lily in a lighter heart than at any time over the last week. She had allowed herself the innocent dream of an end-game approaching, in which their lives were restored, by the deft wrong-footing of an inexorable but overconfident adversary. The nearer they came to this first seat of Saleem's dominium, however, the more Lily's impressible spirit was wrought by thoughts of his insidious power and control. He was not overconfident, and, like any evil dictator, every conceivable threat to his security, real or imagined, would be removed.

'Delhi Road was the address,' Lily said, a tremor of apprehension in her voice. 'Delhi's where we've come from, so this must be the road.'

They saw a large sign swinging from a mast above a complex of silver-cladded buildings, looking efficient and business-like on their landscaped site. The sign said Ramachem and could be visible from all directions. A road led off to the left of the site, and then wound around to the rear of Ramachem. It served a collection of old workshops, and modern commercial buildings with vacant lots for future phases. Lily's phone rang; Mahinder slowed to a stop on the side road.

'Lily, this is Ravi, Phil's colleague. I have a name for you, could be Saleem's depot.'

'Hi, Ravi, nice to speak to you. Fire away.'

'It's Haryana Box and Packaging.'

'Mahinder, don't stop here. Keep away!' Lily gasped the

words as if some unutterable terror was upon them. She had just looked out to see, only a few yards away, a small plastic notice on the side of a brick pier: **Deliveries Please Ring**, and under that, **Haryana Box**.

Mahinder drove around the corner, and stopped again by an empty site.

'Ravi, so sorry. I'll call you back.' Feeling both hot and cold from nausea, Lily took two steps from the car to a low wall. Her vomit rose, her stomach turned by the sudden shock of being so close, potentially so compromisingly close. She stooped over the wall, the retching continuing interminably, as if some diabolical bitterness must be expelled. She returned slowly and hesitantly to the car, mentally and physically chastened. As well as the bile induced by malevolent oppression, Lily had left another part of herself over the wall – some of the simplicity and innocence that had supported her conviction.

They sat for some time looking back at the buildings, Saleem's compound. This was a major breakthrough, of that there was no doubt, but it was one of fact, not opportunity. That would require the second location together with the further unfolding of what plan they had – then perhaps they could find a way through Saleem's defences. But this was a chink, observed and recorded by Lily's own astonished eyes.

'Wait here,' Mahinder said. 'It is less suspicious to stroll by, than to drive slowly past.'

He returned with a rueful grin. 'I have another name for you – H.S. Global Sourcing – it was above a door just inside the gates.'

It was a relief to leave what felt to Lily a danger zone, although she knew in her heart that their quest for Saleem's other lair was beset with a precipitous jeopardy now more real than imagined. They pointed the car west and, subject to the twists and turns of the country roads, which called wherever random settlements demanded, they maintained their bearing for the next two hours.

31

Olly did not expect his father to return in any particular time frame, and he had no way of following or anticipating the progress of his friends. He had just to wait for time to pass, but it was the worst kind of time: it was indefinite. Minutes dripped slowly into hours, but at the end of each day there was no collection to carry forward, nothing to measure. He tried to pace himself, mentally adjusting to increasing spans – daily certainly, weekly probably, monthly possibly. But the burden of the daily unknown was also a comfort – each day he was left unmolested marked his continued service as his father's guarantor, and therefore his father's security.

Olly was grateful for the tools that Ashish had found, and for hauling over lumps of fallen masonry. Whittling sticks gave way to more drawn-out pursuits: the time-transcending activity of sculpture, a perfect way of dealing with virtual solitary confinement. A few hours at least were chipped away from each long day, and those, paradoxically, were the ones over which Olly would have been content to linger. He was carving the figure of Lily. Like Pygmalion's ivory statue, maybe Aphrodite would come and breathe life into her. Olly had told Ashish about Lily and also about the legend of the Greek sculptor and Galatea – his sculpture made flesh. Olly took his time – to finish the carving would take away his one diversion, and leave him back in a void.

Ashish brought food, and, apart from a short time in the

251

evening, was allowed to stay only long enough to complete his chores. For the hour before he was required to draw the bolt on Olly's door, however, he would sit on the step and relate stories about his childhood and his family. They were happy-turned-sad stories, always brought to an end in the same way: his father's induction into Saleem's influence.

Whether he knew the name of the *haveli* or the village, Olly could never make him speak of it. He spoke instead of Saleem's cruelty and his single most paralysing deterrent: the cold, crawling terror induced by the threat of a ride in his helicopter. The fear of flying – the fear of falling, can be rationalised, but the thought of someone being pushed into the dark air a thousand feet up had secured absolute abjection in Ashish. It mattered not who was the pushed or pusher – himself, his father, or any other innocent. There were stories of this happening, and of one family member being required to push another. The intimidation could not be more complete.

Frank was secure, at least for as long as he dispensed mastery over his subject. It was a specialism that Dr Chinn seemed willing not only to defer to, but also to learn from. Dr Chinn organised the printing and packaging for the anti-retroviral tablets – a function the main and legitimate occupants of Saleem's factory were well set up for. He became quartermaster for Frank's needs: solvents and chemicals for his testing procedures, and also for the ever-increasing quantities of material coming from Mr Gupta. At an unguarded moment, and with a bitter tongue, he expressed concern to Frank at the alarm bell this excessive diversion would eventually set off.

Frank tried to probe Dr Chinn's relationship with Saleem. He had read into his reproach, and other comments, a clear antipathy to Saleem and his methods, and the possibility for an allegiance. But in this regard at least Dr Chinn was a closed book. It was Dr Chinn's interest in the spectrometer and its uses, however, that gave the lie to his apparent confederacy with Saleem. Not yet entirely proficient at the methodologies of spectroscopy, let alone the arcane complexities of Frank's tables, Dr Chinn's attempts at analysis would have faltered but for Frank's intervention. The subjects of his trials were samples of the ATS: the amphetamine-type stimulants that his laboratory had been producing – ecstasy and crystal meth in the main. It became quickly apparent to Frank that four out of the six samples had been severely adulterated, the essential ingredient cut back and replaced with material ranging from inert to downright lethal.

'Did you know about this?' Frank had tested countless examples of spiked drugs, but nothing as reckless as this. His accusatory tone caught Dr Chinn off-guard.

'I ... I ... knew they had cut some back.'

'But what about the fentanyl and the PMA? You must have known about those. They don't have molecular structures that compound by accident. Is making money so much more important to you than the suffering you cause?'

Dr Chinn looked down at his clipboard – not only a chance to avert his eyes, it also held the test results.

'Nothing like these figures. I knew nothing about these quantities.' He looked up and somehow Frank believed him. 'I agreed only to the slightest traces, to make up for the shortage of ephedrine. We cut back too much with previous batches – the dealers were complaining.'

'But you have loads of ephedrine, and other precursors come to that. I saw them myself in that store.'

'We have now, but there was a time when supplies dried up, and Saleem was desperate to keep up production.'

'Why so desperate? Who's cracking the whip?'

'Oh they don't know, but I think Saleem has other problems.' Dr Chinn let out a sigh, partly of pity and partly of anger. 'But I have difficulties too: Saleem passed some money through my account – for convenience he said – but I now understand it was to set me up. He has now someone to blame if the truth comes out, and a hold on my silence if it doesn't.'

'Who's they?'

'I have said too much already.' The clipboard was shaking, 'My life is worth nothing to that man.'

You could argue that Hinduism, an eclectic collection of myths, beliefs, and ideals, is more philosophy than religion, with too many interpretations for a zealot to flourish. A Hindu might worship a tree, an animal, or any mystical entity, there being a god for every human endeavour or predicament, but the personal search for immortality, a Nirvana where the soul is eternal, cannot be tied to some prescriptive manifesto, or be lorded over by one magnificent, omnipotent power.

The same argument would not apply to cricket, however. It is a religion – one that unites a nation in its traditions and creed. Its tenets and dogma provide an outlet for personal expression and the desire to win, which the more self-effacing faith would deny. Every match is a rite, winning its celebration, winners its gods. It was natural for Phil to reflect on this, sitting in front of the twenty-four-hour cricket channel. He had observed on his many visits to India how cricket had become the most abiding, obsessive pursuit for young and old. Every square yard of a park or playing field would sprawl with overlapping games. On every scorched patch of earth, backyard, or narrow street, you would see boys and men bowling balls at batsmen holding anything from the finest willow to a chair leg or barefoot urchins playing hour after hour in the dust, padding home sadly as the light failed.

The television showed back-to-back cricket: live tests, one-day or 20/20 matches, re-runs of India victories, or endless variations on the statistical absolutes so loved by the scorers – best last-wicket stands, fastest centuries, bowling routs, and boundary records. Phil wallowed in the novelty of it for most of the day, and was grateful for the diversion. A particular doubt had been gnawing at him, perversely let in by good news. He had passed Gus's tip to Lily, the name of the packaging company, and within twenty minutes had received the news that Lily had found the factory, plus another name for Gus to frisk. Lily was now bound for the second location, and even with the rough coordinates she had, surely it would now be only a matter of days ...

Not without allusion to his current trials, Phil's thoughts returned to cricket, and hoped that in this orgy of sporting abandon, the five-day test match would never die out. To Phil these matches were the apogee of the sport, the highest expression of the first-class game. They were a true test, enjoyed not only by watching, but also by just following their course: reports of ever-changing prospects, accounts of valour and endurance, dispatches from the front – everything for the genuine addict. He preferred the complete test, the trial of skill, patience, and strategy that could turn a well-timed declaration into a victory, or a painstaking defence that could turn a looming loss into a draw. The test was one of a series and a draw was still a result. Watching two batsmen digging in, not going for runs, just holding their position against every bowling and fielding ploy was satisfying, if not exciting.

Phil wondered what Saleem made of cricket. How would someone so devoid of humanity be disposed to any fine human endeavour? He would prefer cruel sports, which were as much about power as winning. Playing for a draw would be too subtle for Saleem. The television demanded his attention again – he listened to the strident roar of a winning crowd, the triumphal chanting at each falling wicket; for them it was all about winning and only that. For some it could even be life or death – maybe he was wrong about Saleem's sporting preferences!

As for this present test, Phil feared that they were homing in on a draw. Soon, with both addresses known where Saleem had hidden away Frank, Olly, and conducted his clandestine activities, it would be a simple matter to blow the whistle, let police procedures take their course, and sit back. Frank and Olly would be freed – unhurt, he eagerly hoped – but that would not secure Saleem. Phil had no doubt that contingent plans would protect him, and leave him free to wreak vengence on the dismantlers of his empire. They must not play for a draw, and no move should be made against Saleem until he was cornered – and that, Phil was convinced, would come out of this Africa venture.

He called Ravi again. 'Remind Lily to take her time, be very careful, and not to do anything precipitous. Ravi, she's burning up.'

'Phil, if she finds the other hideaway, one word and we can get out the police – they could raid Saleem's lairs before you can say …'

'No police,' Phil cut in, 'unless I give the word. Whatever happens. That's vital.' A plan was taking shape in Phil's head that depended on this, although too insubstantial a thing to bring out of the shadows yet. 'I have my reasons.'

Mr Gupta had indeed been increasing his supply. The extra material produced a delivery of 750 kilos to Bishen's lock-up on Tuesday – probably one and a half million tablets. Phil was impressed with the professional packaging: blister packs of ten tablets each, generic-sounding names, and instructions for use. With the delivery was an envelope containing copies of an official-looking analysis table confirming the exact makeup of the triple dose tablets. Attached to it was a note from Saleem.

Further consignment on Friday, approx. same again, need more medical supplies, plus another next week. All arranged with Lamumba, more cash and instructions later.

By midnight they had finished the re-packing and Phil left to catch an overnight plane to Mombasa. The pallet stood ready for collection, to be just one of millions traversing the globe, but not, Phil hoped, one of the few that were inspected. He would arrive in Mombasa tomorrow, a day before the freighter, to see Mr Lamumba, and presumably Saleem's cash would reduce the likelihood of any detailed scrutiny. Saleem seemed confident that the money was enough for a good commission, as well as any more personal import tariffs officials might demand. Phil checked out of his hotel the next morning, this would be more than a day trip – further dispatches for Africa seemed to be coming with almost wanton speed. Ravi was instructed, Bishen knew the form, Phil was prepared for chicanery. By any calculation, if things went smoothly, Saleem would slip four or five million dollars into an account somewhere, and he seemed in a hurry to do so, regardless of overplaying his luck back home.

By the time Phil had crossed the Indian Ocean to Ethiopia on the first leg of his flight, Lily was starting the fourth day of her search. Guided by Mahinder, they had driven on to Jhunjhunun – a town famous for its *havelis*. This would be their base, and appropriately they checked into a hotel that had started life as the home of a rich merchant and his entourage, an exquisite *haveli* now staffed almost exclusively, Lily observed, by a gentle male personnel. A far cry, Mahinder reminded her, from the patriarchal tyranny of the past. The *haveli* was eighty miles from Rewari, outside the furthest of Lily's arcs, but they had driven nearly seventy miles in the two hours. Their logic now was to add a margin, and work back from that.

A series of reasonable excuses evolved for their search, the rationale refined to suit the circumstances. In some places they would find a local acting as a guardian to a particular *haveli* or a collection of them, happy, for a small fee, to show them round his lonely domain, and talk freely about others. In these cases the pose of a tourist was enough to open doors and mouths. In other villages with no guardian to entice, they would enquire about property to rent, for a school, a retreat, or a commune. By day four, their excuses seemed to wear thin, and their circumspection increased. They had crossed the seventy-mile line, and if only by the law of averages, they knew they must be within stumbling distance of Saleem's *haveli*. Stumbling into it, however, was not to be advised.

32

Phil hadn't been to Mombasa for many years, but just as one mentally ages an old friend and a reunion holds no surprises, so it was with this, Kenya's second city. Civic decline and decrepitude were expected to have gathered momentum, the general assumption was that threads would be barer, the once bleached and worn but presentable streetscape more pockmarked with decay. Twenty more years of tribal politics, a world bristling with competition to their staple exports, and corruption based on hopelessness for the poor and greed for the rich had left the country paying the price for the lack of investment. As usual, people got along as best they could, but the economy was all local, an alternative economy that kept mouths fed, that could afford a tarpaulin for the roof or a bucket for the water, a subsistence that left nothing for maintenance or infrastructure.

Mombasa therefore held no surprises for Phil – it had simply continued its mouldering journey into decay. Individually the Kenyans were assiduous in their labours, and with the meagre resources at their disposal, but collectively they were working against the odds. The odds were that any surpluses would be siphoned off by corruption or the enrichment of the few in control – for many years the same politically dominant Kikuyu, plus other smaller tribes who best responded to their patronage. The first sign that caught Phil's eye at the airport was advice to ring a telephone number in case of corruption. On a world corruption scale of one to ten, Kenya would score nine.

Phil had arrived in Mombasa in the early hours of Wednesday afternoon – in time to go straight to see Mr Lamumba. His office was just off the coast road north to Malindi, one of the only two major routes that served the city. The other major road – that which connected Mombasa, the largest port north of Durban, to Nairobi and the central African interior beyond – met the coast road in the centre of the city, where caravans of over-laden trucks snaked through side-streets, markets, or the ubiquitous roadside repair and recycling yards. With all airport traffic converging here, too, Phil sat patiently as his taxi joined the slow procession. The air was thick with the pungent smell of burning metal, cutters and grinders reducing vehicles and machines back to their component parts. Clever mechanics could keep the wheels turning, the pistons firing, and the torn and pummelled chassis welded on vehicles with a then better life expectancy than their own. Phil's perennial philosophy was that trade and enterprise would always find an outlet, a force for the good, if only to provide the basic necessities of life, and it certainly held up its tattered colours on the grey streets of Mombasa.

Leaving the city, Phil's taxi drove along roads with potholes the size of motor cars. Either side were sisal or oil palm plantations – good cash crops – as far as the eye could see. It would have been easy for Phil to break out his usual protest about governments letting the people down, being a party to the corruption. He was, however, here to corrupt some officials himself. His indignation would have to take second place to his duplicity.

Mr Lamumba was a large man with a disconcertingly mask-like face. His dark skin was stretched shiny and taut

260

over his skull, with only the slightest crease as it skirted his deep eye sockets, and around his mouth, which, containing a palisade of perfect but gappy white teeth, smiled without constraint. It was a face with nothing to hide, no furrows of guilt, nothing to declare.

'I have no qualms about taking your money,' he said as Phil pushed the envelope across his desk. 'As compared to my superiors, it is food for the monkeys.' And as if to justify himself further, 'I would like a better country, but until then a little extra means will keep my options open. Unlike the rich, I will keep my money in a Kenyan bank for someone else to use, not taken out of the country, out of circulation.'

'Fine with me,' said Phil, 'and it's good to work a flanker on the devious pharmas who drag out every quibbling bloody excuse to prolong their patents.' His echoing sentiment, of a man who wouldn't be doing this but for the failed system, seemed the right form, the right format for a working relationship.

'The stuff that's arriving tomorrow is a perfect generic copy. Here, you can give this to your lab; it'll help them with their testing.' Phil put Frank's analysis results on Mr Lamumba's blotter. 'And I am pleased we are able to supply you with further deliveries – they will be arriving later this week and another next week.'

'It is an opportune time – my political masters are being taken to task over their response strategy to the HIV problem. As you know, our government is a sensitive coalition that must maintain a delicate balance of interests. They are learning that it is as easy to subdue people with a little hope as to counter violent dissent with suppression. In areas or times of tension the balm of a little extra health care saves lives in more ways than one.

'Please leave me with your hotel and contact details and

we will contact you when we have tested the drugs. We will take care of the import procedures so you will have nothing to do. Some of this,' he said, holding up Phil's envelope, 'will complete the necessary forms, but I will need you to sign other documents for our files.'

'And payment?' Phil was under no illusion, it was all arranged, but Mr Lamumba might let slip a little detail.

'I will get authority for the transfer to H.S. whatever it was after the tests. My discretion,' he said with a mixture of pride and humility, 'extends only to a million dollars.'

'Good, good, that's all understood,' Phil replied, still fishing. 'Was it the Delhi or Dubai account?'

'Whatever you asked for,' he replied, but turned the page in a small notebook. 'Actually neither – here in Mombasa. There's less red tape for us to transfer money internally, so we insisted on a local bank. Payments can be arranged instantly in our own currency.'

The slightest eddy of satisfaction washed over Phil's face. It must have registered as a ripple of concern – Mr Lamumba continued conspiratorially, 'Less, of course, your own invoice for medical supplies as per manifest. I will arrange a bank draft in US dollars for that.'

'Of course,' Phil replied incuriously. Of course – this time he smiled to himself – of course, he gets paid effectively his commission, the rest goes to Saleem, just for an internal supply. What fictitious goods or services they had sanction for was anyone's guess.

Mr Lamumba insisted on a complete tour of his depot, a distribution centre for the coastal region. The warehouse was stacked high with boxes and crates marked Red Cross or UN or other aid agencies that preferred to send goods rather than cash. A large workroom housed white-shirted scribes recording transactions and orders, on its walls charts and maps – graphics for the many diseases endemic in the area. Mr Lamumba stood by one. 'You can die of many things in Africa, Mr Donahue, but the rarest is old age.'

Phil had heard the aphorism before but somehow Mr Lamumba imbued it with less resignation.

'We have over a million people in Kenya suffering from HIV and as many orphans,' he said, and continued with a sad simplicity that revealed the human side to his maps and graphs, 'and we have to help them.'

Phil left, sober with the pitiful statistics, but replete with information. Mr Lamumba had an aura that stroked Phil's own benign disposition, but where on a line from mercy to mercenary he stood, he would reflect on later. For the moment he might just have enough details to point Gus to the right bank account, dealings in which could be of special interest to his Chinese friends. He should let Saleem top it up before declaring its contents.

Over a million dollars was the inference – a tidy sum though still a bargain for a million doses of the latest state-of-the-art triple-therapy drugs. But the quantities were actually quite small, and even with another few deliveries Phil knew that the trade would be short-lived. Eventual discovery, together with his strategy to entrap Saleem, would leave Mr Lamumba's new supply chain looking elsewhere to secure its promise of hope. At least, Phil ruminated, some little good would have been done, some tens of thousands of people would have a few more years to hope for a cure.

He then remembered that the first load now contained a million and a half, not the original million, with the same again on Friday, and more next week. Dr Chinn must be having kittens, and what unyielding force was pushing Mr Gupta to these unsustainable levels was hard to imagine, without admitting the presence of some dark compulsion.

He called Gus: H.S. something or other must have opened an account in Mombasa; find it and look out for lodgements from some Kenyan quango.

By Friday, he'd been called to Mr Lamumba's office to be given a draft for $80,000, had received a call from Ravi that the second load was en route, and had had a short message from Saleem saying, rather boyishly: *How's that Mr 10%!*

'I am pleased to say,' announced Mr Lamumba, 'your drugs have proved the highest quality in our tests – all in line with your own readings, of course.'

'Never any doubt.' Phil waved a confident dismissal.

'I am pleased also that you have been able to expedite further deliveries. Having discovered this affordable new source, I am being pressed to get the drugs into the field as soon as possible – we need to be seen to be building up stocks for a credible campaign.' He put both hands on his desk with a sigh of resignation, 'A campaign I have to accept – just as political as medical.'

Phil heard himself reciting platitudes about political realities. Then in a more practical tone he said, 'Second load arriving in the morning.'

'Indeed, and with the tests complete, I shall be able to arrange immediate transfer of funds. You may care to call here at midday for your second draft.'

Of course, of course, it goes without saying, one would expect no less – Phil hoped that his countenance still projected these sentiments as he nodded assent.

'The third and for the time being last consignment must be here by Tuesday, and I believe this is all in hand.' Mr Lamumba felt comfortable with Phil's worldly-wise demeanour, his easy grasp. 'The other dimension to this, Mr Donahue, in case you are wondering, is a fiscal one. We have to spend our allocation by the end of the month, which is Tuesday.'

264

Perfect, thought Phil. If he could get hold of Saleem's account in Mombasa, then he could make his move. This was definitely money not being declared to his sponsors. He found himself thinking of his own account – 10% of Saleem's millions would do very nicely ... although how much he would be able to keep if he managed to expose Saleem was an open question.

It was Monday afternoon, a week after they had set out, when Mahinder and Lily entered a barely signposted village, a settlement of cottages and houses inexplicably come to rest on a dry and unyielding plain. It had been a long, eccentric, and so far fruitless quest. Day followed day, but their methodical sweep, met with either shrugs, suspicion, and incomprehension, or friendly but misguided direction, threw up no clues. Their energy and spirit dimmed by each blind alley, they drew encouragement only from the numbers – statistically they were getting nearer, the process of elimination must be narrowing their search.

The buildings were scattered haphazardly as if fallen from some giant passing conveyance, the road now barging through them when seemingly it could have easily travelled around the empty hinterland. In the centre was a triangle of ground with a well surrounded by stunted acacia trees, the thorns on their lower branches carded with the wool of grazing sheep and goats. An old man sat in the shade, chewing khat. He didn't look up when Lily and Mahinder approached – content to let his animals greet his visitors with their own watchful eyes.

Initially the old man had been pleasant enough. Mahinder had asked him in Hindi about properties to rent – he looked up from Lily's pink feet and replied in English.

'No, there is nothing here to rent or buy.'

'But surely,' Mahinder pressed him, his arm taking a

265

sweeping measure of the abandoned-looking houses dotted around the village, 'some of these properties must be available. They can't just leave them.'

'But they do,' the old man sighed, 'apart from that one.' He nodded over to the only other road in the village. It travelled north to the deserts, and before it disappeared into the shimmering distance, it stopped by five or six very large houses on the edge of the village – deserted *havelis*, faded and peeling but their grandeur unblinking in the overhead sun.

'Good. It could be what we're looking for. Are you the guardian? Could we have a look over it? Which one is it?' Whether it was the questions or their intensity, the old herder recoiled, and, looking away to his animals, he seemed to wrestle with some embedded scruple.

'Best you look somewhere else.'

'But surely we could have a look if they let it?'

'No, no, it's already been taken.'

Words of deliverance, they hung in the air like the cry of a lookout, after casting around a lonely sea. Those were the words they had been waiting for all week, they went to the root of their enquiry. Lily and Mahinder had lost count of the times they had asked the question, but now by sheer numerical weight their persistence had elicited an answer. Lily was wide-eyed and spellbound with unutterable joy – the words must mean she could unbind Olly from the cold grip of an indeterminate future into her own warm and unconditional embrace, and what little doubt she had about their significance she could soon remove ...

'Oh, is that the one the Chinese have moved into...?'

'Best you look somewhere else,' he repeated, this time with a hint of suspicion – the matter was closed. The old man's retrenchment confirmed the answer, and their need to be wary.

'Ah well, never mind.' Mahinder caught Lily's eye. 'Maybe somewhere else. Let's go further east – apparently they've got plenty available there.'

They drove east, out of the village without looking back, without seeing the old man walking his goats up the north road, maybe to better fodder, maybe to earn a tip for his watchfulness. A mile later they found a track leading north – it led to some brick-works, the seam of clay long since exhausted, leaving only a layer of fine dust over the track and surrounding land. The track went on further, bending round to the right, promising to deliver them to the cluster of *havelis* in the far distance. They stopped in a clump of trees. The habit of instruction and the pleasure of sharing knowledge prompted a short aside from Mahinder; it would in any event give their rising expectations a chance to acclimatise.

'These are khejri trees,' he said. 'They share the landscape with the acacias – the only ones that can find the deep water and stand up to the hot dry winds. It is said that in a severe drought, survival depends on three things: having a goat, a camel, and a khejri tree.' Lily nodded sagely. She wouldn't ask him to elucidate; it would spoil the image.

'If we are to get closer,' Mahinder said, returning from his adage, 'it must be up that track, on foot and after dark.' He looked back down their trail. Their car sat, out of sight, behind the trees, but its presence was heavily advertised by the plume of dust that had followed them. 'I don't want to drive through the village again past that old man.' Their joint understanding of the potentially miraculous find was unspoken, a spell not to be broken.

'Also we'll be able to see lights. Empty houses don't need lights.' Lily was still collected, keeping her excitement wrapped up in more practical thoughts. It wasn't till they had passed through the next village that she let out a whoop. Mahinder slapped the steering wheel and looked to the sky – there would be a god to thank for this.

The moon rose in its fourth quarter, a pale imprint over the eastern horizon, like a silver rubbing on a cloth of blue. It was little more than a crescent, but would be more than enough to light their expedition tonight.

33

Frank found it hard to connect his new existence with any move to secure his and his son's salvation. He trusted Phil implicitly, but after days of working and sleeping in locked rooms under constant surveillance, the world was closing in on him again. Mercifully the shutters on the otherwise barred window of his bedroom – the room of his original confinement – were left open. But the Ramachem sign hanging in full view across the way now haunted him with a reminder of his isolation. Was it lax security or a lack of concern? Was this little clue to his location of no consequence – his having no one to pass it on to? Cruel doubts played with his loyalties. But he held faith in the strategy to inveigle Phil into Saleem's confidence. He still trusted Phil, even though the easy realism of their spurious antipathy and Phil's comfortable bonding with Saleem gnawed at the edges of his certitude.

This idea for a new line of drugs had certainly enabled Phil to gain access to Frank and Olly, and, apart from the chicanery, had allowed fleeting words of communication – enough, Frank hoped, to identify the locations he'd been taken to. The rest of it, though, was surely irrelevant, just a matter of following through for appearance's sake – not that he had any choice, with his son locked away. At night Frank fought back his tears when he thought of Olly and his sacrifice; he was scared, the pit of his stomach churned with the thought that they should hurt his son. During the

269

day the routine of his allotted tasks relieved the tension – feeding the tableting machine, running tests, supervising production – and he could not deny a certain satisfaction with the end product, and the end result: the knowledge that there would be more vital medicine in the world than otherwise there would have been. But despair waited for him in his room at night, harrying and threatening, breaking his hope with that blunt instrument of fear – the sound of his son's distress.

Frank worked abjectly, though eventually not questioning the point of it all, and Dr Chinn, bustling nervously between the production room and the unsuspecting packaging team, oblivious to the fraudulence of their labels, was sinking into a cold sulk. The two men, watched over constantly by at least one of Saleem's minders, slumped into a grim acceptance of their situation. Saleem's visits, his self-satisfaction perversely bringing a chill to the already manifest gloom, seemed to scour any concord between him and his head chemist, and by the end of the second batch – the second enlarged batch – the abrasion had worn away any pretence of cooperation. Before Frank could take in any particulars of the argument they were rehearsing, Saleem held up an imperious hand to declare, 'I don't think we need Mr Landing here. He may go to his quarters.' He meant be taken away – pushed along to his cell by a minder with a key.

'What do you mean, Gupta has run out?' Saleem was full of vitriol, 'He can't just run out – unless it's of his will to live …'

'You may threaten him all you like, but the simple fact is that one more gram of the compound will lead to his discovery. I need hardly remind you that we rely on him for much of our other materials, and the last time we ran low he came to your rescue.'

'He gets paid well for his diversions.'

'Not as much as your diversions from Triad funds. They'd cut you to pieces if they knew.'

'I assume you mean our diversions?'

Dr Chinn was incandescent. Saleem's stretching of the raw materials together with his own share of the proceeds had not been hard to discover, but he then found his options spiked by one of Saleem's devious designs. Saleem could only say this because he had planted money in Dr Chinn's bank account from an unknown source, and Dr Chinn had been stupid enough to acquiesce in further regular payments – to maintain his silence over irregularities. He would keep silent, he had resigned, unless the flow of money stopped, or the adulteration of the drugs became more serious. How much more serious he would have to decide – the quotient of suffering he could condone for each extra dollar would be less than Saleem, but still, he would arrive at a figure. He realized too late, however, that his calculations would be academic – the very record of payments was enough to condemn him regardless of any whistle-blowing.

'You're evil, Saleem, black evil.'

'We are both evil, Dr Chinn, in an evil business with evil sponsors, and the sooner we can finish this order to Kenya, the sooner we can both get out of their clutches.'

'I'd sooner be in their clutches than yours.'

'But you are in mine, so I suggest you get Gupta round here and sort out another delivery. I don't care what it is,' Saleem said into Dr Chinn's defeated face, 'so long as we can press it into tablets, and it's the same colour as before.'

Dr Chinn's face was written over with shock – he had not expected this – but Saleem had misread the shock for defiance. 'Be careful,' he said, 'you have not yet made yourself indispensable,' and, turning to his minders, he added, 'and there's nothing that these two cannot do.'

Actually Dr Chinn would carry on, even without the threat – he reasoned that it could lead to Saleem's downfall. Suddenly he felt calm.

Saleem also became calm – he had had his way. Carrying on production with worthless fakes was not perhaps the best outcome, but Lamumba's people weren't testing subsequent deliveries, so what did he care? He would have the money and Donahue would face the music when the fakes were eventually discovered. It would take a little time at least for the inefficacy of his pills to be noticed. That this would not register before some poor wretches were denied any remission, and reach a point beyond further treatment, was of no concern to Saleem. That they would then be tipped into a deadly decline was a fact of their lives not of his.

A downfall … Saleem was also thinking about a downfall, this one literal and physical – for Dr Chinn.

Frank was left in his room; whatever the argument between Saleem and Dr Chinn, the production continued without him. He was still at their disposal but … but ultimately disposable. The old man, Ashish's father, brought him food and water and what encouraging words he could whisper. Days went by – Frank made no count, each one would only add to his burden of uncertainty, and there was no countdown to a day of release. The open window was his saving: if he stood close enough he could not see the bars, he could see outside spaces and of course the Ramachem sign. He wondered ruefully, knowing the Indian's penchant for deities, whether this could be Rama the god of good chemists; he would say a prayer.

The moon was shining on only quarter-power, not enough, Lily and Mahinder calculated, for their approach to be observed, but enough for them to make their way from the group of khejri trees to the *havelis* standing darkly in the distance, the only interruption to a faint horizon. The track which had promised favourable access earlier in the day ended after a few hundred yards, giving way to the broken crust of the old clay diggings. They battled commando-style over a course of trenches and walls of rejected bricks for over an hour, before they found themselves on open ground, scrubby with coarse grasses and low, thick bushes. Still no lights advertised occupation of any of the dim silhouettes ahead, no beacon raised their hopes that they had found the only inhabited *haveli* for miles. Soon, impassable thicket prevented their advance, manoeuvring them into a traverse of the unyielding terrain, but with their veering angle of observation the distant roof-scape changed shape until the furthest building, no longer eclipsed, came into view. A light flickered, just a pinhole piercing the blank canvas, then another – divining, defining lights bringing resolution to Lily and Mahinder's theory of how they should find their quest.

They set their heads to this glimmer of hope, tacking where necessary against the ever-increasing press and pull of the undergrowth, until they could discern a back-lit window or an open door. A hundred yards away, seeing a flash of movement followed by the sound of voices, they stopped. Also they were downwind of creeping and sluggish air on which wafted a sour odour, with a withering choking pungency, into which further advance would be ill advised.

'We should go back,' Mahinder said, breathing through his sleeve. 'I think all is confirmed.'

Lily did not demur. They could have skirted the toxic fumes – presumably from a chemical dump outside the grounds – got closer in, spotted an occupant, been spotted themselves. It was time to withdraw. They had achieved a 90% certainty – enough for the moment. It would take some hours to make their way back in the dark, and their next visit should be with more light and fewer obstacles. The crescent moon had long since slipped away in the night, making their return journey slow and hazardous. It was nearly dawn before they returned to the car, cut, bruised, and exhausted, but jubilant.

A late breakfast found them studying the map to find a route that led to the northern exit from the village, without passing the centre and the dark hooded eyes of the old herder. It was worth the considerable detour to find, a short distance above the group of abandoned buildings, a stopping place behind some shrub-topped hummocks beside the road – a perfect vantage point from which to watch the comings and goings from the one occupied *haveli*. They sat for four or five hours through the fierce midday heat into the late afternoon. Not a single vehicle disturbed the dust on the road which led to the Rajasthan deserts to the north; no animal, human or otherwise, found a reason to pass by. There were sounds, natural rustling and murmurs – the hum of insects, the trill of a bird or a flutter of wings, a distant tractor – but the sounds to which Lily's antenna was tuned came from the *haveli* down the road. The walls looked thick and the windows were small, but some clatter of human occupation escaped, just the sharp frequencies – kitchen noises, pots and pans being handled, doors slamming, an occasional voice raised for attention. The only large openings onto the road – balconied windows either side of the great wooden entrance doors – were boarded up as if for a siege. It could have been buzzing with life inside, but whence the buzz …? This was not a happy place.

*

274

When she was about twelve, Lily and a boy in her village had a crush. It was an exquisite period as dewy new sensations introduced her tender heart to the pain and pleasure of yearning for another human being, not the comfortable warmth of a parent, or for any wanton interest in the opposite sex, but an unaccountable yet overpowering need just for contiguity and attachment. The boy understood, even less than Lily, the confusion of every feeling he had taken for granted – hitherto straightforward affections transcended by some delicious new stirring. They both sipped deeply on a taste previously unknown – an intoxicating essence that left their hearts racing. They shared a desire that had no comparison, their days a series of pretexts for innocent union, with the need to snatch moments to share, perhaps to overcome their shyness, or just to bathe in sublime anticipation.

It was in this state of mind that Lily set out to make a closer inspection of the *haveli*. They were just seeking the last piece of proof that this was the second of Saleem's hideaways, but Lily was already convinced she could feel Olly's proximity, and she was drawn to the walls of his prison with a heart fluttering not with fear, but with a need just to be close.

'If you're not back in ten minutes I'm coming looking,' Mahinder said when Lily held up her hand to his accompaniment.

'If I am not back in ten minutes,' Lily replied, holding Mahinder in a steady and insistent gaze, 'it will prove our theory. The last thing you must do is to follow me. You must leave immediately and report the location to Ravi and Phil.'

Followed initially by Mahinder's watchful eye, and accompanied only by her shadow, now released by the abating sun, Lily made no sound as she approached the expressionless walls. Recent use had beaten down the undergrowth that had assailed a side wall, and leaving the road she followed the rutted track that passed along to the back of the building. She was no longer a twelve-year-old girl in a dry-mouthed, heart-stopping rapture, with just the thought of seeing her young valentine, risking the frowns of parents, or the sport of siblings, for a moment of new-fledged intimacy. Now she was a grown woman. This was no transient infatuation warmed only by its novelty; it was a passion from determined adult conviction, a passion prepared for suffering and danger.

Now turning to the rear, she remembered the light of an open door, the only gap she had seen in the perimeter at ground level. A gap to listen by, to look into, possibly to slip through ...

Phil was sitting on the hotel terrace when they came for him – two burly policemen with guns, batons, and unpleasant manners. He was just ending a call from Gus – shooting the breeze after a more intense briefing on money movements – when Ravi's name came up as a call waiting. Before being able to answer, Phil was marched out, arms pinned to his sides, and forced violently into the back of a car. Even without the physical aggression and verbal threats, he was too surprised to resist. His mind was now intent on solving this sudden riddle; something had gone wrong, Saleem was turning the tables, everybody was in danger. He would have struggled, though, if he could, to answer his phone, now urgently ringing again in his pocket. When they drove him to Mr Lamumba's office instead of a police station, the list of potential explanations for his arrest grew longer, if no less vague.

'This is just the beginning of a long and unpleasant period of your life, Mr Donahue – a life,' he said with a truly terrifying plainness, 'to which you may well wish an end.'

Mr Lamumba sat heavily behind his desk, a constriction in his chest added a wheeze of deep emotion to his voice, his hollow eyes swirling red with anger. He was smarting from the attempted deception – a random test had revealed the third and last batch to be coloured chalk and gypsum. They were safely impounded, but until he received the retrospective results from the second batch, which had already been distributed, he was in mortal fear of the consequences. To recall the drugs would be to advertise ineptitude; his position, his career would be crushed to nothing, ground down in the mill of recrimination. Even his life, what part at least was worth living, could bite the dust, trampled under the feet of a baying crowd. Or he could brazen it out, hope that the distribution was thin and not concentrated, and that the harm would be minimised. The fact that at heart he was a moral man only inflamed his dilemma.

Phil sat opposite, flanked by the two officers. He knew he was guilty – guilty of anything they chose. He said nothing – he was too busy running through the possibilities, running through permutations of responses depending on the charge.

'Have you nothing to say?'

'I have a great deal to say, but first you must tell me why I have been brought here.'

'I should have thought that this was obvious,' Mr Lamumba hissed through his ivory, now bared, teeth with a venom that stunned Phil into further silence. Only Saleem, he thought, could induce this level of malevolence in an adversary.

'But then if you are stupid enough to supply me with fake medicine, perhaps I'll have to spell it out for you.'

Phil's expression changed, confused with consternation at the news and yet clearing with understanding as the penny dropped. A smile of grim irony would have been a natural progression, but Phil, recognising in time that this would have further enraged the official, managed to erase from his brow anything that could be interpreted as insolence. In any event the Saleem poison had just reached him too. In a gall of bitter memories, Phil leapt forward, and, too quick for the guards, brought his great fist down on to the desk.

'That serpent, that vile black-hearted, evil, snake ...'

His phone was ringing again. Mr Lamumba held out his hand.

'Listen,' Phil urged, 'I don't know whether you are dealing direct or through some Nigerians, but I knew nothing of this shameful treachery, and this call could be vitally important to you.'

'Hello.' Mr Lamumba held the phone away from his ear.

'Hello, is that Phil?' Phil heard Ravi ask doubtfully.

'No, he can't speak to you right now. Who's calling? Is there a message?' Mr Lamumba decided that at least he should attribute the call. Through the red mist he could see the hapless side of Phil's reaction to all this – maybe the call would be of some significance.

'This is urgent ... tell him ...' But Ravi was torn. It was nearly an hour since Lily had walked around that corner; anything could have happened to Phil also ... somebody had his phone...

'Tell him...' – Ravi was still unsure.

'Tell us, Ravi, it's ok.' Phil's distant voice confused him, but Ravi was reassured by its assertion.

'Lily has disappeared into Saleem's lair,' he blurted out. 'They found the second place – she went in and didn't come back.'

Something about Phil's demeanour suggested to Mr Lamumba that he was an unlikely party to the fraud; he might even be a party to the justice that needed to be

278

exacted. When Phil reached out for the phone he placed it in his hand.

'Ravi, it's Phil. Tell me what's happened.'

Ravi went through Mahinder's account, the conclusion being that, with the two addresses, they could and should bring in the police immediately. Mahinder was acquainted with the Deputy Police Commissioner in Delhi, who had a reputation for a quick and aggressive response to drug rings.

'There is one thing I have to do before any police raids. Ravi, this is absolutely crucial, please assure me that no contact will be made until I give the word.'

'I will do my best, but Mahinder is as deranged as the parent of a lost child, I can't promise to hold him off for more than an hour. What's so important anyway?'

'Ok.' Phil had worked it out. The stakes were already high, but the only fulcrum to raise them to the extra level of his now maturing plan was a lie. Time to be devious himself.

'Let him talk to the police straight away,' he continued. 'Get everything in place. They will understand that there should be no raids until I can get the head man on one of the two premises – he must not escape the net. No one should move until Saleem is cornered.'

Ravi concurred and Phil repeated, 'Remember, I must be kept informed. Please, you or Mahinder call me with a report.' He said this with an appeal on his face to Mr Lamumba, who had listened with a look of distracted forbearance.

The appeal was to keep the phone. 'This is a lifeline,' Phil said with enough gravity to displace any possible objection. 'It may save us all.' He put the phone on the edge of the desk, and, looking straight into the pained red eyes, asked, 'Would you like to hear what I have to say?' And then after the slightest inclination of Mr Lamumba's head, Phil said, 'Would you mind if we were alone?' Another nod bid the two policemen to leave the room.

Time was of the essence, but Mr Lamumba was quick on the uptake, and in less than ten minutes had agreed to Phil's plan. He didn't care if the story was pure invention – the core part of the plan was to get this Saleem apprehended. He had spoken to Saleem only once – to cement the deal and run through the financial arrangements. The introduction and set-up were by people with reputations to protect, albeit with no more probity than the officials they served. It was unthinkable that they would be so short-sighted. No, Saleem was his man.

34

Phil dialled the number; he had carried it around for weeks – in his head. It was on divert – a mobile picked it up, no answer, just a curt instruction: *Leave a message or call back.* He left no message; he would call back. He kept trying – that wasn't Saleem's voice, but it must be his number, it just must be. He had rehearsed what he would say, how he would explain the inexplicable, how he would ...

'Hello.' It was Saleem. Phil could hear the slowing blades of a helicopter. Saleem was on his way to the *haveli*, just dropped into Rewari to rattle Dr Chinn. Phil braced himself.

'Saleem, this is Phil Donahue.'

'What the hell ... where the hell did you get this number?'

'Listen there's no time to explain. You've got to get out of there. There's about to be a raid.' Phil, it would seem, had no intention of letting Saleem be cornered.

'How do you know where I am?' Saleem sounded off-balance, almost a little nervous.

'I don't know where you are. I mean get out of the country – out of India. You have to get out as soon as possible ... it's not just the police.' This was the extra barb on the hook from which Saleem might otherwise slip.

'How do you know this, and how did you get this number?' He was wriggling.

'Oh I checked up on you. I always like to know who I'm doing business with – I liked what I heard. Anyway that little shit Liu called me. She says she's worked it out, got

281

someone snooping around. There's trouble on the way, said she'd see us in hell. Speaking of which, what the hell's going on with her? Is there something I should know?' It was good to goad Saleem with talk of Liu, who, apart from being a useful source for all unexplained information, was clearly an elusive, ratty little shrew who gnawed at his composure.

Phil hoped that his faux indignation would provide a smokescreen for his dubious claims; however, at the mention of Liu, on top of the suggestion that more than the police were to be feared, Saleem swallowed deeper on the hook. It was Liu, she was the lure, and, unbeknown to Phil, more mesmerising than, at his most artful, he would have wished. An hour ago Saleem had been told of the girl who had crept into the *haveli*. He hadn't waited for a description; he knew who she was – the mystery girl who seemed to know so much, the girl he had tried to capture. 'Keep her under lock and key till I arrive,' he'd commanded. The inference now, that it was not her, but someone snooping on her behalf, didn't reduce the menace he felt in any way. He squirmed with the thought that she was still at large, and with the notion that had often crossed his mind, but that so far he'd dismissed, that she could be his undoing.

'You don't have to worry about her,' Saleem said, stiffened by his hatred. 'We have caught her accomplice, and as soon as I get to her I will extract the information I need. I assume,' he said, 'you have no objection.' There was a challenge to this, a test.

'I want to say help yourself, and if you find that Chinese witch let me know, but it may have to wait for another day. I'm telling you, you have to get out of there now, you've only got a few minutes.'

Saleem made no reply. For all his bluster he was still dangling uncomfortably, twisting on fine threads of doubt.

'Look, I've got Lamumba eating out of my hand. He's just paid over for today's delivery – he's desperate for more bribes and reckons he can stockpile tons of the stuff. We can work him over for millions. We can do it anywhere, but for Christ's sake jump on a plane and get over here. And bring Dr Chinn – we'll need him; leave the rest.'

Saleem had walked into the factory, and standing in front of Dr Chinn, held out the phone 'Can you repeat that last bit?'

'Bring Dr Chinn. We'll need him; leave the rest.'

'Come,' he said to Dr Chinn, 'we have to meet Mr Donahue.'

Saleem ended the call – he had taken the bait, he was on his way, even, it sounded, bringing Dr Chinn, who Phil had only suggested come to add some textual verity to his claims. He hadn't really believed that Saleem would want to save someone he had shown only antipathy. Dr Chinn would surely fall foul of Saleem's tumult and be left behind. Phil allowed himself a little anticipation, cautiously enjoying thoughts of Saleem's fulminations, his angry strutting demands, flights, hasty arrangements, and complex logistics. He could feel Saleem thrashing on his line, and it would be some hours before he was truly landed, but in the meantime he must tell Ravi to let the raids commence in the hope that Saleem, far from being cornered, had escaped.

Saleem, now back in the helicopter, still hadn't made up his mind. He didn't distrust or trust Phil. Then again he had tried never to have to rely on anyone whose compliance he had not secured in some way. He was inclined to believe that Frank and his son meant nothing to Phil – indeed the obvious scorn between them would suggest more indifference, than concern that could be exploited. What drove this small-time dealer was money, a plain one-dimensional greed that was easy to pervert. It would make sense therefore for him to secure his new source of riches – he, himself, Saleem. He would consider the other side of the matter as they flew – the extent to which this Liu might have done what she seemed to have told Donahue, and with whom she might be in league. Delhi – she had worked out where he was, and '... who your bosses are' – another of her 'hunches'. The disappearance of his man in London poured more into the foundations of his bafflement, and everything associated with this woman seemed to raise another level of paranoia.

No matter, he resolved, he would continue his journey to the *haveli* as planned; he would wring the truth out of her accomplice. He had made up his mind and he would take no summary action. Donahue's warning was probably misguided – a panic to protect his new benefactor. Saleem would not run on one person's word without very good reason.

As the churning blades lifted them above the home-going rush around Rewari's commercial areas, Saleem scanned the activity for the presence of police. What would a raid look like? Flashing lights ... commando units ... cordons ...? All looked normal. Yet there was nothing normal about Saleem's afternoon – two phone calls, both linked to that elusive girl, had instigated his extreme state of disquiet. These were threatening events outside his normal web of control. He felt snagged on something he didn't understand, and was unable to shake off. Some manipulative entity was ensnaring him. Donahue had said it – she wanted to see them in hell.

But then he rationalised the purpose of his mission, and his confident defiance returned. After all, the vigilance of his well-trained men had caught an intruder, just a young woman, hardly the forward party of a police raid – a tender

284

young woman who would lead him finally and fatally to Liu – the Chinese witch, as Phil Donahue aptly called her. Saleem's sense of control returned; this was, after all, a beautiful game. The flight was almost over when he remembered Dr Chinn strapped into the seat by the door, unaware that Saleem's distractions had earned him just a temporary reprieve.

'Looks like a welcoming party,' Saleem's pilot said as he arrested his descent, Saleem's self-belief now suspended over the scene below.

From five hundred feet the ground seems to lose a dimension. They looked down on the flat graphics of an early computer game. The *haveli* looked like a disturbed nest with small creatures scattering in all directions. Their usual landing place, just up from Lily's earlier vantage point, was a corral of cars and trucks from which were fanning out more running figures, forming themselves into a broad cordon encircling the building. Loud cracks and smoke from stun grenades left no doubt as to the overwhelming determination of the raiding party, and no doubts for Saleem to controvert about his predicament. His beautiful game was over – he swallowed deeply on his pride, and choked on the humiliation of being worsted.

'Up, up,' he barked, 'go back up, go back.'

The slightest adjustment to the pitch of the rotor blades and they were sucked back up into the fading light of the ending day, into a slaty sky of gathering cloud. The gloom suited Saleem's temper while they headed back east to Delhi, his capricious mood darkening as he let in the full enormity of his defeat, as he let it displace all other considerations but vengeance. She had won the game but she was no match for his omnipotence. No one with his guest list of the great and good, the rich and powerful who had visited his needs, who had provided dispensation and cover in return for patronage, payment, and privacy, could regard this as other than a temporary setback. She would live in fear when she heard of his escape – Phil Donahue was right, and Saleem reviewed himself favourably at having cultivated Phil's dependency. The man was right about getting out of India, if only while the dust settled, but not right about taking Dr Chinn.

Dr Chinn ... Dr Chinn ... Liu ... Saleem recalled his earlier thought – with whom was she in league? His seat-belt checked the shudder that would have propelled him across the cabin as the revelation hit. The underlying evil that streaked his soul seemed to loose a hideous creature, half-bird, half-snake – he saw his hands as talons and could feel a darting venomous tongue in his mouth. In an instant the clasp of Saleem's harness was undone, the loose straps tightening around Dr Chinn's neck. Saleem was too strong for him – in a few moments his air-starved brain had shut down and his head fell limp over his convulsed body. A moment later the door was open and Dr Chinn sat slumped on the floor. Saleem waited for the fresh air to restore his consciousness, for Dr Chinn to be alive to his own death, before pushing him to it.

'We found the H.S. accounts in Kenya,' Gus had said earlier, 'Looks like he opened in three separate banks – two international and one local Kenyan bank. That's where the money's been transferred from – 135 million Kenyan shillings to Barclays Kenya and another 200 million to Standard Chartered, all in Mombasa. H.S. has myriad accounts in India – you'd need a lot of time and a forensic accountant to decipher them.

'Apart from stuff washed through the *hawalas*, which you'll never see, his accounts are peppered with transfers for quite small amounts. Apparently anything under

$10,000 gets under the money-laundering radar these days.'

This was all before the *haveli* was found, and Phil was disappointed they couldn't delve deeper, find a pattern of inflows and outflows that might profile his business dealings. It was interesting, though, to see Mr Lamumba's deposits, and also that they had not been transferred beyond other Mombasa banks. Perhaps it was naïve of Phil to think he could unearth proof of Saleem milking the Triads' profits, but as it turned out, Saleem had delivered his own indictment, and if Phil could play him in, Saleem would seal his own fate. A little later that evening, before Phil could tantalise him further with another call to his private number, Saleem called him.

'I'm making arrangements – I'll call you with details.' No mention of the reason, or acknowledgement of the warning. Phil rejoiced in Saleem's terse message, in the delicious hubris. He hoped it was not premature.

Saleem had a house and a safe near the golf links in New Delhi. Not a large property by the local ambassadorial standards of this most elite of prime areas, the exquisite colonial bungalow sat on sprinklered lawns in a compound of high bougainvillea-topped walls. Saleem ran his affairs from here. He lived alone, attended on by a family of five who had lived in the grounds for generations. They were there before him and would stay on, he reflected dispassionately, when the over-mortgaged property was repossessed.

He was in the house for just thirty minutes. Going straight to his computer, he checked for the last payment from Lamumba, for what amounted to worthless gypsum. The sight of it, timed in to his account at six that evening, another two hundred million Kenyan shillings – another one and a half million pounds – took away any doubts about his destination. The secret of control was always to have choices, never to be imposed on by others' advice or circumstances, and even in this sudden flight Saleem knew he had choices. That last lodgement endorsed his prowess and settled his choice – not Europe or the USA but the dark continent of Africa. There he could disappear, prosper, and live like a prince.

He checked the airlines – there was a seat to Mombasa in just a few hours' time via Addis Ababa and Nairobi, and another via Mumbai. He chose the first; he did not want to touch down *en route* still on Indian soil. Opening the safe, Saleem took out two bundles of banknotes and three passports: one for the journey and the others he secreted, together with the dollars and the pounds at the bottom of a suitcase otherwise full of a hurried selection from his wardrobe. In the next fifteen minutes he had moved crucial files to his laptop, and transferred three substantial deposits to his Mombasa accounts.

It was now almost ten o'clock. He made two calls. The second was to Phil. To a casual listener he would have sounded confident and at ease, even ebullient.

'I'm on the 02:45 flight via Nairobi, arriving Mombasa tomorrow at 14:40. Book us both into the best hotel – it's time to celebrate.'

It was a defiant swagger, however, that Phil heard – it induced the same blithe sentiments, though in Phil's case it was that delectable pause before the coming *schadenfreude*.

'Brilliant' was Phil's reply, and he really meant it, 'absolutely brilliant.'

But Saleem's outward act of imperturbability masked a bitter, spiteful, and malignant tantrum, which could only be soothed by the sweet balm of revenge. His first call had been to London. He'd posted a reward on Liu's head of such an amount that those two young cavemen would tear the city apart in their efforts to find her – starting with that flat that they had been pussying around outside for the last week.

'"It's time to celebrate," he says.' Phil was still with Mr Lamumba – now under no more persuasion than the offer of a pleasant dinner. His host was content – the second batch had proven genuine, and the third was on the way to an incinerator. He had kept a small sample back as a reminder and a warning to himself. Also there was a lesson to be learnt. They were both relieved that Saleem hadn't tried to transfer that last payment; their gamble had paid off – finding withdrawals frozen would have had him running to a different continent.

'To be exact,' Phil expanded, 'that time will be at midday tomorrow, when Saleem arrives at Nairobi.'

'His final transfer to Mombasa,' Mr Lamumba beamed, 'will not be the flight on his ticket. Once he steps into my country, he will be subject to my own arrangements.'

35

'OLLY ...' Olly heard a shout, then another muffled cry, then silence. He had never heard Lily's raised voice, but there was no mistaking her essential timbre.

Olly's thoughts had wandered much into the prospects of his and his father's rescue and especially at its advent. If and when it happened, it would be a sudden event, a snap announcement of diametric and immediate change. With no advance warning of their rescuers' progress, there would be no early signs to watch for, just a quick commotion, the sound of running feet, raised voices – word of their location had got through, Phil had worked his magic, a relieving force had been mustered, Saleem cornered and neutralised. But in Olly's unempowered state, suspended between daytime hopes and the darker foreboding of night, the waiting was torture. Efforts to contain the agonies of continual expectation that dogged his confinement did produce an occasional oblivion, yet in these periods he knew the surprise would be greatest, and it was such when he heard Lily's distress call. He was sitting on his stool with the familiar feel of a hammer and chisel in his hands. Lily's statue had passed the blocking-out stage and he had abandoned his thoughts just to dreamy details, the easy grace of her informal stance, the set of her head, her beautiful gamine presence.

If he had been holding his breath, tipped off about an imminent escape, he would still have been unprepared for this. He had not expected the plaintive cry of the girl who lived in the other half of his soul. It was like a pressure wave from an exploding shell – Olly's head jerked up from his work, spinning him back, a hot surge of adrenaline prepared his body for action.

'LILY ...' Where the air, or the despair, came from to produce such a fervent reply, Olly was slow to understand, but his mind was now ahead of him; it had registered danger in her second call – smothered by an unknown hand perhaps, or just fear. Reeling from reflex, there was no time to consider a cerebral mode; his calculating left brain stood aside and gave full flow to his right, and its intuition required a spontaneous response. Realising that her call came from the other courtyard, Olly picked up the unfinished statue and ran towards the only opening in the dividing wall. The momentum of a hundred pounds of cold marble was not equal to the strength of the great door, but enough to shatter the bolt. Olly pushed hard, but the door, sunk by time on its hinges and stuck in its jambs, was resistant to change.

'Please don't go in there.' It was Ashish, alerted also by Lily's cry and then the assault on the door. He pulled at Olly's sleeve. The tug brought a pause to Olly's headlong tilt, a few seconds for his left brain to intercede. It had been balancing the probabilities – Lily's arrival must herald a rescue effort, the location discovered, others must know she is here. But however imminent the consummation of his hopes, Lily was still in immediate danger.

'Ashish, did you hear the girl's cry?'

'Yes, what does it mean?'

'It means that this is the beginning of the end – depend on it, help will soon follow, but we must find her quickly.'

Ashish wavered – he had his own calculations to make. He didn't bother to finish them, and although his mind was fettered by Saleem's psychological dread, he found his body turning away from the opening, turning enough to face his shoulder to the door. Olly crouched with him. Their combined strength, surging with the pride of confirmed comradeship, overcame thirty years of settled inertia – the heavy timbers swung open with an arthritic crack. The closed years had also added growth to the climbers on the other side, their creeping tendrils cloaking the forced opening of the door and clogging the arches around the cloistered square.

'Wait here,' Ashish whispered, heaving the door closed behind them, 'I won't be noticed.'

He moved swiftly from arch to arch until he could emerge from his usual direction. A frequent visitor to this half of the haveli, he would regularly collect food for himself and Olly, plus sometimes also for Saleem's security men patrolling the premises. One of them was standing, arms crossed, outside a door on the far side – Ashish recognised the stance of a man on guard.

'You caught her then?' he said as he approached the guard.

'What do you know?' The words were contemptuous as well as suspicious, but it was his involuntary backwards glance that answered the question.

'Only what Saleem told me.' Ashish paused more for inspiration than effect – also he had not expected confirmation so quickly. 'He told me that he knew she had been snooping around.' The completely accidental accuracy of his answer was enough to elevate his status – an unlikely confidant, but Saleem was full of surprises.

'Yeah, that old boy in the village spotted her. Anyway we've got her now. Saleem's on his way.'

'Good for you.' Ashish's plan was to ingratiate himself with the guard, send him off for a break, and release the girl. It might well have worked but Olly, with no knowledge of the subtle details, but aching with the need to get to her, and racked with fears for her safety, stole impatiently around the arches, fired up and intent on a more physical strategy. The guard was turned to Ashish and didn't see Lily's head coming – it was a useful chunk of her statue that had survived the earlier battering. It was battered once more – this time against the guard's skull.

They drew the bolt and dragged the unconscious body through the door. Lily stepped out of the shadow at the back of the room and, as Olly looked up, a charge passed between them – weeks of suspense, a lifetime of waiting if necessary, a whole world of bliss, everything that needed saying compressed in a mutual instant. Neither spoke, but Ashish understood, and, dry-mouthed with his now irreversible commitment, he led them silently out of the room and back around to the veiled door, every second expecting discovery and unthinkable consequences.

Between them they pulled the door back into its tight frame, and Ashish, commanded by both fear and hope, took control. He spoke in a low voice, its grim urgency not to be denied.

'Go back to your room,' he directed Olly. 'They will look there, but you will know nothing,' and grabbing Lily's hand he said, 'We will hide elsewhere.'

Olly watched in disbelief as the two ran around the courtyard and disappeared. He sat inert on the stool outside his room, his feet in the circle of chips from his earlier carving, his mind lost in wonder at the sudden acceleration of events, as if dropped back to earth after some whirlwind. Now he was rooted to the spot by interlacing forces, of exhilaration, anticipation, and dread. That madcap girl had found him, but what had gone wrong?

Nearly an hour passed before the desperate search reached him. The felled guard had either been discovered or had recovered consciousness, leading to a hue and cry of manic proportions. Every inch of accommodation around the second square had been scoured and probed, every yard of the grounds outside combed for the missing girl. The main courtyard had been discounted as the panicky search flailed around – after all, access to it had to be past at least one sentinel watching the only entrance at the top of the stairs. But finally the most feared of Saleem's cohort descended those stairs – the two martial-like individuals whom Olly had seen flanking Saleem at Phil's visit.

'Where's the girl?' one screamed at Olly.

'What girl? There are no girls around here.' Olly remained on the stool.

'Where's your boy, where's that boy?'

'He went for food. I'm sure he'll be back in a minute.' Olly started to rise up from the stool, but was met by a flash of feet to his chest and stomach. They were soft shod but the weight and accuracy rendered them hammer blows. Olly fell back winded and bruised; it would be some time before he had gasped enough breath to move.

'Stay there.'

They were now looking for two people. Olly could hear the hollow shouts in empty rooms as they worked around the apartments; he prayed that their quarry had escaped, that Ashish knew where to go to ground. The search effort was to look behind every door, into every usable space off the colonnade – every space, that is, except for a small recess beneath the stairs ... Their otherwise thorough search finally led them to the door through the wall, overgrown and invisible from the other side. The newly shattered bolt confirmed its recent use, the door opening easier this time. Amid loud oaths of realisation, one of the two thugs dived through the opening, shouting for reinforcements; the other turned and, with a face twisted from the deception, advanced on Olly, who was now back on the stool, his breath returning in what minimal sips his broken ribs could produce. He had watched the discovery of the connecting door and braced himself for the consequences. He knew that any resistance offered would be swiftly countered, but he needed to slow their progress. He must take his punishment and then exchange information for time, from what little time was left, he hoped, for this evil crew.

The guard knew where to hit him: a sickening blow to the side of the head that would leave a recipient conscious but disorientated and deeply nauseous, with the conviction that a second blow would be fatal. Olly hit the ground again.

'They came through here. Where did they go?'

Olly saw the raised hand. How could he stall? How could he say he didn't know?

'They went up the steps ... must have slipped past your man. If they didn't get away, they're on the roof.'

A search party arrived through the door: some of the young student chemists, and an old local man whose services had been 'retained' by Saleem. They were all driven along furiously by the other of Saleem's two vipers. 'Come on, you idiots. They're here somewhere. I don't care if they've crawled through a crack in the wall – find them.'

He looked up at the guard at the top of the staircase, who was turned away from them, smoking a cigarette, heedless to the action below. Yes they could have slipped past him.

'You,' he commanded two of the young students, 'get up on the roof.'

Lily and Ashish had survived the first round, but this was a fingertip search and they could hear its slow and deliberate approach. Crouched beneath the bottom steps of the stairs up to the exit they could see just a small wedge of the ground outside. Their contorted bodies recoiled even further when a pair of feet arrived. The owner hesitated, then crouched to his knees. A hand appeared and then another to support the bending body. A head looked in. It was the head of Jitendra, the old Rajasthani who, like Ashish and his father, had been wiled into employment and then secured by Saleem's axis of fear. Ashish met his astonished gaze, both pairs of eyes blazing with terror – the old man's coming from the decision he had just taken.

'Nothing around here,' he reported.

Ashish let out a silent gasp of gratitude. He had staked his own risk at least on a breath of encouragement, but the old man had no hint of any improving prospects; it was an act of dangerous and pure benevolence.

Ten minutes later the search was called off, and as one last initiative, Olly was dragged to his feet by the two bellicose enforcers.

'If you can hear me,' one shouted to the four walls, his arm around Olly's head, 'you have one minute before I break his neck.'

The total silence which fell on the drama was in contrast to the screaming inside three heads all being crushed in the vice of decision. Lily and Ashish knew that their emerging would mean a cruel retribution on the old man, but he in turn knew that it was inevitable, and, doomed anyway, he needed to save them from the responsibility.

He stood forward and said, 'I know where they are.'

Why he decided to point toward the door through the wall will never be known, his gesture lost among others' hands pointing to the figures on the roof, men with ropes and guns.

Saleem's enforcers, his two infernal lieutenants, looked up – the world had turned in the last seconds and left them facing the cloven hoofs of reprisal. The one holding Olly tightened his grip as the first stun shells exploded, as if to secure a shield. The pressure on Olly's ribs was excruciating, but it reminded him of the feet that had done the damage, which, in contrast to his own feet in their hard-heeled boots, could creep and dart about silently in soft slippers like the pads of a gecko. The association was crucial as it inspired Olly's only defence. He brought his heel down with crushing force on the soft pad, grinding down further between the instep and toes. Olly was released as his captor fell into the grip of his own pain, but his partner, now at heightened levels of belligerence, felled Olly with a screaming blow to his head.

Olly was back in the dust, barely conscious, but aware enough to absorb the generality of the scene around him, that scene he had dared to imagine so many times – commotion, running feet, barked orders. He prayed he wasn't dreaming, but then there was Ashish, helping him to his feet, and there standing in the ring of marble chippings was Lily – not a lifeless statue, but a live girl, a beautiful live woman, from the tender mercies of her head, down to her determined feet, perfection to every last animate detail.

Olly and Lily clung to each other in the mêlée, and when the smoke and confusion cleared, a dejected and beaten crew sat under close guard in the centre of the square. No one had escaped: Saleem's workforce awaited transfer to an unending legal hiatus, starting with the crowded cells of one of the largest prisons in the world – Tihar in Delhi. The unlucky ones would be sent back to China. The police had clear orders; Olly and Lily were the only ones not swept into custody. They both felt ashamed of the few seconds it took them to see Ashish in the group, and behind him Jitendra the old man who had thwarted the search for Lily and Ashish.

'Wait,' Olly said to the policeman about to march them out, 'some of these men are innocent. Only we know who they are.'

'They will all be subject to the full process of the law – any innocence will soon be established.'

'No,' insisted Olly, 'they were just as much prisoners as we were – they must not be subject to any process.'

'I have my orders'

'Well you'd better check them if you don't wish to look foolish.' It was Mahinder, just arrived with a more senior officer. The officer stepped forward and addressed Olly.

'Your request will be granted, but first I need to know which one of these is the chief man. We were told to hold off until he was here.'

'He is not among them,' Olly confirmed, and noticing his recent persecutors, the only two not downcast in supplication, but spitting hatred at Saleem's mention, and it would seem his escape, he added, 'but those two are his seconds.'

'No Saleem,' Olly continued dejectedly. Then with his mind overloaded with fresh worries for his father, urgent questions came in rapid fire.' What about the other place? My father is there. You raided that too? Is he ok? Who was there? Was Saleem not there?'

'This Saleem,' the policeman revolved the name round his mouth and spat it out, 'was not found there either.' He looked accusingly at Mahinder. 'Perhaps we were held back until he had got away.' Then, turning to Olly with a gentler tone, he continued, 'Your father is well; he is half-way here already, with an old man also – like you, he wanted to identify the blameless. The rest are in custody.' Turning to the prisoners in the dust, he asked, 'Which are your innocents?'

'Him,' said Olly, pointing to Ashish.

'And him,' Lily was pointing to Jitendra when she noticed his hand was holding that of another local, just a youth, 'and him.'

36

Some time later, Frank was brought into the courtyard, together with the old man who had shown him kindness in Rewari – Ashish's father. Olly and Ashish leapt forward to embrace them, the filial and paternal bonds that had been so abused now unfettered by Saleem. No chemicals were needed to induce the rush of euphoria as the jubilant four danced around the square, tears of joy flowing from uncapped springs, down cheeks flushed with relief and gratitude. Olly fell to the ground exhausted – even gaiety is a labour to a man with broken ribs. He laughed painfully as Lily, Jitendra and the youth – his nephew – joined the circle, skipping round him until, giddy from the heady relief, they, too, collapsed. Lying on the ground, they looked up at the heavens through watery eyes, the night sky swimming with stars – which ones had guided the extraordinary combination of people and events that had conspired for their good fortune? Olly sat up, and, looking at Mahinder, who had stood back shyly to let them enjoy their triumph, said, 'We have no fallen comrades to sadden the moment, but others yet to thank for it.'

'Hear hear.' Lily endorsed the point with a beam of gratitude.

Mahinder nodded his head genially to acknowledge their recognition of his part, and then self-effacingly said, 'I have spoken to Ravi, who called your friends Phil and Gus, with news that you are safe.' He came closer to the company and continued in a confidential tone. 'Phil will call tomorrow morning after he concludes some unsettled business. Ravi said he would not be drawn about Saleem's whereabouts, except to say that there was a difference between an escape and non-appearance.'

Olly's and Frank's ingrained confidence and trust in Phil sat easily with Lily's own cast of mind. She had met him and heard of his exploits, and it was enough to allay any wisp of confusion or suspicion that may have floated by her; but Mahinder, who knew little of Phil's qualities or abilities, was clearly discomposed.

'Forgive me, but I am a little confused. I had to wait over an hour after Lily disappeared before being allowed to call the police, and then another hour before the signal to commence the raid. In the circumstances, surely Saleem's non-appearance is just the same as an escape.'

At the allusion to Saleem's escape, the sky seemed to darken as if a cloud was blotting out a trillion hopeful stars. The Europeans derived some comfort from the long arm of justice that they were used to, but to the locals, his non-capture red handed meant that he could turn the scales; he would slip behind a screen of obfuscation and judicial casuistry, abetted with malign influence over any who might bear witness to his vile criminality. For all the euphoria of their reunions, they would not breathe the clear air of unthreatened lives whilst Saleem was still at large. Ashish, his father, Jitendra, and his nephew might return to their villages, but with futures blighted by the same fear that put them at his mercy in the first place.

Olly now stood to speak. 'I'm sure we are all very tired, but let's not assume the worst. I suggest we all stay in Jhunjhunun tonight, we can rest in the hotel and hope for better news tomorrow. Our colleague Phil will have his reasons for his guardedness, and don't forget we are all here, free to go, thanks in part to his delightfully devious plans.'

'I bow to your belief in your friend,' Mahinder replied gracefully. 'I didn't mean to sound faithless.'

His quiet equanimity and the earlier mention of tired-ness seemed to pull another string of their susceptible mood. They would accept the day for what wide-eyed joy it brought and let sleep close their minds to darker concerns. 'One more thing before we go,' Mahinder added. 'Gus said call him when Frank gets here.' He handed Olly his phone.

The journey took less than an hour, probably the max-imum time that the eight occupants of Mahinder's small car could withstand their compression, but the amusement that came from their discomfort lightened their spirits. Lily sat as gently as possible on Olly's lap, fending off swaying bodies from his injuries, their closeness bringing immeasur-able tenderness, and an intimacy that normally followed moments of passion. In this case their passion would not be rushed, but it fizzed between them like a long, slow fuse.

The phone rang in the flat. Gus ignored it, then his mobile called for an answer – he switched it off. Gus was in no position to respond to either – he'd just had a more urgent call, this from the front door, and he knew he would have his hands full. He'd heard earlier about the rescue, and after jigging and whooping around the flat, had turned his attention to the van outside. Did this mean that the hatchet men would stand down? Would their mandate expire? Ravi said Phil had been cagey about Saleem – more news in the morning. Was he still on the loose, controlling these ugly customers? There were then two in the van – the first time they had doubled up. He saw them step out and with furtive glances cross the road and disappear out of view. Gus had expected no less; they were bored waiting, they were coming, and he had his plans. By the time they rang the downstairs intercom Gus had opened the bookcase just enough for notice and had drawn the blinds to keep the afternoon sun out of the atrium.

'Hello ... Interflora.'

'How nice. Come on up.' Gus thought it would reassure them to hear a feminine voice – he did his best. Leaving the front door ajar, he climbed the darkened stairs. He checked the now downward-pointing up-lighters, and with a mixture of relish and trepidation awaited the intruders' arrival.

You can close your eyes, or look down, but you can't look up at a thousand watts of light. Eyes cannot accommodate that amount of sudden glare from just a few feet away, and it can take the brain a second or two to adjust to the danger that lurks behind. In American football a wild throw in the closing seconds of a game, with just a hope and a prayer that a forward will catch it and touch down, is called a Hail Mary Pass. Gus was a quarterback again, waiting at the top of the stairs, but this time he would be throwing himself not the ball. He heard low voices, the slip of the front-door latch – they were staying. They were moving around downstairs, the drag of slouching feet on the carpet, controlled breathing. Why the stealth? Gus mused – they were invited up. A perceptible stir of the bookcase on its heavy hinges, the tread of a ponderous boot on the first of the sixteen wooden steps, and Gus started his count and the Hail Mary. The delivery boys were coming, and they were not smelling of flowers. The leading boot continued its clumsy ascent followed by its partner and then the echo of a second pair. Three ... four – Gus was half-way through his prayer – five ... six – they were so slow, as if expecting a trap. What were they carrying? Guns? Coshes? Seven ... eight – another Hail Mary, one for each. Nine out of sixteen – time for lights and action.

Gus flicked the switch and launched himself onto the

landing. Two startled and blinded ruffians stood side by side, their faces level with the two heavy boots now looping toward them. Gus swung from the handrail and performed the drop kick he had prayed for. Already bloodied and stunned by Gus's attack, their backward freefall onto the bottom step completed the battering, leaving them broken and defenceless, long enough at least for Gus to put some bonds on them. He had seen it done in the westerns – the villains finally bound and gagged. He left them feet lashed tightly, hands tied behind their backs, mouths taped. He would release them, of course, but into whose hands depended on news from Phil on Saleem.

'Gus, you ok?' It was Olly's second attempt, 'I tried earlier.'

'Olly, you hero, you ace, you did it!' Gus had been elated by the news from Ravi, but now he was flying. He wanted a blow-by-blow account, but was content with a one-minute explanation. All would be revealed tomorrow – Phil's unfinished business. He was too excited even to mention the business in the flat just then – that he'd tied up some loose ends of his own.

Only Phil and Mr Lamumba knew precisely what they were waiting for – they had devised a perfect end-game. The others were left with just the impression and the hope that one more resolution was coming. The how and when would ensure that they slept uneasily that night. Saleem, though slept evenly, and, barring the interruption to change planes at Addis Ababa, he arrived in Nairobi with a mind eased by rest and reflection. He had consulted his fears but concluded that their nervous petitions were beneath his natural mastery, and what weariness he may have felt was laid to rest as he touched Kenyan soil with that wonderful feeling of elopement and rebirth. Saleem walked with a light step to the terminal building, stopping to savour the warm African morning – not so different climatically to India, but there was something more primeval in the air, and it suited him, it suited his predatory nature.

He thought satisfyingly of Liu. His hag-ridden obsession with that wretched Sibyl had haunted and nearly defeated him, but now he could ponder the inevitable and glorious retribution awaiting her. There would be nowhere for her to evade him, especially when her friends returned. His watchers would watch them; his followers would follow them until she was found ...

'Good morning. Ticket and passport please.'

Saleem was one of just fifty people on that early morning flight, and just one of seven or eight non-African faces. Without a name the immigration official had to rely on a description of the passenger to be detained, and if in doubt hold anyone approaching the likeness. The paler skins belonged to four Europeans and a young family of Gujaratis, but in any event only one passenger was in transit to Mombasa.

'Mr Samudra, please step this way. The porter will help you retrieve your bags.'

Not a scintilla of suspicion clouded Saleem's brow as he followed the loping steps of the porter to the carousel – he was used to VIP treatment. Most of his assets were in the laptop hanging from his shoulder, but when his bag came around, he patted it with affection. It contained a useful amount of cash, but more importantly two further identities. He walked imperiously behind the porter as he was led back to immigration – a visa formality, no doubt.

'I'm afraid there is a problem with the Mombasa flight. You may care to call anyone who is meeting you not to set out till an arrival time is declared.'

Saleem's mood was still too light to be over-vexed by this

minor hitch – he had all the time in the world. Turning his phone on, he called Phil.

Mr Lamumba and Phil had written the script the previous evening for this little charade, and as they lingered over breakfast, Phil's phone was propped against the coffee pot. They knew the plane had landed, there was only one passenger who could be Saleem, and if they were right he would call to confirm. If Phil's mobile sounded, the play would become a gothic drama, cued in by the main protagonist. They sat in silence, minutes ticked by, long minutes but wickedly enjoyable. Then it rang ...

'It's me,' he said with not so much as a good morning. 'I've been delayed – you'll have to check arrival time later.'

Phil nodded to Lamumba, who made his own call.

'I already know your arrival time.' Phil was toying with him – pausing long enough for little stabs of doubt to prick Saleem's confidence. 'It takes eight hours by road to Mombasa.'

'What are you talking about?' Saleem had recovered his indignity; he was now affronted.

'Did you ever wonder how I got your phone number?' Phil said no more. They would be words that Saleem could chew over during his ride to Mombasa; words no doubt he would grind into a bitter curse. Phil heard a scuffle and ended the call.

Saleem hadn't noticed his escort falling in behind him. Phil's words hung in the air for a second before a shudder of suspicion spun him round to face the absolute certainty of his ensnarement. Like a drowning man whose whole life was flashing through his mind, in one or two seconds every detail, every nuance of the trickery of the last weeks added to his comprehension until he was just an animal caught in a trap, howling and struggling insanely against the vicious jaws.

*

In the event, none of the eight new guests in the hotel had slept till almost morning. The locals' agitation, returning with the spectre of Saleem on the loose, had disturbed even the relative equanimity that Olly, Frank, and Lily had previously felt. They were all still in their rooms in the early afternoon when Mahinder took Phil's call. He knocked on each door in turn with the news – Saleem is captured; he won't ever be coming back.

Lily had lain beside Olly's pained and restless body all night, a mixture of pride, love, and worry for him confounding her already fitful sleep. The message was perfect – it was a signal to cast off into a deep and blissful repose, to float in a dreamy oblivion. Frank got up and went to their room. There was no sound of reply as he knocked gently, then quietly opened the door. Olly and Lily were lying in each other's arms, peaceful, careless, and confident. He backed out of the room, proud and thankful for them both, and touched by their condition. He went back to his bed, happy yet sad to share it with just memories of Biddy. She still orbited his heart like a celestial body. Her elliptical path seemed to be drawn into closer transit at times of great joy or sadness.

Ashish, his father, Jitendra, and his nephew each turned back in their beds, for the first time aware of the clean white linen, the first they had lain their bodies in for a long while, at last to bask in that delicious pre-wakening sleep, that restoring, healing sleep that repaid the debts of lost nights.

Mahinder alone had come down to spend the morning in the hotel gardens. A pair of tame mongooses gambolled around his feet as, sitting quietly, he reviewed the extraordinary adventure that he had been brought into. It was later, while watching a mongoose circling a bush, that the call came through from Phil. At that moment the creature dived into the undergrowth and came out with a snake in its teeth.

Whilst Mahinder was not a religious man, the coincidence of the two events allowed him to be moved, at least by the face value of the spectacle. He delivered the news in turn to each of these people who had touched him so, and returned to sit in quiet contemplation of their rewarded spirits.

37

Saleem's journey was long, hot, and uncomfortable. Chained to a ring in the floor of a truck, escape for him was impossible. He hoped the two in the cab could hear his extravagant promises – more money than they could spend, girls, luxury, and a life of ease. Just to leave him beside the road with his bags. They did hear, but followed instructions and ignored his pleas. Had his bags been with them they would have been tempted, but Mr Lamumba appreciated the frailties of a poor man's conscience. Saleem's laptop and suitcase were put in the hands of a separate and special courier – there was now a spare seat on the Mombasa flight.

The drivers' silence fuelled Saleem's blazing temper as he thrashed and kicked at his chains. He was aware that he was becoming a wild animal but could do nothing to prevent his boiling rage. A wild animal … but he doubted he would be let loose on a reserve. He slaked his fear and his dehydrating body from a jerry can of water that had been left within reach, drinking down the tepid liquid unaware of Mr Lamumba's tribal remedy. The emetic worked slowly and accumulatively, and by the time the truck pulled into Mr Lamumba's compound Saleem was too weak to struggle.

Only his bloodshot eyes hinted at the demons within, demons too weak to fight but desperate to avoid a diabolical fate that only they could imagine. Mr Lamumba's prescription had worked.

'If you are to live, we must get you to hospital as soon as possible, but before that there are conditions to be met.' Mr Lamumba put the laptop on his desk. He placed a piece of paper beside it. 'Two accounts, two transfers. The first account will receive the return of moneys transferred to you yesterday, and the balance of your accounts will go to the second.'

Saleem managed a grin – as always, money takes over the negotiation. He sat shaking from a fever but financially unmoved.

'There is enough for all of us,' he said defiantly, 'but if I die you will get nothing.'

'If you die we will simply confiscate the money as illicit gains,' Mr Lamumba replied – he held Saleem and his deposits in check. 'And,' he added, 'knowing the poison you were given, this will be in just an hour or so.'

Poison is a terrifying word – death from the inside out. But still Saleem held out. He knew he was good on the brink. He looked into Mr Lamumba's face, his taut expressionless face, and waited for a blink from those deep, deep eyes. But whilst none came, the poison was working its bitter ruin. Seeing the retch of fear take grip, Mr Lamumba looked at his watch slowly and leaned forward.

'I give you my word – you will be taken straight to a hospital as soon as these transfers are cleared. We are not barbarians.'

Poison … hospital … two trigger words, pressing down on his resolve, squeezing the stiff neck of his stubbornness. He opened his computer – the operation was completed in a few minutes – funds out, funds in. The accounts were in the same branch, transfer was immediate.

Long into the night Phil and Mr Lamumba had debated how the world spawned and then nurtured people like Saleem, how they relied on others' greed to feed their own.

There were enough ways for misery to be visited on people, but the heart of them was ignorance. Yet ignorance should be stifled not tapped. Mother Nature had her own rigorous rules, but it was human beings who created the climate for perverted exploitation. Maybe it was the survival of the fittest, but why had our enormous brains evolved other than to receive some sort of enlightenment? Insights other than a succession of heart-stoppingly naïve religions in which perfectly intelligent social or spiritual guides were trampled underfoot, soured by divisive partisan cant.

'Oh don't get me going.' Phil had heard himself ranting again.

But he had touched Mr Lamumba's conscience, and between them they had worked out an equitable solution to the distribution of Saleem's deposits and cash. Of the two accounts credited by Saleem, the first was Mr Lamumba's ministry account, into which yesterday's payment for the fakes would be returned. The second, a new account set up for good causes, would receive the balance: payments from the two genuine batches, plus the additional deposits that Saleem had transferred before fleeing – a total of well over £5 million. In addition Phil would pay in his surplus on the dealings. This amounted to £25,000 – the same amount as in the envelope that he had passed across the beaming quartermaster's desk, which Mr Lamumba graciously consented also to deposit in the good causes account. Withdrawals and distribution of any moneys would require both signatures. Mr Lamumba had looked wistfully at the funds, but there was something about this Phil Donahue that suggested that cooperation would be good for more than just his soul. He was a trusted civil servant, but he knew that any impeachment proceedings would be summary and decisive. And to be a trustee of this new munificent foundation would be good for his esteem.

Saleem, who had dragged himself into the corner of the room, directed his venom at Phil. 'You and that witch,' he snarled, 'will live to regret this ...' He wanted to say more but choked on his foaming rage.

'If your threat refers to young Garry and Len, well they too have fallen under her spell.' Phil had the names from Gus. When Gus had explained the demise of their patron, they had been only too pleased to be released back into the wild.

Saleem was defeated, he had no bite left – all he wanted was not to die. 'Take me to the hospital.'

The HIV/AIDS sanatorium outside Mombasa was built for TB patients. Now the surrounding walls were raised to confine sufferers in advanced stages of this new scourge, this latter-day Black Death. The sign over the entrance made this clear and advised precautions for all who should enter.

'But this is an AIDS hospital,' Saleem protested, he lay secured to a stretcher. 'I don't have AIDS.'

Phil felt a shiver of pity, but then remembered the million fake tablets; he remembered his wife's village – he couldn't ignore the comparison; he remembered Saleem's treatment of his friends, his total disregard for the sanctity of anything. His recall was long enough, his reply short ...

'Not yet ...'

The world stopped for a while, allowing them all to come to terms with a new order. Ashish, his father, Jitendra, and his nephew returned to their village. Phil had given them Saleem's suitcase; he hadn't counted the cash it contained, but however much, it would be small recompense for their pains and their courage.

Phil followed the line back through Mr Wei to the Chinese. As he suspected, they had their suspicions, and it

311

would have been enough to show some of Saleem's banking for them to heed the whistle, had Dr Chinn blown it. Instead, Phil painted the picture of Saleem's fakeries, their discovery by the Kenyans, and the bust by the Indian police. He hoped he had created an impression of himself as a man let down and out of pocket, especially by the confiscation of all Saleem's deposits. The publication, thanks to Mahinder, of the details of the raids and press speculation about a local magnate behind the operation being spirited away to rot in an African jail brought final closure – the Triads had other dark corners to inhabit, other hands to deliver their plunder.

Phil and Frank, Olly and Lily returned to London, still suspended from the great hand of chance that had swung their way. The only place to get back down to earth was Arthur's, the only place where their earlier memories, whether old and abiding, like Olly, Frank, and Phil's, or newly experienced, like Gus, Liu, and Lily's, could mingle and bond with the haunting retrospect of the last few weeks.

But they were all children of their own time, and when it restarted they had to go along. They had time to thank for creating the sublime moments of juxtaposition when their presence or talents had coalesced, but they had to return to their own individual specialties and circumstances – circumstances now irrevocably entwined. They returned, they hoped, better human beings – perhaps their actions and loyalties had encouraged betterness, perhaps, too, they had discouraged badness, much of which had challenged their own ignorance of the world.

Frank and Phil went on a journey, first call to visit Mr Lamumba, to see about some expenditure and some good causes, then ... who knows. But would Edmund Burke's admonition apply to them? Could they not do more than a little? Probably, but when their spare millions seemed

312

inconsequential amongst the outstretched hands, they should remember the wise man's words.

For Gus the boy from Montana, meanwhile, wild horses could not tear him away from London and Liu, Olly, and Lily. He had anyway a new job – his past and recent experiences made him the perfect candidate. He would be working for Frank and Phil's new foundation to confront, not the entrenched attitudes of a corporate workforce, but the entrenched ignorance of the western world about illicit drugs. His brief was to propagate an intelligent debate about the legalisation of banned drugs, thereby to cut away the ludicrous support given to the finances of an evil trade, which at every level encourages corruption and enslavement. What was needed was a groundswell of enlightenment for the politicians to align with. This was an adventure for which nature and events had designed Gus Hampton.

As for Olly and Lily themselves, they finally found time for their passion, their breathtaking desire no longer teased by chance or doused by cold alarm.

Lily stepped out onto the terrace; it was the end of a warm June day – she looked up at the great night sky. She was not overwhelmed; its infinite possibilities had assured her she was not dreaming, that this could really be happening. She looked at Olly standing just inside. 'Tonight,' she said, 'I want to make love to you under the stars.'

With one bound he was by her side ...